I Do?

Edwardo Jackson

Published by

JCM Books
a division of JCM Entertainment, LLC
15228-B Hawthorne Blvd.
Suite 203
Lawndale, CA 90260
USA
Tel: (818) 231-2397
E-mail:JCMEntLLC@aol.com

In association with:
The X Press, PO Box 25694, London, N17 6FP
England. Tel: 020 8801 2100 Fax: 020 8885 1322 E-mail: vibes@xpress.co.uk

Distributed in UK by Turnaround Distribution
Unit 3, Olympia Trading Estate, Coburg Road, London N22 6TZTel: 020 8829 3000
Fax: 020 8881 5088

ISBN 1-902934-43-1

Printed and bound in Great Britain by Bookmarque Ltd, Croydon, Surrey

To Mom –and anyone who's ever had love, lost love, and fought like hell to get it back.

"Destiny is not a matter of chance, it is a matter of choice; it is not a thing to be waited for, it is a thing to be achieved."
— William Jennings Bryan

"You either love or you don't... Thin love ain't no love at all."
— Sethe (Oprah), "Beloved" (the movie)

"I have to know I am the only one."
— an actress, of course

1

I HAD NO IDEA LOVE would taste so much like blood. Shortly after being knocked on my butt by a two-fisted, kicking flurry of white wedding dress, somehow, the beating stopped. Shakily, I regained my footing, bleeding slightly from the mouth. I had no idea what to be madder about: that I bled from the mouth and had a perfectly done bob ruined, or that this woman in the white wedding dress was an impostor.

And she was an impostor. This Tabitha, this "Souldance" creature was as phony as a pair of Guccis bought in Times Square. She was an impostor because she had fooled her fiancé all the way to the altar. She was an impostor because she was marrying my man.

The scene must have looked ridiculous, I'm sure. Here I was, fresh off a four hour flight from Atlanta, having barged my way in on my ex-boyfriend's wedding, stopped it, and received a physical beatdown from the bride-to-be for my efforts. There she was, Tabitha Washington, only a few feet away from me, tempestuous fists balled up, ready to finish what she had started.

And there stood Nick. Only a few feet away from us, Nick's sharply attired, tuxedoed, dark brownskin form stood in the priest's chambers inside the church, bisecting the distance between the two of us, forming the perfect love triangle. If you liked your triangles in Bermuda. He looked so handsome. He also looked confused as hell.

The fact that he was confused was a small victory for me. Six years ago, I had broken his heart. Now, he was in a position to break mine. I had put it all out on the line, flying in at the last second to be one of the people who objected to the wedding ceremony by having decided not to "forever hold my peace."

It all had been priceless: Ex-Girlfriend Breaks Up Nationally Famous Columnist's Wedding. Sounds like the sort of headline I'd read on the job. His mother's eyes had rolled up into the back of her head. Malloy, his best friend, had looked like he was about to punt me out of the church personally. And let's not even talk about how the bride had looked standing at the altar.

But now we were in the relative safety of the priest's chambers, away from the prying eyes of an expectant wedding crowd. All of my last minute theatrics had come down to this. It was crunch time, and the stakes were higher than stripper heels.

"Everybody just try and calm down," Nick tried pathetically to referee.

"You don't love her, Babyluv!" I pleaded with Nick. I admit it—it was a shameless tug at his heartstrings by calling him the name I had once emblazoned upon his heart. He would always be my Babyluv.

"You don't love her, Babycakes!" Tabitha threatened me.

"I love you!"

"No, I love you!"

Something had to be done, something drastic. So I ran over and kissed him—again. Actually, it had been my kissing Nick earlier that had earned me the beatdown from an ill-tempered Tabitha.

Well Tabitha did not disappoint. The next thing I knew, I felt an open hand knocking me off of Nick's face.

Nick's fiancée countered by kissing him as well.

The dazed look on Nick's face was photographic.

"What's it gonna be, Nick?" spat Tabitha. "Her or me?"

"We were meant to be, Nick!" I lobbied. "You're my Babyluv!"

"No, we were meant to be!" challenged Tabitha. "You're my lobster!"

Lobster? What the…

Tabitha and I stole one loaded, testy look at each other. In unison, both of us hollered at Nick: "CHOOSE!"

One of the things I have always loved about Nick was his ability to choose. The man was decisive as the day was long. It had been his preemptive decisiveness that ended us six years ago. And for the first time in the almost nine tumultuous years I've known him…Nick could not… choose.

Luckily, he didn't have to. A piercing scream shattered the delicate, fragile peace. A general murmur went up outside the door to chambers.

A man who looked as if he could be Nick's brother—Nick's height, Nick's walnut brown skin, and Nick's charming dark brown eyes—burst into the room without knocking. Malloy.

"Nick, dawg—your moms fainted!"

An expletive slipped Nick's lips as he barreled past the stunned expressions of Tabitha and me. Briefly casting me an evil look, Malloy led the charge out the door.

I started to follow when Tabitha slapped me back, forcefully.

"Stay away from my man, bitch."

Even if I had wanted to respond, she was out the door before I could.

*

Nick's mother had breast cancer. This wasn't exactly public knowledge but I'd found out nevertheless. Nick, I assumed, had known for a year, having largely kept her illness a secret. I wonder if even Tabitha knew. From what I gathered, Mom didn't have much time left, about two or three months left to live. She needed very expensive, experimental treatment that Nick hadn't been able to afford to provide her. Without using the treatment, Mom would most certainly die. In that brief moment I had walked down the aisle (in pursuit of my man, not with him, unfortunately), the glimpse I had seen of her had shown her looking remarkably fresh. But, in the excitement, I guess she had fainted.

I followed behind the caravan of cars from the church in my own rented Camry. Although the trip to the hospital only took ten minutes, it felt like a mini-eternity. Or a reading of one of those crappy, street fiction novels. Funny, but love always does. Maybe it was because Nick had stalled on making the biggest decision of our lives. Or maybe it was because he was about to make the biggest mistake of his.

Not even the Secret Service guarded the President as well. I sucked my teeth with rueful impatience as a thick shield of family and friends stood between the hospital room door and me. While Nick was nowhere to be found, Malloy made himself real easy to find, informally running the familial SWAT team. He was being a real ass about it, too.

"Go home, Jasmine."

"No."

"You've caused enough trouble for one day. For one lifetime."

"I care about her, too, boy," I countered defensively.

"Well I care about her and him—more than you ever could or did," he sneered derisively.

Not true, I wanted to scream in his ignorant little face. Instead, I curbed my efforts and returned to the thick of the concerned wedding guests who had dared brave out an outcome on Mom's health.

The remaining wedding guests were a diverse mix of darkskinned Cuban and Dominican-Americans from Tabitha's side and just plain 'ole black folk from Nick's. I tried to be inconspicuous. Fat chance. Everywhere I wandered, the sea of humanity parted for me. I was as recognizable as Jesus—or a leper.

After four tense hours even Chairman Mal had to go to the bathroom. So I seized my opportunity. Taking advantage of my leper-like stride, I marched right up to the closed hospital door. Winnie would've kicked my tail had I not knocked first, which I did quietly. Not waiting for a response, I barged into the room.

When the door opened, I could have been Shaquille O'Neal and nobody would have noticed. At first. A doctor and two nurses hovered around an uncurtained bed area, obscuring who lay there. Nick paced around, talking to a nurse very intensely.

10

The tie from his tuxedo shirt was undone, shirt askew. His tuxedo jacket lay in a heap near some bland orange plastic hospital chair.

I furrowed my brow. Where the hell was…

A tap on my shoulder. "Excuse me."

Tabitha.

Before I turned around, I concocted the meanest, nastiest face I could, a face I hadn't had to use in over a decade, not since my impetuous, partially misspent, borderline hoodrat youth. I had had enough of getting beat down by this shorter, younger, unprofessional chick. So when I turned around, I was ready for her, for anything. "What."

In a voice that teetered between calm and crazy, she uttered plainly, "There is nothing more I would like on this earth than to beat you into another dimension, ex-girlfriend. Believe me."

After what I've put up with from her today…"The feeling's mutual." Bitch.

"You have ruined my wedding, the happiest day of my life. You have ruined it out of your own regret, selfishness, and bad timing. Nick is marrying me, not you. You don't belong here."

Just when I had gritted my teeth, readying to go Brooklyn around-the-way-girl on this little pecan slice of the Valley, someone grasped my arm.

"Jasmine…Let's talk."

As my eyes visually challenged Tabitha's, I mumbled, "Okay."

Before Nick led me out the room, I stole a glance in Mom's direction. The human shield around her bed had dissipated to reveal her lying in the bed, asleep, oxygen mask over her face. She drew in deep, sleepy breaths. Mom was a short, squat, lovely, darkskin Panamanian woman who neared sixty. Sporting the remains of her wedding day makeup for her Handsome, Mom still looked beautiful. She was going to be okay.

Out in the hall, Nick led me by the wrist—not the hand, the wrist—past the hospital guests. As my reputation preceded me, they made way like we were cops in the projects. A general gasp arose from them. Nick. With her.

An aborted charge in my direction by Tabitha's mother—Blanca, I think her name was, said the report—was headed off by a cousin or something. Blanca jabbered angrily at us in Spanish, then English, then in the universal language of Cuss. She hollered down the hall after us. I was rattled, but I let Nick lead me wherever he needed to.

While we waited on an elevator, I found the temerity to ask him, "Where are we going?"

His words were clipped, his tone short. "Someplace we can talk."

*

I hugged that white paper cup of Maxwell's House as if my life depended on it. In all actuality, it did. Sitting across from Nick in the hospital cafeteria, I could feel a judgment brewing on the events of today…on me…on us.

Nick stared intently into his cup of Hawaiian Punch. He had never been big on coffee, usually just when he was depressed or something. From what I had heard, he had met this Tabitha woman in some coffeehouse not far from the church in San Diego's North Park district, Clair de la Lune. She had been performing during some sort of poetry open mic night and he had bought it. He had bought her whole act—hook, line, and faker. Nick was always quite the romantic.

In the tense silence, I observed Nick deeply, through those light brown orbed windows to my soul. It had been five years since I had last seen him. This was almost like seeing him again for the first time, as I soaked him into my consciousness with intimate detail. He looked older, for sure. For the first time, I could see the light formations of wrinkle lines in Nick's forehead. I suppose he was allowed; I mean we're both thirty. His haircut was trademark Nick: the low cut, lightly greased, well-lined "even Steven." All the features I loved still dominated his face: the broad nose, the Van Dyke style goatee-moustache, and the sensitive dark eyes. Dark brown, thick-lipped, and broad-shouldered—even more so than I remembered. Nick had been working out, having added at least fifteen pounds more muscle to his lean, firm, six-foot mass.

Babyluv was handsome, but no Adonis. Hell, nobody's

perfect. I had to learn that the hard way. But he was perfect for me.

I could have looked at him all day long.

Should I have been the first one to breach the fragile peace? I didn't dare want to find out. But all this silence—dead air, we called it—was killing me Roberta Flack style. I felt as if my very existence hinged on these next few moments. I would be right.

"Mom's gonna be alright," Nick said, saving me from opening my foolish mouth.

I sighed. "That's wonderful to hear."

Nick finally gave me his eyes. Shrugged them off on me like cement shoes in the East River was more like it. "I'm glad you care."

"Look, Nick, I didn't come here to—"

"Don't speak."

I obeyed. I wasn't the most obedient girl in the world, but I knew when to shut up and take the Fifth.

"Tabitha and I are postponing the wedding."

The reaction was natural. As much as I tried to control it, the look of surprise/false hope sprang to my face.

No matter. Nick crushed it swiftly, joylessly, like a Nazi Panzer tank. "We're getting married in a month."

I had to say something, right? I just didn't know what it was to be said. "Wh-Why?"

"Why am I getting married?" Nick's ire was raised. We had already covered this topic earlier today when we had been alone in the priest's chambers.

"No," I amended quickly. "Why in a month?"

"Thanks to you bogarting my day of supreme happiness and ultimate commitment, I lost the one-week window I had to get this done and go on honeymoon before principal photography started."

His tone had lightened enough for me to venture another question. "Principal photography?"

"Shooting, Jasmine. I start shooting a movie next week."

I felt dumb. Of course. "Oh."

"Well, I'm not shooting it, but I'm starring in it. It's the first lead of my career and it's a big budget film. It's a major deal," he explained patiently.

"Sand Adventures, I know. I'm proud of you."

"Thanks, Baby—" Nick stopped. He almost called me it. Those words, the name I had longed to hear for five, long years. His equivalent of "Babyluv" for me: Baby J.

I had almost seduced him into being comfortable with me again. There was something still there. It felt so big, it made the elephant in the proverbial room look like a plush toy souvenir.

He got mad at himself for being so easy. "Jasmine, go home. Just go… home."

A look of confusion and hurt registered on my face. "That's it? Just 'go home?' I expose myself to you, a church full of people, and God and the best you can do is 'Go home?'"

"Don't you dare turn this around on me," he threatened. "Not now. Not this time."

"I love you. Do you have any idea what I gave up to realize that you are the only one I need? Do you know what I gave up to be here? I really, really love you!"

If I could tear out my heart to show how it bled nothing but love for him, I would have. But even if I could, it still wouldn't be enough.

"That's not my problem, Jasmine. This ship has passed and you know it! Too little, too late."

"It's not too late, Nick! I felt something in there, and I know you felt it, too. When I kissed you—the first time, before Tabitha came in and hit me—I know you felt something."

"I used to love you, and you had your tongue in my mouth," Nick countered clearly. "Of course I'm gonna 'feel something.' But whatever it was, it wasn't love."

Nick drank down the last of his Hawaiian Punch and stood up, ready to go. I was running out of things to say to stop him.

"Nick…I…you…"

"Go say goodbye to Mom," he instructed. "I'll be back to the room in ten minutes—with Tabitha. Don't be there."

With that, Nick walked away.

*

Standing by the edge of the bed, I couldn't do it. She looked

14

so peaceful, so serene, oxygen mask and all. I felt ashamed that I had had something to do with her collapse. That shame was amplified earlier when I had to fight my way past Tabitha's angry mother and relatives in the hallway outside the room.

Even in denial, Nick was generous, gracious. He didn't have to let me see her. He didn't have to let me see this woman, his mother, one last time. I grimaced sadly. That was the sign of a great upbringing. Good home training. A good mom.

The few times I had met the woman, she had welcomed me like a daughter. Even before he'd proposed, I could sense that she knew he would to me. I wonder to this day if she truly knew what had happened between her son and I. I wonder if Nick had ever opened up the scab on his heart to tell her the whole painful, silly truth. Now here, all Nick wanted to do was to get married before she died. Here I was trying to deny her even that.

I sighed. I had caused enough damage for one day, even if it was well intentioned. The embarrassment of this defeat ranked up there with Waterloo, my very own Bay of Pigs. I had no idea if I would ever see her again—alive that is. I just knew that I couldn't disturb her for the second time that day. Quietly, I turned away from the bed and made my way to the door.

When I opened it to come out, I saw Nick and Tabitha sitting in adjacent hospital chairs. They held hands as their foreheads leaned against each other. She had been crying. Nick softly, tenderly comforted her. It was as though they were the only ones in the hall—in the world—even though family and friends milled about. Talk about your postcards of love.

I wanted to cry out of my own selfishness.

Somehow, Nick felt my gaze. Gingerly, he gave Tabitha a peck and helped her up. The swishing sound of Tabitha's big white wedding dress accented my humiliation. It was as if I were stuck there in that doorway, awed by the strength of their love. Nick had loved me once. But he had never loved me like that.

Wordlessly, Nick led his fiancée past me and into the room. I watched them huddle by Mom's bed, with Tabitha's crying waking her up. Weakly, Mom placed a soothing hand on Tabitha's tearing face.

I saw all of this in that brief moment that door to the hospital room closed shut. Closed shut on Nick's mom. Closed shut on my future with Nick. Closed shut on my dreams and me.

First Goodbyes

It was a snowy December day in Central Park at twilight. On an ordinary day, I'm sure this would have been a romantic, beautiful setting. Instead, I had come to deliver bad news. News that I feared would affect our relationship.

I watched him approach from a distance. Nick came straight from work at Chase Manhattan Bank in Downtown Manhattan to come see me. It had been my request that he come see me, for I knew better than he did that he needed an answer. As he approached, with his six-foot tall, dark wool-coated form, I contemplated the best way to break the heart of the one you love.

And I did love him. I loved Nick with all a heart and soul could afford, and then some. If love were a credit card, I was maxed out. He was the most perfectly romantic man I had ever met. Our worlds meshed completely, from a mutual love for sports to the simple appreciation of Bath and Body Works massage oil. He was sincere, intelligent, attentive. He loved me; I knew this. That I loved him; he knew this. These past two years, these past two and a half wonderful, wonderful years, my heart and spirit had been filled by his love. With him, I never wanted for anything.

Then why were we here? Why had I summoned him back to the scene of the crime, the reservoir in Central Park, where I first began to fall for him? Where he'd made that impromptu little speech about everything that he wants in a woman? Where we'd held hands and had walked all around the park, oblivious of everything and everyone? Where our lives had begun their life-changing, life-reaffirming, DNA-like grapevine?

I had brought us here.

And now he was there, five feet away from me. I embraced him with my love debt—more than my soul could spend. We must have hugged there for a full minute, our emotions syruping like hot molasses over buttermilk pancakes. I have been in love once before, but never quite like this. Nick made love so simple and easy for me.

Which made what I had to say next all the more

16

disconcerting. Too bad I never got to say it.

I didn't dare give him a kiss. I was too scared. He didn't give me a kiss either. Maybe he was too scared. Scared but in love, scared but in love. The story of every healthy relationship.

As he let me go, my eyes began watering against their will. I hated my lack of control around him. I looked cute as hell today, too—wearing my gray Elmer Fudd hat, dark blue scarf, and my diva-like gray wool coat. I wanted the package to look as good as the presentation, so there would be no question about my decision. So, of course, I started crying.

He hugged me again, and I silently thanked him for it. Gave me an opportunity to quit my boo-hooing.

"Jazzy...I'm moving to Chicago."

Say what!

Someone turned off the faucet of my tears. "What did you say?"

Nick disengaged me just enough to peer seriously into my eyes. "I'm moving to Chicago. There's a position for me at Harris Bank as a credit analyst. Same thing as I have here but they're paying me more. Also they're giving me a tuition waiver at DePaul University so I can get my MBA and advance within the bank. I'm leaving, Jasmine."

Whoa, whoa, whoa. I backed away from my boyfriend, never breaking eye contact. He had just said a mouthful. A heartful. "When did you decide this?"

"Last night."

This was not how I had envisioned this going down.

Our relationship was a partnership. "Without talking to me?" I protested.

"It's not like we're married or anything."

Ouch. I felt that one. I was too stunned to put together coherent sentences. "It's-it's- it's just so sudden, that's all. I...when do you leave?"

"Two weeks."

I felt my legs go. Something outside of me kept me standing upright.

Meekly, I said, "What about us?"

"What about us?" His response was cold, before he had a chance to regulate it.

17

"I—" I had to act fast. Smart and fast. "I've never been in a long distance relationship before." Good. That was diplomatic, leaves him an out, and doesn't play myself, either.

Too bad he did that for me. "And I wouldn't want you to start now."

What did I do, Nick? What did I do to make you do this to me, Nick? I wasn't ready. Someday I would be, but not today! I came to give you an answer, Nick! I came to tell you that I love you very, very much but I couldn't give you that right now. Could that decision hurt you so bad? Should that decision seismically alter our relationship? Should that decision destroy all the love we've enjoyed for the past two years? Two years, Nick?

I wanted to say all of this, but couldn't push the words out of my mouth. Call it inner reflex, call it instinct, call it basic black woman survival, but I resorted to saving my ass. My first, most costly adult dealing with the dreaded DFP: Damn Fool Pride. If this could fail, anything could fail. When it all boils down to it, women should never depend on a man for anything—except for him to hurt her heart.

Jacque.

Nick.

They always do.

"So I guess that's, it, huh?"

Nick's eyes searched mine, for weakness, perhaps? None here, baby. No weakness here. I have been weak for you for the last time. I have been weak for a man for the very last time.

Nick, resignedly: "I guess so."

He seemed unsure. Nick had made a big life decision yet he seemed to hedge a little bit. I wanted him to hedge. I wanted him to take back everything he had said these last three minutes. It wasn't fair. There were people in abusive relationships, people cheating on each other, people breaking other people's hearts for pure sport. And here Nick was, voluntarily ending our relationship, our imperfectly perfect relationship. It was not fair.

I turned away because that water flow problem with my eyes had started again. I could not think of anything other than the truth to tell him.

"I love you, Nick."

"I love you, Jasmine."

All this time he had been holding my hand. All this time this man, the love of my life, had been holding my hand, to ease the pain. I didn't realize he had been holding my hand until he let it go. Even when he hurt me, he loved me.

I watched him fade into the twinkling darkness of the night. I watched the man who had proposed to me fade right on out of my life.

2

I NEVER KNEW FLYING first class could feel so miserable. I vaguely remembered the ticket agent telling my tore-down, morose-looking face that they needed to balance the plane so that's why they had put me in first class. Even though I made good money these days, I came from money, so wasting it had never really been my style. Because when Winnie had turned me loose after I'd quit Columbia, I scraped like everyone else. I worked a shitty temp job as an administrative assistant in Manhattan and hustled to get by to pay my own rent. Damnit— I wasn't supposed to curse! At least I was trying not to. That was how miserable I felt.

For a woman crying her eyes out for three straight hours, I still looked good. Maybe it's because Winnie had taught me to always be presentable, no matter what hand life dealt you. Looking pretty was her version of a poker face. Winnie was the ultimate in looking cool, calm, and comely under fire.

Although I no longer speak to my mother, I still respected all that she's done. My parents got divorced and I didn't see her cry once. Raised my sister and me by herself. Moved us from Toronto to New York shortly after the divorce, when I was fourteen. Worked as a mathematician for one of the nation's largest pharmaceutical firms. Graduated MIT when she was still pregnant with Nia. If I was smart at all, I attributed it to her good genes.

I hate the fact that I haven't spoken to her in years.

Nick.

There went the pain again, wracking my heart and spirit. So much I gave up for him, to be with him, to be in love. There's a reason why women are afraid of rejection. It's because the reason always feels like this.

I guess some history was in order. We had dated for two and

a half years. After Nick had proposed to me— and I didn't say yes—he actually did leave for Chicago.

That was six years ago.

The last time I had seen him before this weekend's debacle was five years ago, shortly after I had moved to Atlanta. He and his boys, including Malloy, had run through Atlanta for Freaknik. Well, that was back when the rowdy, citywide black college student party had actually been worth calling a Freaknik.

I don't remember much of what was said during that visit to see me. All I remember was that I made some smartass remark about "not being a nun" when he asked me if I had been dating. We ended up messing around, but we did not make love. If we had, maybe I could have forgotten him like I have the others.

Hm. The others. I could list their names but it would sound like an inverted music video role call. Don't trip now—I am not a slut. Up until Nick moved to Chicago six years ago, I had only had two real boyfriends: him and Jacque.

Nick was my true love.

Don't even get me started on Jacque.

So, as you can imagine, I had a lot of living to make up for. I had met Nick a mere three months after I dumped Jacque for cheating on me. Malloy once said, "Women don't cheat unless men give them a reason to." The difference between women and men? At least we need a reason. Jacque must be the stupidest nigga alive. Because when it comes to sex, you know I put it down.

I wasn't out there-out there…but I was out there. Yet still, in the end, it always came down to Nick. Invariably. The love we had shared was the realest thing there ever was.

Was, of course. It was all gone. The tears were real. Our love, no longer.

*

Charlotte picked me up in her sleek, sporty little two-door BMW coupe. Emerging from the baggage claim, I could hear her before I saw her car. Jay-Z. She's a hustler, baby. She's a, she's a hustler.

21

Charlotte sang along, sunroof open to embrace the afternoon autumnal sunshine. Better ask about her.

I smiled. Charlotte was a trip, but a trip worth taking. Born Charlotte Royer in Brooklyn, New York—check that: Flatbush, Brooklyn, New York—she fiercely clung to any vestige of her New York upbringing, particularly the music. At twenty-seven, Charlotte had a dark brown, Rand McNally-curvy body that men and women would pay for. Well, in fact they did, or had. During our last year at CAU, Charlotte had danced at this cigarette-and-stab-wound hole-in-the-wall strip club called Body Tap. With her daughter's name tatted on her chest and a crouching lioness on her shoulder (she was a Leo, natch), Charlotte barely made the two-tattoo minimum to dance there.

The reason why we had bonded so quickly was because we had been older than everyone else in our class. My last year at Clark Atlanta University was when I met Charlotte. She was twenty-three and I was twenty-seven, still taking what was essentially a freshman class in our Communications major. My excuse was that CAU was my third school in eight years while in pursuit of that elusive bachelors degree, dropping credits like dominoes along the way. Charlotte's excuse was better—she had a baby girl to take care of.

As she bobbed her head to the seductive hip hop beat, I slid into the seat next to her, tossing my daybag in the back. Charlotte stopped singing long enough to give me a hug. Damn, I needed that.

"Dang, ma. You was back quick!" Charlotte teased, peeling off from the baggage claim curb. "One day out there and you're back?"

"Tell me about it," I brooded.

I knew she was trying to be helpful, but her curiosity got the best of her. "So did he marry that chick?"

"Damn near. My flight was late and I had to interrupt the wedding."

Charlotte nearly veered off the road. "You busted up the wedding?"

"Not exactly. He's still marrying her," I sulked. "Just not now. In a month from now. It's over."

"No it's not, ma! He didn't go through with that wedding

22

because somewhere inside him, he knows he loves you! That's the deal right there, girl."

I stared blankly at the cars we passed on I-85. I knew the deal. "He didn't go through with the wedding because his mother fainted."

Charlotte started. I could see her suppress a giggle. "Oh."

We rode in silence for a full minute. I could have rode in silence for a full hour.

"Don't trip off him, J. Don't ever let no man get you down," she supported.

Here we go...

It was as if Charlotte could read my mind through my eyebrows. "I'm for real. Boys suck. That's all men are—overgrown boys. They are mentally and emotionally inferior than we are; therefore..."

"Charlotte," I interrupted, eyes half-closed, "could we save the sermonizing for another day?"

"I am not sermonizing; I'm tellin' it real. Look, Jasmine, I am not gonna let you piss and moan over some guy you dropped some six years ago," Charlotte rationalized. "So get over that shit. I already know what to do to make you feel better. I already called Nadine, and we're gonna..."

"Nadine. Great." As if I needed her judgmental mug in my grill right now.

"We goin' to the spot, J, we goin' to the spot. Just cool out, ma, and allow your girls to take care of you." Charlotte turned her attention back to her favorite pastime: breaking down men.

"Now in the case of Anonymous—"

"Nick," I adjusted.

"Marriage Boy," she amended. "In the case of Marriage Boy, we have a clear cut example of how men are like children, drawn to women as kids are to candy, requiring constant supervision and instruction if we ever hope for them to be responsible, self-governing adults..."

I groaned inaudibly and made like I was asleep.

*

23

But she was on a roll. Charlotte continued to preside over the court of her opinions later on that night, as we sat at a table in one of our favorite hang out spots, ESPN Sports Zone. Located in the tony, party section of Atlanta known as Buckhead, the Sports Zone had been our informal gathering spot for about a year, as we dissected our lives over some mediocre chicken strips but in front of a bevy of TVs. While Nadine and I were the sports fans and enjoyed the various sporting events on the ubiquitous televisions, Charlotte pretty much only liked the place because she actually did like the mediocre chicken strips.

I have to admit, we looked cute. Charlotte, ever the fashion and style guru of our troika, was studded out in a form-fitting, V-neck evening dress. I was killing 'em in a hot little sheer top number that stopped above my navel, giving a hint of the small, cursive tattoo that read "Jazzy" on my tabletop tummy. And Nadine was, well, Nadine.

Nadine Montgomery was my friend. Nadine Montgomery was also my boss. She was the producer of the morning news show I co-anchored for WAGA TV, Fox 5 News. Just before I had finally gotten up the nerve to push for my promotion from production coordinator to on air personality over a year ago, my former boss, a stodgy, visionless white guy, was replaced with hotshot defector from WSB Channel 2 News Nadine Montgomery. In the interests of having newscasters that reflected Atlanta, Nadine sacked several of the lazy, underwhelming anchors and replaced them with young hungry talent like me. Basically, she gave a hardworking assistant a chance to anchor the graveyard shifts of the weekend morning shows. Soon, my training and skill had impressed them enough to expand my responsibilities to the weekday morning shows. After winning Atlanta Journalist Society's New Television Anchor of the Year, I proved Nadine to be the genius she was. She saw something in me that I, at times, didn't even see in myself. That's why we were friends. I owed my career to her.

In and of herself, Nadine was a special woman. She was not particularly striking. When she tried dressing up (tonight was not one of those nights), Nadine looked decent. Not fine, not drop dead gorgeous, but decent. But when she didn't try, as was the case tonight, her short, close-cropped hair and blue-black skin did not do her light pink eye shadow any favors. Yeah, Nadine's my girl and all, but she had all the fashion sense of the preacher's daughter she was. With her conservative, top buttoned blouse and her prim, ankle-length skirt, Nadine could make a nun look like a porn star. From Albany, Georgia (Albinny, to locals), the woman was as prim and proper as a Jane Austen novel. However, what my girl lacked in style, she made up for in personality. Nadine was honest to a fault, and I loved her for that. While she could be dowdy at times, she was equally as ambitious. She was honest, yet tactful, and always saw the best of a situation. Nadine was the perfect counterbalance to Charlotte.

But that's not to say I didn't have issues with Nadine.

"So he's going to marry her, huh?"

"I thought we've covered that, Nadine." I focused on a far off TV that broadcast a Braves-Marlins game.

"I'm sorry. I didn't mean to overstate the obvious." Nadine turned her attention back to her drink.

Running interference for us, as usual, was Charlotte. "I was tellin' her earlier that she's better off without him. A man ain't nothin' but trouble."

"Then why do you have so many?" rebutted Nadine.

"Please. Ain't no man with me right now."

"Excuse me. Then why have you had so many?" Nadine restated.

I covered my drink with a snort.

"Don't get me started, Virgin Mary…" sniped Charlotte.

"Heffas…please. This is not helping me," I said.

"Moping over him isn't helping either," Charlotte pointed out.

Nadine dove into her chicken strips. "She's allowed. She gave up so much for him."

I glared my instantaneous hatred for her. Sometimes that bitch could be so shallow. "I know you're not talking about Rodney."

Charlotte could see this one coming, so she averted her gaze. This would forever be a sore spot between Nadine and me. I mean, it was a unique situation, having had my ex-boyfriend, who had once proposed to me, end up going out with my friend—and end up proposing to her. The wedding was set for October 18th, in three weeks.

The cheap bastard had even used the same ring that he used with me to give to Nadine. Every time I saw that shiny, one-carat promise of forever sitting snugly on her fat little finger, I wanted to expose her fiancé. But I wouldn't. No matter how much this short, self-righteous, little woman would test me.

"I'm not. At least not by name," Nadine defended. "I mean in the year and a half I've known you, your best shot at happiness was Rod. But ever since then, it's been all about Nick. No guy you've dated since then could hold a candle to Nick. Quite honestly, you never gave them a chance."

Charlotte continued her suddenly newfound interest in NASCAR.

I stirred my drink violently. Now I may not be the most tactful girl in the world, but even I knew when to shut up and take the Fifth. Because if I did open my mouth, I would tear her apart—or add more fuel to her fire.

"Listen Jasmine, Charlotte and I both care about you. We do," Nadine expressed earnestly, her Georgian accent sounding folksy and prominent while simultaneously dragging Charlotte by the hair into the mix. "I'm not telling you all this to hurt your feelings. I'm telling you this because it's the truth.

"When you told Rodney no after he proposed to you, I didn't say anything. When you called Nick the same day and begged him to take you back—and he said no—I didn't say anything. When you raced out after the show on Saturday to catch a plane to San Diego to go stop the wedding, I didn't say anything. I cannot continue to be a silent friend, Jasmine. You need to let Nick go."

I didn't want to say it, but she was right. She was always right. Even though she was a mere five months older than I was, Nadine was always right. The practical, no-nonsense, bottom line one. She rationalized before she felt. She was the perfect TV executive.

Playing peacemaker/tiebreaker, Charlotte added, "Fuck a man, ma. Make business your man."

"Right!" agreed Nadine. "You've been doing some spectacular work, Jasmine. The station loves you. The people of Atlanta love you. And, most importantly, the ratings love you."

Nadine stole a moment to collect herself. Daringly, she added, "'Fuck a man. Ma."

Charlotte broke into hysterics. For the first time that day—from that miserable four-hour flight, to the ride in Charlotte's Beemer, to the impromptu shopping trip at Lenox, to the dinner at the Sports Zone—I finally cracked a smile. Virtuous little Nadine cursing was enough to do that to you.

"You're stronger than that, J; you know it. He may have once been the love of your life, but now it's time to love yourself just as much," Charlotte advised. She flicked her bob-style micro-braids behind her neck with authority. "No man makes or breaks us. Even as childlike and simple these men can be, I know that you will end up with the man who was meant for you. We all will. But until they find us, or he finds you, you have got to make yourself happy. You should be doing that anyways. Nick was never gonna make you happy. He was gonna complement your happiness. Just make yourself happy, Jasmine."

I took a look at my girls at the table. Both pairs of their comforting eyes encouraged me. I could appreciate this kind of support.

I forged a simple smile. "Fuck a man. Ma."

*

The next couple days passed without incident. I gradually reintroduced myself to my life. I slipped back into the work routine on Monday, waking up at my normally obscene four A.M. hour to throw on some jeans and a blouse and head down to the station. In an act of rebellion, I went out and chopped off four inches to my hair, and had it spiral curled to within an inch of its life. While Nadine was initially shocked, she warmed up to it. I mean Monica Kaufman at WSB was always changing hairstyles; it's not like I bleached my hair blonde like that sista did. New hairstyle, new start.

My life wasn't bad these days. I maintained a cute little townhouse out in the upper-scale but overpriced Virginia Highlands area of Atlanta. Driving to work meant pushing the

Lex, a shiny, champagne colored four-door sedan I had bought three months into my anchor stint at WAGA. Hell, I deserved a decent car—I had been roughing it in a Geo Tracker throughout my last year at Clark in my production assistant days. I kinda missed my pink pseudo-jeep. Her name was Wylona, like Ja'Net DuBois' character on Good Times.

Yep, I had a lot to be thankful for, I convinced myself. That brass ring of college, one I had been chasing through eight years of school off and on, had finally paid off after over two years in the trenches. I had a job I loved, a nice house, a beautiful car (I called this one Alexia), and supportive, if not diverse, friends. If I wanted it, there was a slew of brothas left over from my college days that wanted to holla at me. The professional men had some flavor, too, as the occasional guest to the morning show would subtly flirt with me on camera and then unabashedly follow it up off camera. Every once in a blue moon, I would let the random professional-looking black man in Lenox get far enough along in his impossibly scripted patter to ask for my phone number, even though I always, always took theirs. I wasn't doing this just because I was a local mini-celebrity. This had always been my rule—and it worked. Life was good.

That was why I didn't see this day coming.

"Jasmine."

Nadine called me into her office with all the authority her position commanded. See, we had two kinds of tones at work. There was the "Hey, gurl, I wanna talk to you" voice and then there was the "Hey, Jasmine, I need to talk to you" voice. My boss was calling for me.

I shut the door behind me, as per her instructions, before sitting down. Her clear, glass, diamond-shaped Heritage Atlanta Radio and Television award bounced light from the open window a million different directions. As I had so many times before, I read the smoke gray inscription on the glass trophy. Nadine Montgomery, WSB-TV. Producer of the Year. I won't even front—I wanted one of those trophies, one for Anchor of the Year. I wanted one bad. Someday.

Nadine read my mind. "You want one, don't you?"

"So what's up, boss?" I changed the subject smoothly. It was a quarter after nine A.M., and I was already changed out of my on

28

air top and back into a relaxed, dress casual blouse.

She grinned. "I know I gave you the rest of the morning off last week, but I want you to stick around for the ten A.M. production meeting."

I groaned. "Oh, come on, Nadine! I was gonna go get my teeth bonded by Dr. Ainsley at 10:30! Do you have any idea how long I've been waiting to see this man? The reason I only had to wait two months for him is because Toni Braxton cancelled at the last minute!"

"Get over it."

"Two months, Nadine!"

Nadine smiled sternly, her sparkling white overbite taunting me like Bugs Bunny did Elmer Fudd. "I need you at this meeting, Jasmine."

The boss had spoken.

*

"…And our last order of business…"

I was practically asleep on my feet. Or in my chair. I privately fumed that I had missed out on Atlanta's dentist to the stars for this wholly uneventful production meeting in which the only input I had contributed was agreeing to switch from donuts to muffins for craft service. Nadine was so getting a toaster for a wedding gift.

"…is to announce one of the five nominees for the HART Award for Broadcast Anchor, a professional in our own midst…"

I began to tune Nadine out, stuffing a jelly donut in my mouth. Just what Derek, the two-time HART Award winner, seven-time nominee, and all around egomaniacal five P.M. anchor needed—yet another HART nomination.

"Jasmine Selene!"

The donut fell out of my mouth—right onto my blouse. Now I see why we were switching to muffins.

"Me?" I squeaked, amid thunderous applause and my jelly stain.

Nadine led the charge, as she walked over to where I sat among glad-handing, backslapping coworkers. I just sat there, stunned as everyone there, who were proud of me.

Uncharacteristically, Nadine reached out and gave me a hug. "Congratulations on a brilliant first year, honey."

I sat there as speechless as a whore in confession.

*

"So what does this mean?"

We sat in a booth at the Cheesecake Factory in Buckhead. Lunch was on Nadine, or, rather, on the station. Everyone remotely involved with my on air performance had shown their excitement for me via phone and fax. My email box was blowing up, too.

Nadine popped the cork on the champagne and began to fill her glass. I watched on with horror. Nadine was having a drink? This was a special occasion.

"This means the beginning of the rest of your career. Jasmine…I don't think you understand how big this opportunity is."

"Opportunity? This is just a nomination. There are four other anchors up for the award," I reminded my boss. "Besides, I'm the new kid on the block. The Heritage Club members will hate on me just for only doing this a year. Ain't no way I'm winning this thing."

"Ain't isn't a word. Neither is lose," Nadine stressed. "You have to win this thing."

I smacked my gums with glee as the waiter escorted a huge plate of cajun chicken pasta my way. I wasn't paying Nadine no mind. "I thought you always told me that 'the only thing I have to do is stay black and die.'" Nadine was always good for these useless yet colorful little expressions.

"Look, Jasmine. There is an opening coming up for a nighttime anchor position at Fox Headquarters in LA in November. Fox is actually gonna try its hand at doing a national evening news show on the network, apart from Fox News Channel, like CBS with Dan Rather or NBC News with Peter Jennings."

Taking a moment to chew, I glanced askance at Nadine. "Fox

Nightly News with Jasmine Selene?"

"It could happen," opined Nadine, starting in on her oh so exotic dish of biscuits and gravy.

"I think we're making an evolutionary leap on the career path. How could I go from a local anchor to a national one without having had any real field experience?" I rationalized. "Every time you look, Brian Williams is running off to Nepal or somewhere, saving the yaks. How do you know they'd want me?"

"The word is out. They are looking for you!"

I mouthed the word, "Me?"

"Practically," she amended. "They want someone young, beautiful, ethnic, professional, who is versatile. Now tell me that 'ain't' you."

"You just described every third graduating Broadcast Journalism major," I dampened.

"Look, you're the hottest rookie anchor in the whole Fox network, whether you know it or not. You've already won the Atlanta Journalist Society's award, the Society for Excellence in Broadcasting award…"

"I have?" That was news to me.

"Oh yeah. Sorry to spoil the surprise for you. They're making their announcement next week."

"How do you know?"

"I'm on the board."

"Oh. Um, thanks."

"And winning the HART will give you the trifecta," Nadine finished, gushing. "With all that hardware from the local level—in your first year—I would be shocked and horrified if you didn't get this job. If the folks out in LA don't see how much talent you have and hire you, I may just sue the network myself."

I sat there, stunned and stuttering. "I—I…well…Why do you care so much? Why are you so excited for me?"

"You winning the HART as a rookie anchor will look good for everybody," confessed Nadine. "It'll generate great publicity for the station, make a local celebrity out of you, and make me look platinum as a producer. Wouldn't you want to hire the producer who took raw talent and molded it into the consensus Atlanta broadcast journalism anchor in one year?"

"Hey, I wasn't 'raw.' I'm always refined—and a lady."

"You win this thing, Jasmine, and we come out looking like champs. Super Bowl champs." Nadine sank her teeth into the gravy laden plate. "And also, Jasmine…Focusing on this award will keep your mind off of the triflingness of life."

I smiled ruefully. "You mean Nick."

Nadine smiled. "I mean men."

*

"So explain to me how this works."

Walking up an infinitesimal staircase to the top of the BellSouth Building, Charlotte and I worked out side by side on dueling StairMasters at Run 'N Shoot down in southwest Atlanta, the SWATS. My slim, elongated, five-foot nine-inch frame put the pedal to the metal. Sweat glistened off my honey brown face. It was hard work staying so beautiful.

"Basically, five anchors each year are nominated for a HART award."

"Which stands for?"

"Heritage Atlanta Radio and Television award." I stole a glance at my picture in the Atlanta Journal-Constitution under an article explaining the very same thing. The paper was propped up on the machine's bookholder like the trophy it was. "It's basically like the local Oscars for news broadcasting."

The actress in Charlotte could feel that. "And you was one of the five nominated? That's tight, ma. When do they pick the winner?"

"The awards ceremony is a month from now, October 26th." I began pumping my legs even harder. "I have a month to do something newsworthy."

Charlotte was distracted. Another guy, sculpted of pure cinnamon granite, had glided into the weight room, in all of a tank top and shorts. "Newsworthy?"

"Yeah. For whatever reason, the HART Club always chooses the winner based off of something extraordinarily newsworthy they do during that month between nomination and the ceremony."

I snorted, legs operating at peak efficiency. "Monica Kaufman screwed up the whole process five years ago."

Charlotte was very talented. She established eye contact with the big, brown Adonis while somehow maintaining a conversation with me. "The lady with all the hairdos on Channel 2?"

"The very same. She went out and did some exposé on teen sex slavery in the West End right before the voting submission deadline and walked away with the HART in a cakewalk. Ever since then, everyone nominated turns it up a notch that month. You should've seen the work that Steve Coetzer and Michelle Hollister did four years ago! I thought I was gonna cry during Fiona Washington's piece on unwed teenage mothers on smack two years ago. And Lisa Rayam raised the bar last year with her groundbreaking feature on the state of the forgotten Georgia Indian reservations. October turns into kinda like a sweeps month for Atlanta news broadcasting."

"That's cool," mumbled Charlotte, visually luring the guy over in her direction.

I confined my disgust to a happy little smile. Char was Char. I gathered my breath as the StairMaster began to slow to cool down rate.

"Shit!" she cursed, as the beautiful, buff, brown man was met halfway to Charlotte's StairMaster by his girlfriend, who bounded into the room by hugging him up.

I laughed.

"Niggas and flies, niggas and flies," Charlotte groused. "The less I like niggas, the more I like flies."

"Don't sweat him, Char. He was too pretty for his own good."

"You know I don't sweat no man, ma." She pumped along in silence for a moment. "I'm glad how you handled Nadine the other day."

"You mean over at the Zone?"

"Yeah. Not everybody could take that kinda mess from their girl who's marrying their ex."

I shook it off. "I figure Nadine's gonna be pretty unbearable between now and her wedding day so I just better get used to it. Maybe when she finally gets some, she'll quit telling people how to live their lives."

"Okay?" Charlotte amened. "I mean a thirty year-old virgin? No wonder she's so damn uptight. It makes my coochie dry up just thinking about it!"

I huffed, but really didn't have much to add to that. It had been a few months since anyone had earned entrance to my own Cupid's Grove.

"So it still doesn't bother you that Nadine's marrying Rodney?"

"Why should it?" I shrugged.

"Because we're less than a month away and it looks like they're actually gonna do it." Charlotte wiped the sweat from her brow. "I've said it before and I'll say it again: if that were me, I would be straight buggin'. If you went out and married Sperm Donor, I don't know if we could be cool anymore. Date him, fine. I think that'd be kinda foul, but that wouldn't really irk me. But marry him? Oh hell no!"

Sperm Donor was Juan, the Puerto Rican father of Charlotte's child.

"Look, if marrying Rod makes Nadine happy, it makes her happy. Am I supposed to hate on that?"

"Atlanta ain't filled with nothin' but men. Single, fine, professional, black men," Charlotte pointed out. "She couldn't find a man you didn't date?"

Despite the cool down speed, I worked my legs faster.

"Rodney wasn't the first. Don't you ever get tired of Nadine going through your leftovers?"

*

This time when I sat down in Nadine's office, I looked at her HART with a little more than admiration in my eyes. I looked at it as if it were going to be mine.

"It's strategy time, honey," Nadine said behind the closed door. "Bump that 'It's just a pleasure being nominated' stuff. We need to start putting you out on assignments that will raise your profile, give you added exposure."

"What did you have in mind?" I asked.

"Well, the team and I are putting our heads together to come

34

up with a story sexy enough to win you that HART. But for now, we're just going to reintroduce the people to Jasmine Selene."

"What? Am I finally moving to five o'clocks?"

"Get real, Jasmine. Derek would have both you and I fired. He's one of the few anchors in town who could practically earn a co-producer credit on his show."

"I'm teasing, Nadine. But I'm listening."

Nadine hopped up and began to pace the room, in thought. "I know this isn't much, but it's a beginning. We've gotten you an interview with a young dotcom mogul from DC who is really creating a stir with his company."

The idea had me bored just hearing it. "Come on, Nadine. Nobody wants to hear jack about some dotcom millionaire whose company is probably gonna burn through its venture capital in three weeks! The story'll probably be dead before we air it!"

"Listen, Jasmine, the company is sound. Check it out for yourself. They're called 4sight.com. The company is already turning a profit and East Coast Capital just gave them another infusion of funds to the tune of thirty-seven million dollars. Now if ECC is shelling out that kind of money to a company that is already making money, obviously there's some merit to their business."

"Which is?" I asked, stifling a yawn.

"Building programming for high speed wireless networks." I shot Nadine a quizzical look, who shrugged in response. "I don't know what that means either. But he's gonna be here in four hours so hit the 'Net and find out."

I rose out of my seat and stopped at the door. "Who is he?"

Nadine smirked to herself. "He's the CEO of the company. A real tall, smooth looking brotha. Real polite and charming when we met for drinks last night, shortly after he got into town. You'd like him."

I rolled my eyes. Whatever. "What's his name?"

"J. Anthony Daniels."

My brow furrowed. For some reason, that name sounded real familiar.

"It'll give you something to do while we piece together a plan to get you that HART."

"Right." I started out the door.

"Besides...It might be an interesting interview," Nadine grinned.

"I can hardly wait."

*

Actually, I could. Four hours later, my Internet research had yielded very little. There was a lot of technical mumbo-jumbo on the 4sight.com website, but little in usable information for me. The company appeared to be committed to creating original programming for wireless Internet devices such as cell phones and Palm Pilots and the like, as well as helping shape the infrastructure of these wireless networks. While there were short, paragraph-long bios of the 4sight team, not much was said about its CEO, Mr. Daniels. Just a short blurb about how he was originally from Philadelphia but resided in DC. I really didn't care too much either, seeing how I was out to put in my fifteen, twenty minutes, and be done with the interview.

I consulted my notes on a clipboard as I strode through the hallways snaking toward the studio interview room. I was already dressed in a professional, conservative navy colored business suit-skirt combination that I made sexy with a splash of color in the form of a red scarf. My curls shined, still a little wet from the spritz of water I gave them moments ago. As usual, Tyrone, our makeup artist, had my face looking as smooth as a sheet of glass and as flawless as a clear lake.

Our camerawoman, Angie, stopped me outside the door to the interview room. She sucked her teeth admiringly. "Gurl, you sho' is a lucky one today."

"Why's that, Ang?"

"Because this dude up in here is foine! I mean slap-ya-momma foine! And he's smooth, too! He just asked me for a glass of water, and I was ready to have his baby! Mm!"

I chuckled. Although only on this job for a little over a year, I had interviewed my share of fine brothas. When I interviewed Maxwell, I was ready to stop the tape and suck his toes. "I think you were ready to have his baby before he asked for some water, Ang."

"Irregardless, you get that man's number! He is too fine!"

"How do you know he's not married? Maybe he has a girlfriend?"

Angie sucked her teeth dismissively. "It don't mean a thang, if he ain't got that rang! Ya heard?"

I smiled. "Ready?"

"After you, Miss Jasmine."

I walked into the room with my head down, reviewing my clipboard notes. When I looked up—

Jacque!!!

"Jesus Christ," I let slip out. Well, I guess it was better than cussing, right?

I stood there like the village idiot, grinning in an attempt to maintain control. Angie stood right next to me, smiling and basking in the glow of his fineness. I clutched the clipboard for fear I would drop it and make an even bigger fool of myself than I was now.

For the first time in eight years, I had seen my first boyfriend. My first love. My first everything.

Jacque stood, crossing over the distance to greet me. It was as if those three short steps lingered on an eternity, I was just so concentrated on seeing him. Jacque was so tall, brown, and broad-shouldered, I hated him for being even finer than he was when we were dating. Only a couple of years my senior at thirty-two, the clean-shaven Jacque was in the prime of his life, looking as handsome as a black Ken doll, wavy, pretty-boy hair to boot. I barely registered the impeccable Christian Dior double-breasted suit that hung comfortably on his lean, built, six-three frame like a bathrobe, it just fit him that well. Jacque topped off his look with a stylish, thin moustache, no goatee.

I hated him because he still looked incredibly handsome. I hated him because I knew that I would always have this reason to hate him.

"Hello, Pre—" Jacque stopped himself. I fed him an evil look, just out of habit. He was about to call me a name he had forfeited the rights to a long time ago: Pretty. "Hello, Jasmine."

"J. Anthony Daniels?" I questioned, tersely shaking his hand. I breezed by to take my seat.

"Sounds real professional, huh?" he smiled glibly. His teeth were white and straight and perfect. I hate you!!!

Still, I couldn't believe I'd missed that. "What? Jacque isn't smooth enough?"

Jacque sat down across from me, comfortably engaging my eyes. "I don't know. You tell me."

I could feel myself withering, so I snapped to attention. "Angie! Angela!"

Angie snapped out of her waking dream.

I gestured toward the camera. "Do you mind?"

"Oh! Right." Angie reluctantly scrambled behind the camera and prepped herself to begin shooting. She commanded the floater camera on me while another camera opposite her was preset to record all of Jacque's responses.

As I busied myself unnecessarily with arranging my already pinhead-neat notes, I could feel Jacque's intense gaze boring a hole into my head, if not my heart. "What?"

He shielded a smile. "Nothing."

"How long did you know you were going to be interviewed by me?" I demanded. Then, I saw Angie's camera red light go on.

"We are rolling!" cried Angie.

As Jacque started to answer, I hissed out, "Never mind."

Just as I had performed countless times before, I turned my head toward the camera and the cue card guy standing next to Angie.

"In five…four…three…two…"

"Well, good morning Atlanta. Glad to have you with us. For our featured news special today we are speaking with J. Anthony Daniels of the innovative 4sight.com, a dynamic, high flying online technology company that has survived the dotcom purge of the last several years."

I swiveled to face Jacque, and his beautiful, brown, bad, lying, deceitful, cheating…FACE!

"Now, Mr. Daniels…What is it that has kept 4sight.com afloat while many, many other dotcoms have folded and gone under in this highly volatile, continuously risky, cybertechnology landscape?"

Jacque seemed a bit blown away at how freakin' professional I truly was. Sure, if he were having this interview with some other journalist, he wouldn't have mentally half-stepped. But with me…well…I guess he was surprised to see how much I've grown up since we last talked.

"Well…uh…Jasmine…"

"Ms. Selene," I adjusted firmly.

"Sorry. Well…uh…Miss Selene…" He looked so uncomfortable, I wanted to pull up a couch and a pint full of Haagen Dazs.

"Ms.," I corrected, hammering his toes.

"Ms. Selene," recovered Jacque professionally, "what has kept 4sight.com financially solvent and profitable is our sound business model. We have a five point, four phase business plan that not only focuses on our long-term possibilities, but also our short-term realities. We are in Phase Two of the plan."

"So what is 4sight.com's product? What is your hook?"

"4sight is dedicated to providing original programming for high speed wireless networks, as well as the infrastructure for those networks."

"When you say the 'infrastructure,' do you mean the actual hardware, such as satellites and cell towers, or do you mean the software programming infrastructure that creates the virtual networks?"

Jacque cracked a thin smile. He had no idea I was this smart.

I could tell he was warming up to the interview. "The software, Ms. Selene. We have developed a high speed operating system that we anticipate will become the Microsoft of broadband wireless devices."

"And by original programming, you mean that 4sight is creating content, correct?"

"Providing content, yes."

"Well that's ambitious, Mr. Daniels." I was setting him up. "Do you think it's wise for an Internet start-up to be in the entertainment and technology industries? Aren't you afraid of spreading yourselves too thin?"

That question zinged him. He blinked twice before answering. "Actually, Ms. Selene, we pay licensing fees to obtain the rights to broadcast the content on our website, as well as for our high speed wireless network, when it is up and running."

"With all of this licensing and network building…Just how does 4sight.com expect to make any money?" I challenged.

Jacque flashed me a coded look that read Damn, woman! I smiled serenely. Yet he was up for the challenge.

"Advertising revenues. If we are the gateway to wireless device interconnectivity, then we will be the sole provider for advertising space for cell phones and personal digital assistants on a high speed, national level. And with all the wi-fi hotspots popping up at malls and Starbucks and the like, that's one huge gateway."

"Very well," I accepted, ceasing fire for the moment. I could swear I saw a glimmer of something in his arrogant eyes. "On your website it says that you're from Philadelphia. According to my research, you're actually from—"

"Shit!" cursed Angie. "We have to cut. Film difficulties. Gimme two minutes."

As Angie darted out of the room, cue card guy in tow, I gained a newfound interest in my clipboard.

"It's nice to see you," Jacque said.

Silence.

"How've you been?" he asked.

Nada.

"I'm sorry," he offered.

"You damn right you are!" I snapped. "You're sorry and you're tired! What part of 'Don't call, write, fax, or email me' did you not understand!"

"Well aren't we the Big Headed One, Ms. Selene?" Jacque teased. "Believe it or not, I had no idea that you would be interviewing me. As a matter of fact, I had no idea you worked for this station, let alone were even in Atlanta."

"Until last night," I surmised.

"Until last night," he agreed. "She really is a nice woman, Nadine. She speaks very highly of you, Jasmine Selene. And why in the world are you going by your first and middle names?"

"I like the way they sound."

"I like the way your last name sounds."

"It doesn't matter what you like anymore!" I burst. Once again, I shut myself up. Control. You're on my turf, Jacque.

"It's been a long time since Toronto," he said quietly. Jacque was talking about the time he'd come up to the University of

40

Toronto to steal me away from Nick while I was at journalism camp. He had been assisted by my mother, who hated Nick like the sun hated the horizon. That was when I told the lying bastard that I never wanted to see him again.

So why was I seeing him again???

"People grow a lot in eight years."

"People don't grow out of cheating," I shot back.

Disarming me, he said, "People don't grow out of love."

Before I could sass him back with "Yes they do!" Angie was upon us. I shut my trap as she shuttled around behind the camera. I could see Jacque admiring me in the periphery of my vision. I wanted to gouge his eyes out with the heels of my Kenneth Cole pumps.

"Okay, we're ready," Angie sang out.

Good. Time to get this nonsense over with. J. Anthony Daniels.

"And we're rolling in five, four, three, two…"

"Mr. Daniels—" I was unnerved by the way Jacque kept smiling. Threw me off. "Mr. Daniels, what would you say is 4sight's greatest asset?"

"Its people."

I gulped. That stupid smile was getting to me. So much so, I ignored his junior high business class canned answer. "And with a background in international business, how did you come about becoming CEO two years ago of this start-up based in Washington, DC?"

"Will you marry me?"

An audible gasp escaped from Angie behind the camera. I was too shocked to be angry. Hell, I was too shocked to close my barn door for a mouth.

The next thing I knew, I looked down and this fool was on his knees. One knee. With a ring in his hand.

"Jasmine Selene…Will you marry me?"

"So that was Jasmine?"

"For better or worse," answered Nick, missing the irony.

Nick and Tabitha lay in the Jacuzzi tub in the master bath of their comfortable, Playa del Rey home in Los Angeles. The bubbles obscured their bodies, soaping them down in the warm water. She held his walnut brown body close against her creamy

41

butterscotch one, grazing her hand lightly over his curved, firm chest. Tomorrow was his first day on set and she was taking care of her little movie star.

"I'll take worse," muttered Tabitha sourly. "What did you ever see in her?"

"I was young. She was my first love. What makes anyone fall for their first love? You're just too young to know any better."

Tabitha smiled sweetly. "You're my first love."

Nick leaned back and gave her a peck. "I know. I won't let you down."

"I know you won't, Babycakes." She gave him a peck back. "I love you so much, Nick...I don't ever want to lose you."

"You won't," he soothed. "You won't."

"Good." Tabitha shifted her body in the bath water. "So you promise me you'll never see Jasmine again?"

Nick angled to face his fiancée. "Why do you say that?"

"She's bad news, Nick. Just promise me, please."

"Well, I had no plans on seeing her again. But I can't help it if the girl's at the same place I am."

"I know. But if you have to see her, leave her alone. In fact, run."

"Precious, everything is over between Jasmine and me. You're the woman I love. The woman I'm going to marry."

Tabitha cocked her head cutely. "Say more things like that."

Nick grinned. "That sounded like Rachel. You've been watching Friends, haven't you?"

She sighed. "I figured I was gonna have to if I had to cohabitate with you a month from now."

Nick rearranged himself so that he was facing his bride-to-be. He studied her eyes deeply, admiringly. "You know how much I love you, right?"

"Enough to marry me and live with me forever?"

"You damn skippy." Nick engaged her in a passionate, soulful kiss.

When he released her, they hugged. In his ear, Tabitha whispered, "I don't want you to ever see her again."

Back in her ear, Nick whispered, "Done."

3

"YES!"

"Angie, shut up!" I ordered. "And turn that thing off!"

Smiling like a drunken angel, Angie was reluctant to comply. "But this is historic! This is romantic! This—"

"Can be edited around," I finished firmly. "Turn it off, Ang."

I turned my attention to the fool on his knee. "Boy, get up."

"Not until you say yes" was Jacque's response.

"Then I hope you brought kneepads and a sack lunch."

I made to get up, but he grabbed my hand. "Jasmine, I want to marry you."

"Where the hell is this coming from, Jacque? I haven't seen you in eight years! Now, all of a sudden, you want to marry me? And get off of your knee!"

Not letting go of my hand, Jacque climbed back into his seat. "Look, Pretty—" My skin crawled when he said that—"I know this is crazy, but something bigger than us is working here! I didn't even know you were going to interview me until last night, when Nadine mentioned it. That's when it struck me that we were meant to be together."

"If we were meant to be together then you never would have—" I stopped. A professionally composed smile to my camerawoman. "Excuse me, Angie, but could you give us a few minutes, please?"

Her smile faded. I kept mine plastered until the door shut behind her. Then, back to business. "If we were meant to be together then you never would have cheated on me!"

"You're right," Jacque agreed. "We weren't meant to be together—then. But it's been eight years, Jasmine. Eight years! A man learns a lot in eight years. He learns what it's like to be in a room full of people and still feel lonely. He learns what it's like

43

to compare every woman to only one woman—and find them all lacking. He learns what it's like to miss the only woman he ever truly loved."

Here came the hate again. I used hate as a defense mechanism because Jacque could be so freakin' smooth at times. He could also be as disingenuous as a telephone psychic. "You don't love me, Jacque!"

"Of course I do. I always have and I always will," he professed. "After Nadine told me yesterday that you were interviewing me, I just knew it had to be fate. Of all the people in the world to interview me…Of all the people in Atlanta to interview me…It had to be you. That's the story of my love life: it had to be you."

Touching story, I'm sure. "And the ring?"

"I bought it this morning. Is it sufficient?" Jacque plied the ring case up under my nose for a closer look.

Wow. I lost all sense of standoffishness when I became trapped in the hundreds of tiny, naturally shaped prisms reflecting within the clear, shiny stone.

I can admit it took me a minute to catch my breath. "Is it…"

"Four carats? Yes it is," answered Jacque nervously. "But if it isn't sufficient, we can take it back to Friedman's at the Galleria this afternoon and get you a five."

"Five?" I croaked. A five carat diamond? Was Jacque acting out of love, bribery, or just plain foolishness? "Uh, yes. It's more than…sufficient."

"Good," smiled Jacque, taking the ring out of the box.

Then I realized what I had just said. "No! No! It is not sufficient. None of this is! Jacque…this is crazy!"

"It wouldn't be love if it weren't crazy."

"Jacque…Put the ring back."

"Pretty…"

"Put it back," I commanded forcefully. "And can I have my hand back, please?"

"Sorry." Jacque released my hand. Reluctantly, he put the ring back inside its maroon colored box.

"Look, Jacque, I am very flattered that you feel this way about me. But I don't fe—"

"Don't say it," Jacque hushed me, placing a finger to my lips.

"Please don't say it."

"Jacque, this is neither the time nor the place for this! And I just don't fe—"

"Don't say no. Don't say anything. Just think about it," negotiated Jacque. "I know it's all kind of sudden, but just think about it. I'll be back in three weeks for your answer."

"Three weeks, three days, three hours from now, Jacque, it's still going to be no."

"Just think about it, Pretty—"

"Will you stop calling me that?"

"Just think about it, Ms. Selene. Just think about it."

Jacque placed the ring box in my hand, despite my attempts to refuse it. He wrapped my hand around the box, and gave it a pat. "It always came down to you, Jasmine. It always came down to you."

*

The girls were mesmerized.

"And what did you say?" creaked Nadine, all misty-eyed.

"What could I say? I had to take the damn thing."

"Lemme see the ring," Charlotte demanded coolly, businesslike. I complied. You should've seen the look on her face when that maroon, felt-covered box opened up. And then she dropped it. "Shit!"

The box slipped and hit the restaurant table, ricocheted, and landed on the floor. The ring slid out and bounced an additional ten feet. Like pigs in a trough, all three of us hit the floor, diving for the ring.

Nadine found it. "Got it! Got it! I've got it."

As I rediscovered air in my lungs, I shot Charlotte a look.

"Sorry, ma. I ain't never seen a rock that big, yo."

Closing one eye, Nadine squinted at the ring through the bottom of her empty water glass. I'm sure the people at ESPN Sports Zone were wondering what the hell was up with those crazy black chicks by the big screen.

"Yep, this is flawless," Nadine assessed. "A flawless four carat diamond."

Charlotte shook her head lightly. "And he asked you if you wanted a bigger one? Where the hell are those men in my life!"

I snorted, taking inventory of my pink lemonade. "Out screwing around on you, like Jacque did me."

"So you wouldn't ever consider marrying him? I mean, that was eight years ago," said Nadine.

"Well look at the Virgin Girl taking up for Satan," crowed Charlotte. "I'm surprised to hear that coming from your mouth, considering how highly you regard the act of sex."

"Yes, sexual intercourse is a gift from God that should be cherished and not entered into lightly. But God also teaches us forgiveness and to be merciful. For those of you who live in the secular world, who do engage in premarital sex and fornication—" Nadine preacher-daughtered.

Charlotte and I shared a quick look from our peripheral vision. Fornication??

"—I'm sure it's not a big deal to forgive sins of the flesh, especially when that person is truly repentant," Nadine finished. "And it was eight years ago. Maybe he truly is sorry."

"The only thing he's sorry about is that he got caught," I said. "He doesn't love me. He can't love me."

Eyeing the ring up close herself, Charlotte, who was temping at a law firm this week, commented with "Well this is a four carat counter-argument, Your Honor."

Nadine fed her palm her chin, leaning forward on her elbow. "Why can't he love you?"

I had no good, real answer. He just...can't.

"What makes what he feels for you different from what you feel for Nick?"

"Nick is getting married," I rebutted. "He's emotionally unavailable."

"So are you," Nadine pointed out. "You're in love with another man. But should that make his love for you any less real?"

I tried shaking off her statement with a nervous twitter. "Did Jacque put you on his payroll or something when you two went for drinks last night?"

Nadine's serious, unwavering gaze insisted upon an answer. So did Charlotte's curious one.

"The funny thing is," I began shakily, "Jacque said something to me that I had always thought of when I thought of Nick."

I fixated on the men running the bases on the television until their uniforms and bodies became colored, visual blobs.

"He said it always came down to me. It always came down to me."

I sighed and blinked the blobs away from my eyes. When I was able to focus, I could see my two girlfriends straight trippin'. Hardass Charlotte looked like she was about to cry. Nadine did—just a tear. But still.

"Oh, come on, girls! It's just a line!" I protested. "It's always just a line with Jacque! The man could lie at confession!"

"Dang, ma. There are women out there who would die to be proposed to once, just once. And here you are, turning down your third proposal?" Charlotte questioned. "I know he's still a little boy runnin' around in a man suit, but…what if he really loves you?"

And what if he's really lying?

"Jasmine…honey…Why do you think you and he are both single?" asked Nadine. "Why do you think both of you have never married? Why do you think that, after eight years, you found each other again? Why do you think that he went out to buy the biggest dern ring I ever seen just to ask you to marry him? Why do you think that, out of all the journalists in Atlanta, you ended up having to interview him?"

"Bad luck?"

"The will of God. You two were meant to be together."

A-freakin'-men.

*

"But I don't love him!"

I was sauced. We were at this bar, Snaky Jake's, just Charlotte and I, tossing them back and flirting with the locals. Or at least Char was. I was trying not to remember what the hell it was Nadine had said. Nadine had gone home to her fiancé, leaving us single girls to fend for ourselves. As I downed drink after drink, Charlotte politely listened, consoled, and, in her

47

trademark way, made herself very available to the attractive, job-carrying men in the hot and happening watering hole. It was Thursday night, Ladies Night, where drinks were half-priced for us, who brought the single, libidinous men out in droves.

"I know you don't, J," Charlotte said vaguely, splitting time between me and her new, butter brown, Y-chromosomed friend seated next to her.

"I love Nick. Nick is the love of my life! Why can't I be with the love of my life?" I whined.

Admiring his sexy, clean shaven features, Charlotte murmured more to him than to me, "That's what I've asked myself all my life, until this moment."

I loosely remembered him smiling back at her flirtatiously.

"I don't love Jacque! I love Nick! That's exactly why I didn't tell Nadine about Jacque before! She thinks she knows the answer to everything!" I complained. "She doesn't know the answer to this thing! She doesn't know who I love!"

"And who do you love?" Charlotte cooed to Bar Man.

"Nick!"

"I'm Rick," Bar Man introduced himself to Charlotte.

"Not Rick! Nick!" I howled.

"Nick?" asked Rick.

"Nick!" I said.

"No, I'm Rick."

"You are not Nick!"

"I'm not Nick, I'm Rick."

   "Nick is not Rick, he's Nick!"

"He's Rick," said Charlotte. "Not Nick."

"Not Nick," I repeated.

"Not Nick," he repeated.

"He's Rick."

"He's Rick," affirmed Charlotte.

"Not Nick," I mumbled.

"Not Nick," he confirmed.

"Thank you and good night." My head crashed to the bar.

I could feel his confused stare. Rick-Not-Nick probably thought I was crazy.

Before I passed out, I heard Charlotte say, "There you have it—

48

your Atlanta Journalist Society's New Television Anchor of the Year."

I snored my approval.

*

This is what my Friday nights had been reduced to: babysitting Charlotte's daughter while watching HBO. Janaya actually was a precociously quiet four-year

old, a beautiful, medium-complected girl with her father's wavy Hispanic hair, her mother's shiny black eyes, and a forehead so broad you could ski off it. She accompanied me on the couch, fast asleep before the clock had struck nine.

Charlotte wasn't out with Rick-Not-Nick but with a guy she dubbed The Mortician. Ever the fair one, Charlotte gave a guy two dates to prove himself. The Mortician had earned his moniker after the first date. If he didn't shape up and show her a pulse, The Mortician would be as dead as his name. Either way, the ever pragmatic "Dating Realist" had a triple date set up for tomorrow night with Charlotte and Rodney, Rick-Not-Nick, and a new guy for me, one she nicknamed "Cornball." He was a little tame for her but "absolutely perfect" for me. Uh huh. Sounds like just what the Love Doctor ordered.

Friday nights at Charlotte's weren't exactly new to me. That girl went out a lot. I know Char's my girl and everything, but I was beginning to think that she was not a good parent. As much as Charlotte hung out with Nadine and me was as much as her mother spent time watching Janaya. Whenever Charlotte had an audition for a commercial or for a play during the week or weekends, her mother was there for her. Whenever Charlotte had a date (which was often), her mother, or myself, was there for her. Whenever Charlotte had to work temp day jobs in between acting gigs, the daycare was there for her. I wondered if Janaya even knew who her mommy was.

Look, I understood that what I did was nothing. Babysitting a child for a few hours a week was nothing when I then turned her back over to her mother for the rest of her life. I cannot imagine being a single mom was easy by any stretch of the imagination, even with such a gem like Janaya. Still, it disturbed me to see my good friend not be as hands-on a mommy as she should be.

See, now this was part of the problem with Friday nights like this: too much time to think. My aching head reminded me of how much—and how quickly—I had become weak. All it took to regressing back into Nick was seeing Jacque, a man who hadn't even registered on my emotional Richter scale in at least six years.

Look, I won't even front—Jacque was part of the reason why I had turned down Nick's proposal six years ago. It's not that I still had loved Jacque then. Hell, I hadn't even seen Jacque since I had told him to get out of my life two years prior to Nick's proposal. Maybe it was just the finality of forever, the lingering doubt of committing to one person for the rest of your life that initially scared me. I was too young to know any better. It was kind of like "be careful what you wish for," seeing how I have always wanted to be married for as long as I could remember. It all seemed too easy, with Nick being too perfect for me. I didn't want to believe that I lived a waking dream.

And now I'm mired in an ever-loving nightmare.

My mind slowed enough to watch Shakespeare in Love on TV. My heart quietly sighed at how much Gwyneth Paltrow and Joseph Fiennes loved each other. Or at least looked like they loved each other. I found it unbelievable that they did not fall in love during the shoot. I was in love just watching them in love. The power, the intensity in their eyes was incredible. Unwavering. Absolute. Unconditional.

It had been a long time since I had felt that power. I wondered if I would ever feel that power again.

*

How did you know when a date was going bad? When you had to ask yourself if a date was going bad.

Cornball was not a bad guy. He just wasn't an interesting guy. In the words of the infamous Charlotte—what had almost been a catchphrase to her these past few years—"He bores me." That's exactly what I thought when I scored my seventh consecutive goal on him, skunking him 7-0 in air hockey.

Yes, once again we were back at the Sports Zone. For our triple date, Charlotte, Nadine, and I decided we needed home court advantage, so we returned to our favorite spot. Upstairs in the Zone was a full-size adult arcade, complete with interactive sports video games such as stock car racing or jetski riding. As usual for a Saturday night, the Zone was alive, with the chatter so loud and thick, being heard was a luxury. A steady flow of people migrated between the games like salmon swimming upstream. The longest lines were for mini-bowling, the basketball shoot on a real life quarter court, and, of course, the booze bar.

Armed with a hundred points each, the three dates went our separate ways. That was when I learned how unathletic my date truly was. After my air hockey flogging, I abused him at skeet shooting, lapped him in stock car racing, and ran him aground on the jetskis. After awhile, I decided to see just how much I could embarrass Old Dude, he was that pathetic. But the crown jewel of humiliation was the Pop-a-Shot. You never would have known that Nick had taught me how to play basketball a mere eight years ago by the way I tripled Cornball's score. This was the last time I went out on a blind date hooked up by Charlotte.

But Nick. I hated how I compared this date at every turn to Nick. He wasn't as tall as Nick. He wasn't as built as Nick. He wasn't as smart as Nick. I felt like a damn lovesick schoolgirl the way I kept comparing Cornball to Nick, just to find him wanting.

I wanted to blame Jacque for my regression, but I had no one to blame but myself. My girls had said it all along: when it came to affairs of the heart, I was as wishy-washy as a Maytag. At times, I could be so decisive with men it would cost me my family, my friends. But there were other times, times inexplicable to me, when I just could not choose. Was this some sort of personality defect or something? When Nick had proposed to me, despite how absolutely perfect our relationship was—I mean, emotionally, I wanted for nothing—I couldn't pull the trigger. I went backward instead of forward.

I remember when I had first begun dating Nick, three months

after having sent Jacque his pink slip. Jacque had started calling me and trying to win me back, telling me everything I wanted to hear. I was buying it, even though Nick was kicking truer, more sincere game. Actually, it wasn't even game at all—it was just Nick. Pure, unadulterated, honest Nick. I will never forget the time when Jacque showed up unannounced at my apartment, crashing my date with Nick. The look in his eyes. The look in Nick's eyes. They both wanted me. I wanted them. And then…I just chose. Nick. It was simple. I made a decision and stuck with it—for two and a half years.

I also will never forget what Nick had said to me, as I cried in his arms on my living room couch.

"I love you," he said.

"But I don't love you," I admitted sorrowfully.

"It doesn't matter. Not now, anyways," he said. "You chose me. Now I'm choosing you."

Choose not to love him anymore! Just make a damn decision, Jasmine!

"Jasmine."

I started. "Huh?"

"You okay there? Seems like you drifted off for a moment." Cornball smiled at me genially.

"Oh. Sorry."

The six of us were seated downstairs now, facing a big screen TV that featured, of all things, Major League Soccer. No wonder I had zoned out.

So here were the dynamics at our table. Flanking my other side was Charlotte, who might as well not have been there at all, seeing how she was dang near in Rick-Not-Nick's lap. On the other side of Not-Nick sat Nadine, who lovingly straightened Rodney's collar for him, as if he couldn't do it himself. And then we came back around to Cornball who marked space in the seat to my right, desperately trying to up his lame-ass profile by showering me with attention. There was nothing that a woman hated more than a guy with no potential giving her even more of that lack of potential.

Finally starting to catch the drift, Cornball diverted his attention to someone who gave a damn. "So, Nadine. When are you two getting married?"

Shining like an indoor sun, Nadine said, "Three weeks from tomorrow. October 18th." Without needing any prompting, she turned to Rodney, who made moony eyes at her while they cooed.

Rarely did I get jealous of them these days, but I wanted to staple their lips shut.

Charlotte, ever the diplomat, eagerly changed subjects. "So what is it that you do again?"

"Accounting," supplied the Cornball. "I'm an accountant for a non-profit organization for the gay elderly with AIDS."

Nobody said anything. I think Rodney and Not-Nick were shocked that there were such organizations. I think Nadine was just plain shocked. I was still unimpressed.

"How noble!" gushed Charlotte, bravely filling the void.

How boring! "Sounds fantastic," I said as dryly as an unwashed chalkboard.

"You have fun at your job?" asked Not-Nick.

I looked at Rick-Not-Nick like he was the dumbest brotha on the planet (well, he at least had to be in the running). Nadine returned to cooing with her fiancé while Charlotte, mortified, sipped on her pink lemonade. But he sho' looked pretty, huh, Charlotte? Having fun working for AIDS patients?

The question caught Cornball sideways, too. "Uh...I guess so."

Just to ease my boredom, I decided to take an active role in the conversation if, for nothing else, to entertain myself at Cornball's expense. "What's your passion?"

"My passion?"

"Yes. What do you feel passionate about? What do you love to do?"

I saw Rodney break through his cloud of pitching woo and begin to take a bit of an interest.

"Well...I like collecting antiques..."

You have got to be kidding me. "Okay, skip that. What is it professionally you have a passion for? Is it your job? Do you love what you do?"

"Working for AIDS patients or accounting?"

"Either!" Cornball was beginning to frustrate me.

"Well...uh...no."

"Well then what is?"

"I...well...I don't know."

That's it. I threw down my napkin just as the waitress arrived with our food. Instinctively, Charlotte jumped up with me.

"No, sit down, Charlotte. I just forgot that I have a plane to catch."

I walked away, leaving the group embarrassed and confused. I, however, was not. I drove Alexia straight to the airport, not passing Go, but I did collect two hundred dollars. I bought a one-way ticket to Los Angeles, California. You know what I did? I got on that plane and made a decision.

Merci Monsieur

"Merci, monsieur."

I could tell he was impressed. "Now why did you take up French in high school? I know why I did. I wanted to do something different. All the brothas were taking Spanish."

I flashed a kind of grin at Nick that signaled I was about to reveal my deep, dark secret. "Here comes the awful truth of it— I'm Canadian."

"Really?" He didn't even flinch. In fact, I think it turned him on. "You were born there?"

She nodded. "Yep. Born and raised there, until my folks got a divorce when I was about fourteen. We moved down here shortly after."

"You and your mom?"

"And my sister."

Nick dropped his jaw with mock drama. "You mean there's more than one of you!"

I hit him lightly, flirtatiously. For a first date, Nick was mad fun. "Yes, I have an older sister. Her name is Nia. As in Niagara."

"Her name is Niagara?" He wasn't making fun, he was just asking.

"Sho' nuff."

"Where did y'all used to live?"

I hid a smile. Damn, he sounded country right then.

"Toronto. But my mom just liked the name. Everyone

calls her Nia, though. It's spelled N-I-A but we say it 'Nyah.'"

"She as fine as you?"

See, this was the type of shit I hate: dudes always creepin' on my sister. I can deal with the fact that she was a pretty girl. Hell, so was I. What I did not tolerate were those triflin'-ass niggas who would bounce from me to her, just because they thought her short ass was prettier. Nia always had my boyfriends comin' after her and I could not stand it!

"What? You tryin' to get with my sister?"

"No no no no no," he said quickly. "Not at all. Just thinking that we could hook your sister up with my boy."

"That fool at the party freakin' everyone in sight?" I laughed in quick relief. Mentally, I apologized to Nick and resumed the playful tone of the date. "Sorry, boy, but I don't think my sister is his type."

"Hold on! Say that again!"

I shot him a puzzled look. "Say what?"

"Sorry," Nick emphasized, stressing his American accent.

"Sohrry," I repeated—normally.

"You've got an accent!" Nick hooted.

"I do not."

"Yes, you do! Listen to yourself! Say 'house.'"

"Hoase."

More giggles. "Now say 'about.'"

"Aboat."

"I'm gonna have to tape record you so you can hear yourself versus myself sometime. You as Canadian as they come, girl."

I dismissed him with a wave. And? I know I'm Canadian; damn proud, too. You're lucky this is a fun date so far. You giggly bitch.

I watched the mayhem occurring out on the skating rink. There were so many people on the roller rink, they had zebra-striped referees weaving in and out of traffic, maintaining order. People skated, danced, and rolled in trains around the rink to a bass heavy, New York-style, hip hop beat. I far better appreciated our seats on the sideline, at a table behind the rink wall, drowning out the music, the people, and the smell of greasy fries and hot dogs, just to be concentrating on each other.

"So why do you say your sister ain't my boy's type? She ugly?"

"Boy, don't make me reach out and touch someone," I threatened. As much as I had issues with Nia, I have always been protective of my family. "Don't be dissin' my sister."

"I'm not," he answered defensively, throwing up his hands in mock defense. "But I don't know if she ugly or not. And my boy don't go out with ugly heads."

I rolled my eyes. "Whatever, nigga. Nia's got a little somethin'-somethin'. She's got a boyfriend anyway. He plays for the Jets."

Evidently a sports fan, Nick knew what I was talking about. "You mean your sister dates someone on the New York J-E-T-S Jets-Jets-Jets!"

Nodding. "Yup. The New York Football Jets. But don't be asking me for no tickets," Jasmine warned. "You can take that up with my sister. That's her department. Nigga."

I loved messing with Nick. Already, with just one (six hour) phone conversation the night before behind us, we already had a cute, light, playful chemistry. I could do no wrong tonight.

"So why I gotta be a nigga?" With a smile. He said it with a smile.

All things considered, this had been a great date. I was feelin' him, to be honest, I really was feelin' him. Now I know I'm not the most aggressive girl in the world, but there are times when you just gotta lay it down. That's right, the gauntlet. This was one of those times.

"Because I want you to be my nigga."

I don't even think he thought twice about it. Before I knew it, he kissed me. Believe you me, I kissed him back. It was beautiful. It was long. It was a kiss.

When we broke away, all we could do was stare at each other. What happened next? There was no rulebook for this. All we knew was that it felt so right. Gazing into the eyes of this stranger from Seattle, this impossibly handsome, witty, intelligent black man, I began to feel something, something real. We held that soul-sstirring connection as if we were clinging to a cliff. Not to be the one to let us fall, I brought us back to solid ground. I made a decision.

I closed my eyes and gave him a pursed lip baby-kiss. Nick did the same. We must have baby-kissed there for the next ten, fifteen minutes.

"NEW YORK!!! Are y'all gettin' jiggy out there?!?" boomed the deejay over the loudspeaker system. "Next up, Couple Skate! Couples only!"

Nick and I missed it. And that was what made it the perfect first date.

4

"STRANGÉ! STRANGÉ!"

I firmly believed that Boomerang pertained to all aspects of life. If you thought about it, it made sense. Made in 1992 by the Hudlin Brothers, those directorial comic maestros who brought you House Party and House Party 2, Boomerang was the quintessential Eddie Murphy romantic comedy. Starring modern day comic geniuses such as David Alan Grier, Martin Lawrence, and Chris Rock, Boomerang fused comedy and drama as brilliantly as an Eddie Murphy riff on Star Trek. As a player who finally gets played, Eddie Murphy as Marcus Graham took you on a hysterical ride of falling in and out of love, dragging every range of human emotion into the process. (God, I sounded just like Nick. Even before he recognized his calling as an actor, he would talk to me about movies in terms like this.) There were still strong remnants of his influence in my life. Regardless, this was an excellent film almost wholly overlooked by the mainstream white media, and I loved it absolutely. I firmly believed that Boomerang pertained to all aspects of life.

So, as luck would have it, this movie was playing on the airplane. Gotta love our multi-channel, satellite TV-equipped world. I've seen this flick so many times, I just mouthed the words while flipping through my O—The Oprah Magazine, without even bothering to look at the screen. I had picked up the magazine during a layover in Houston. I, too, like millions of other American women, had been seduced into buying the mag by its headlines that promised tales of empowerment that lift the spirit. That seemed as close to direct marketing for me as it could get.

Unfortunately, not even Boomerang could pertain to my life

right now. Or at least I couldn't see it. So I'd settled back in my chair, headphones on, blotting out the rest of the plane in my singleminded fog of determination tempered by doubt.

But I couldn't blot him out. A tall, lean, fit, strikingly good-looking man boarded the plane in Houston, sitting next to me. His was a dark, spiky hair, matched with olive-tinged Asian skin. I guessed that maybe he was probably either Korean or Filipino by the tone of his skin and the shape of his eyes. For some reason, his face seemed vaguely familiar, yet I couldn't quite place it. Adorned with an exquisite, loose-fitting diamond bracelet, the man looked oddly placed riding in coach next to me. At least I had an excuse for flying coach besides General Principle: I had just bought this ticket three hours ago.

The real reason why I couldn't blot him out was because he, too, seemed to know all the words to Boomerang by heart. One of my favorite scenes was coming up. By his reaction, I could see that it was his favorite, too.

John Witherspoon, decked out in brown-mushroom flavored suit, sat at the Thanksgiving table in Eddie Murphy's apartment. He extolled the virtues of "whipping pussy" versus being "pussy-whipped" to Eddie Murphy's character, who was reeling because of Robin Givens' who had played him out,

In unison, both the handsome man hollered, "Bang! Bang! Bang! Bang!"

We stopped. Looked at each other. Then we burst out laughing.

"Seen this much?" Handsome Man kidded.

"Only as much as you have," I smiled.

"Glad to see someone has an appreciation of true American cinematic classics."

"It is. Best movie of Eddie Murphy's career," I concurred.

Handsome Man sighed. "I tell him that all the time."

Okay, that was not exactly the subtlest name-drop of all time, but I had to admit he had me intrigued. "You know Eddie Murphy?"

"I've worked with him before."

I squinted at his angularly featured face. For some reason I felt like I should know who he was. "Are you a director? Producer?"

"I'm an actor."

See, I knew it! Everyone jumps to guess "actor" first. I just didn't want to be "everyone." "Theater or films?"

"Some film. TV mostly," he said.

"Which show?" I inquired. I liked the way he made me ask him the questions, instead of proffering the information in the interests of rampant self-promotion Los Angelenos were famous for.

"C-203. You might not have heard of it," Handsome Man admitted with a chuckle. "It's a first year show on CBS Friday nights."

Aha. I knew he had some self-promotion in him. But I intensified my squint again. "Did you ever do soap operas?"

A humble exhale escaped him, as he covered his head with his hand. "Alright, you caught me. I used to be on Days of Our Lives."

"Tommy Chen!" I squealed. "I knew you looked familiar!"

He extended his hand. "Well, my real name is Mark Dietz. Nice to meet you."

"Jasmine Selene," I introduced, using my on air name. I never used my last name these days. We shook hands. "So what were you doing in Houston?"

"Some publicity for the show. I did a few PAs at Wal-Marts, and helped cut the ribbon on a new Circuit City."

PAs. Public Appearances. I was familiar with the term because the station had me do the same kind of deal, on occasion. Sometimes my agent would get me a couple, to add a few dollars here and there, always with an eye on publicity. "A Wal-Mart, huh?" I giggled. "Sounds pretty cheesy."

He wasn't offended; he understood good-naturedly. "It sure was."

"And they're flying you back coach?" I asked incredulously. Just like with my station, whenever you were flown somewhere by an employer in the Industry, you flew first class.

Handsome Man—er, Mark—leaned into me conspiratorially. "You didn't hear this from me, but the show's running out of money."

Shocked, I repeated, "The show's running out of money?"

Mark leaned back. "You didn't hear it from me. I'm surprised

I'm not flying in the baggage compartment."

"But how does that happen? How are you still on the air?"

"The production company took some hits in bad movie investments last year. They have the money to front the show, but they're skimping on the publicity for it," Mark explained. "It's pretty sad."

"How're the ratings?" I, too, knew that we in the TV biz were slaves to the almighty Nielsens.

"Middling. We're somewhere in the high thirties, overall. We draw about seven million viewers a week."

"For a Friday night? That's not bad at all."

"I know. We've recently gotten a viewership bump, due to our show being nominated for an Emmy."

My eyes lit up. "Really? For what?"

Mark turned sheepish. "Supporting Actor in a Drama Series."

"Congratulations!"

"Thanks. I'm looking forward to it. This will be my first Emmy Awards show."

I smiled at him. "Well I wish you luck, Mark."

"Thank you, Jasmine." He studied my face for a moment. "So how long are you in LA?"

"I'm not sure. Maybe a week or so."

Mark produced a card from his jacket inside pocket. "Here's my card. If you're still in town…I'd love for you to accompany me to the Emmys."

I nearly choked on my own saliva. "You mean as a date?"

Forming a sly smirk that had been, essentially, the foundation of his soap opera career as forensic analyst Tommy Chen, Mark said smoothly, "You do date, don't you?"

I wanted to tell him that I had a boyfriend. But that was a lie. I wanted to tell him I wasn't available. But that was a lie, too. I wanted to tell him that I was out here to get my ex-boyfriend back, that I was on a mission to save him from marrying the wrong woman. But that was too much truth. So I settled for a little truth, and a lot of discretion.

Accepting the card, I said simply, without committing one way or the other, "Yes. I do date."

*

As foolish as this escapade may have seemed, I did have a bit of sense about me. I had bought a ticket to Los Angeles because I knew that Nick started filming Sand Adventures tomorrow on the 20th Century Fox lot. Fox was on the Westside, off of Pico Boulevard in a busy section of LA called Century City. Century City wasn't only busy but also it was expensive. Highrises dotted a street so ritzy it was called the Avenue of the Stars. The hotels in that area were comparably as costly. The one LA excess I indulged in was charging a convertible Benz rental car on the company credit card. I had heard so much about the ridiculously phat rides in Floss Angeles that I just wanted to keep up appearances. With a little research in the baggage claim area of LAX, I decided upon staying at the Westin by the airport on Century Boulevard.

By the time I settled into my room, there were a few messages waiting for me on my cell phone. Nadine, of course, squawked guilt and annoyance into my ear. Something about responsibilities and how I needed to call her about work.

Delete.

Cornball left a message, actually worried about me. I walk out on our date and he called concerned about me. Amazing.

Delete.

The last one intrigued me the most. I had to play it twice to make sure I heard it right.

"Hey, what it is, ma. You like a trip, girlfriend. I mean you ain't got no qualms about pickin' up right in the middle of dinner and bouncin' out to Cali."

I frowned. How the hell did she know I was in Cali?

"Yeah, trick, I know you in Cali. I know because you was thinkin' 'bout Nick, huh, ma? That and Maintenance Man, a.k.a. Mr. TSA, saw you go through security at AirTran last night. The only flights leaving that late from AirTran is goin' to Cali."

Damn? Has Char done all of black male Atlanta?

"Anyway, I wanted to holla at you and tell you I'm jettin' out there tomorrow myself. I'm gettin' into LA about 11:35 in the morning. Delta, Flight 203. Meet me outside baggage claim."

Charlotte coming to LA? What the…

"What can I say? You inspired me, J. I gotta admit, it was a mad impulsive thing you did. It took guts. It's time I faced up and did what I had to do, too—

really give this acting thing a try. So I'll see you tomorrow, ma."

I sank down on the bed, laying myself flat. Gazing up at the ceiling, I reflected upon what Charlotte's message had just told me. Hm. I had guts. I "did what I had to do." She was proud of me, I could tell. I would be proud of me, too— if I weren't so scared.

*

There were times when dealing with your boss who was also your friend was easy. This was not one of those times.

"What the holy heck did you think you were doing, Jasmine?!"

When Nadine used "holy heck," she was quite pissed off. As I piloted my rented Benz down Century Boulevard toward the airport, I tried to concentrate on defusing my answer as much as possible. "I'm sorry I left the date so early. It just wasn't me."

"Besides being incredibly rude, what about your job, Jasmine? You're supposed to be doing something special for the HART next month!"

I had thought about this ahead of time. Oh, about the time I was 35,000 miles over somewhere in New Mexico. "I am working on something special."

"Something that can beat Beverly Bradley?" Nadine challenged through the phone.

Working at WXIA-TV, Beverly Bradley was an industry legend in the making. At only thirty-six, she had already won two HARTs, singlehandedly dragged WXIA from the cellar in primetime news show ratings to the second slot, and posed the biggest threat to the HART year after year, outside of the legendary Monica Kaufman. It was something about Beverly's fiery red hair, innate sense of youthful sex appeal, dashed by a serious gravity with which she delivered the news that made her accessible to damn near everybody. I hated and envied her at the same time. Hell, I wanted to be her.

Could I beat Beverly Bradley? Doubtful. But if I couldn't convince my producer, I sure couldn't convince Atlanta. "Sure. I'm working on an Emmy Week special."

I could almost see Nadine sit her squat self down in her executive chair. "I'm listening."

"I already have an interview lined up with one of the nominees for Outstanding Supporting Actor in a Drama Series," I lied, eyeing the card Mark Dietz gave me, lying on the dash. "I should be able to gain all access to the awards show."

Nadine mulled it over momentarily. She couldn't have been too ecstatic about the idea. But at least it wasn't my taking off for an impromptu vacation like the last time nine days ago.

"Look, I know it's not 'Hooker Nuns Caught Selling Flesh to the Pulpit' but it's a start," I reasoned.

"You mean an accumulation effect?" she murmured. "Interview with an Internet tycoon here, an insider's view of the Emmys there...Jasmine Selene walks away with the HART?"

"Something like that," I approved, guiding the car into the curb lane outside the Delta baggage claim. I saw Charlotte struggle past the sliding doors with an improbably large suitcase. "I've gotta go, Nadine. Just hold down the fort for me while I'm gone."

"I'm sure Polly will look forward to the extra work," Nadine tossed sarcastically, mentioning the station's backup anchor/reserve field reporter. Although I liked the girl, Polly was inferior to me and my professional skills in just about every way. Ratings dipped noticeably when she filled in for me.

"Send Angie down here for me. I'll need her real soon," I instructed. "Take care, girl."

Just as I turned my phone off, Charlotte hollered, "That's the last time I hook your black ass up, heffa!"

I smiled as Charlotte unloaded her burden into the back seat of the Benzo. "If that's what you call a hook up, you can keep 'em to yourself, Char!"

"I usually do." Charlotte clambered into the passenger's seat, exhausted. That didn't stop us from exchanging a quick hug. "Dang, ma. You pushin' a Benz?"

"When in Rome," I grinned. A candy red Ferrari passed by on

the left as I pulled away from the curb.

"Yeah, ma, you ain't kiddin'," Charlotte agreed, rubbernecking at all the beautiful cars that ran the streets of LA like free range chickens.

"So who's babysitting Janaya?" I asked pointedly.

"Her grandmother's got her."

I whistled. "Girl, all I've gotta say is that Ma Royer really has your back."

"She's been great, yeah." Charlotte stared out the window as an airplane descended right over our heads, touching down on the tarmac below. "So where're we stayin'?"

"The Westin. It's just a few blocks from here."

Taking a moment, Charlotte composed her thoughts. "So what's the plan?"

"I should be asking you that, girl."

"I asked first."

I studied the windshield. I kinda wish I knew the answer to that myself. "I guess I have no plan. All I know is that Nick's shooting this film over at Fox, which is on Pico, about five miles from here. I spent all day yesterday trying to find out a phone number for him and, of course, it's unlisted. I don't know where he lives. All I know is where he works. That's my only shot."

"Why don't you call your friend?" Charlotte offered.

I started at this. "Who?"

"You know…your friend."

"No," I dismissed. "I'm only using him again as a last resort."

Charlotte showed her palms in surrender. Bravely, she deeply inhaled the LA smog. Char nearly choked up a lung for her efforts.

I laughed. "I thought a big, bad, Brooklyn girl like you would be used to smog."

"What can I say. Atlanta's spoiled a sista."

"So what's your plan?" I asked. "Do you have any particular plans?"

"Yeah. I brought a grip of headshots and I'mma go out to all the agencies and bust 'em in the cranium with them. Show them that Charlotte Royer's got skills. And a whole lotta hustle."

"Sounds like a lot of work." I observed.

"So does Nick."

*

Char and I were a pretty good team. We tag-teamed Rodeo Drive with all the energy of pro wrestlers. Jetlagged for most of yesterday, I hadn't had a chance to go out and buy some clothes like I did today. We also visited this mall called the Beverly Center. As far as I could tell, it was a pasture where the rich and famous could graze among unknown actor-model wannabes, perfectly anonymous in their fame and beauty. In only half an hour of shopping, I counted four movie stars, three TV stars, six recording artists, and one painter (yeah, I got culture, Damnit!). I don't think they let you in there unless you were beautiful. Lucky for us, both Charlotte and I easily passed the price of admission.

I looked pretty tight, too, wearing a tight fitting sarong and a cleavage-enhancing red tube top. My light caramel shoulders were feminine and pretty, not to mention the hint of my flat stomach, with my navel peeking out between the space where my tube top ended and my sarong began. You could catch a glimpse of the curves of the small cursive tattoo on my stomach that read "Jazzy." While I suppose it was a tribute to my rebellious, ghettofied youth, when I'd tried to fit in so much as an American teenager that I ran with a pretty unsavory crowd, I didn't ever try to have it removed. It wasn't like I had Jacque or Nick's name tattooed there; I was Jazzy. And I certainly looked it today.

After posing as perfection for many a Los Angeleno male, I steered us back to the car. Lurking in the forefront of my mind was exactly how we were going to scam our way onto the 20th Century Fox lot. Thankfully, Charlotte was distracted enough with her cute clothing items en route to Fox so I could hash out my plan in relative peace. True, I was an employee of a Fox affiliate in Atlanta, but I couldn't very well call up Nadine to get me clearance on the lot because I wanted to go make my ex-boyfriend fall back in love with me—even if she knew and accepted the truth. The T&A angle of both Char and I looking delectably diva-ish did cross my mind. But this was LA. How many starlets and budding actresses must a security guard deal with every day? What if he was an old, liver-spotted white guy, who had long ago given up enjoying any diversions of sex and libido? So many things could go wrong, yet this was the only way I knew how to get a hold of Nick.

The ride from Beverly Center to the Fox entrance on Pico Boulevard was a scant twenty minutes in heavy traffic. I felt so unprepared. I believed that Charlotte was oblivious to the fact that I had no plan at all. I guess she must have thought that I had thought this all the way through before I stood up and walked out on our triple date or, at the very least, on the five hour plane ride out here. Now, I really wished I had.

I decided to park at a meter on Pico, just down the street from the Fox entrance. As cars raced by under the glinting LA sun, I deposited enough quarters to last the full two hours afforded by the machine. So I was optimistic; this better not be a short trip.

As we approached the guard shack that patrolled the general entrance and exit to the lot, I tightened my sarong and pushed up my boobs in the tube top. I really was killing 'em with my long, athletic, five-foot nine-inch frame, with the tease of my pecan stomach that was so flat you could eat dinner off of it. Charlotte was shorter and thicker than I—tight, not fat—with just enough legs and butt to announce to the world she was a sistagurl extraordinaire. Damn, I envied her butt. Mine wasn't flat now, but it was distinguished enough only to be what I think Nick called "a dress booty." Hence, the tightening of the sarong. Screw it; we looked tight. Who could resist us?

The security guard, that's who. He was a brotha—tall, built, imposing, security-like. Despite my 34Cs winking at him, Security Guard was not moved. I didn't know if Charlotte caught on that we had no business being here, but she was gonna soon find out.

"Who're you here to see?" he demanded.

I stalled with a fetching smile. I thought about reaching for my press pass, but, somehow, I figured that the press wouldn't be able to come blindly on the lot, especially looking like this. "Who?"

"Show?" he asked.

"Show?" I parroted, confused.

"You're background, right? What show are you here to do?"

I can be if it'll get us on the set. I could almost feel Charlotte's inquisitive eyes boring in through the base of my skull. I had to do something.

Fortunately, a model year BMW convertible pulled up on the outgoing side. The actor looked vaguely familiar, although I couldn't quite place the name.

The security guard scurried to the other side of the guard shack. "Leaving early today, Mr. Pitt?"

Char gaped. Brad Pitt! While she was busy stargazing and Security Guard doing a modified version of it himself, I leaned my inquisitive head into the guard shack, glancing at one of his official on-lot papers. My head was back outside the shack the moment Brad Pitt drove his blond head off into the California sunshine.

Security Guard returned. "Well? What show are you working on?"

"That '70s Show," I piped.

"Name?"

"Ana Rodriguez and Marielle Roulet."

He squinted at me. I didn't look Latina and Charlotte sure as hell didn't look French. But those names were all I had.

So Charlotte picked up the ball. "'Tis an is-land name. Me pops is from Haiti, ya know?" she said in her best, affected Haitian patois.

I love Char! That's my girl!

"IDs?"

I smiled, keeping my mouth shut, not eager at all to reveal my definite lack of Latina-ness. Harrison Ford, chillin' in a Range Rover with Steven Spielberg, honked his horn.

"Just one second, Mr. Ford!" He didn't have time for our mess. Security Guard consulted his list, crossed off our names, and handed us laminated badges. "Do you know where you're going?"

"Sì," I lied, ready for this encounter to be over.

He waved us on in.

*

Two hours later, we were quite familiar with the 20th Century Fox lot. We must've been back and forth across the place about three times. I simply had no idea where the hell Nick could be hiding. I knew for a fact that he was on set today because that was when principal photography started on Sand Adventures. And since it was a movie and not a television show Fox produced, there was not immediate signage alerting us what stage it was in.

That's not to say we didn't have our fun. As we strolled down empty mock-ups of New York City neighborhood exteriors complete with brownstones, NY Times machines, and hot dog stands, we encountered every variety of actor. Charlotte made sure that she flirted with every last one of them. Pulling her off of an even-better-looking-in-person Isaiah Washington, I dragged Char toward what looked like a craft service truck, with a bit of a crowd around it. All this walking had made me hungry.

Standing in line for the truck was Nick. I nudged Charlotte. "There he is."

Charlotte blinked twice. "Dang, he look good, ma!"

"That's just makeup," I demurred, knowing 100 percent that she was right. He looked so firm, dark, and fine!

"So what're you gonna say?"

I sighed. "I don't know. The truth?"

Charlotte laughed. "Never that, J. Make that boy want you again. Make him want you."

"Make him want me," I said, pumping up my nerve.

"Be that woman all men wanna fuck!"

I gave Charlotte a look.

"Okay, okay. Be that woman all men desire," she amended. Then, under her breath, she mumbled, "Desire, fuck. Same thing."

"Say no more. I'm good."

I left my girl and crossed the short distance over to my ex-boyfriend. I flew over there like a homing pigeon, of singular purpose and mission. When I tapped him on the shoulder, know what happened? I lost my nerve. "Uh, hi, Nick."

"Jasmine!" I couldn't tell if he was genuinely spooked, upset, or both. "What're you doing here?"

Desire. Want. All else failed me but the godawful truth. "I wanted to see you."

"How'd you even get on the lot?" he asked, a bit paranoid. "You're not supposed to be here."

I smiled cheerfully. "I lied."

Now there was a tap on my shoulder. "Yes, you did."

Caught. Security Guard. I turned around to find him with a hand already wrapped in a steady grip on Charlotte's elbow. "Is she bothering you, Nick?"

His answer caught me off guard. "No, Lerone. But she shouldn't be here."

"Gotcha." Now Security Guard Lerone's beefy hand clamped down on my arm like a pit bull with lockjaw. "You two are coming with me. Sorry for the inconvenience, Nick."

"No problem."

While Lerone dragged us off, I cast a longing gaze at Nick. It was my best I'm-making-you-want-me-desire-me-come-with-me-fuck-me look. Observing me for only another fifteen feet, Nick quickly turned back to the craft service line, waiting on lunch.

Needless to say, we were kicked off the Fox lot, our badges snatched from us in a grand show of vulgarity. Turned out that the real Ana Rodriguez and Marielle Roulet had come to the guard shack about forty minutes ago, spurring Security Guard Lerone to come look for us. Judging by the venom of his tonality, Security Guard Lerone intimated that we were never welcome back to the 20th Century Fox lot again. I think it's because he said, "You two are never welcome at Fox ever again!"

When we returned to the rental car, I found a parking ticket on my car windshield. I checked my watch. Only seven minutes past the time I had paid for. LA's meter maids did not play! Perfect. Just perfect.

Welcome to LA, Jasmine.

*

Stuck in traffic on the 405. How LA. At least it had taken me

70

until my third day in Los Angeles before having gotten caught up in its world infamous traffic.

As Charlotte and I twisted in freeway gridlock in my rented convertible Benz under a sunny, warm, smog-smeared sky, we chatted idly to pass the time. I just hoped that Angie wouldn't be too mad for being late in picking her up at the airport. This was the last time I used the freeway in LA during daytime.

"I hope you haven't given up on him," Charlotte mentioned quietly.

I drummed the beat of a D'Angelo song into the steering wheel with my idle hands. Whatever happened to that brotha? "Why do you say that?"

"I'm just sayin', it'd be a shame to see you come all this way, only to give up so easily."

The woman had a point. I smiled. "No, I haven't given up, Char."

"Good." Charlotte shifted in the passenger seat. "'Cause I'm tellin' you now, it ain't gonna be easy, ma."

"Why's that?" I knew why; I just wanted to hear her version.

"Well, from what you've told me, Nick's a pretty loyal guy. A loving guy. If he's committed himself to marrying this chick, it sounds like he'd actually do it. It's hard to make someone fall back in love with you, especially when they're already lovin' somebody else."

"I hear you." I ruminated. "But I don't think he really loves her, Char. He can't. If he loved her, he wouldn't have stopped the wedding for me."

"To hear you tell it, it didn't sound like the man had much of a choice."

Finally, traffic started moving. For about fifty yards.

"He had a choice," I said. "Charlotte...I kissed him. And when I kissed him...I swear that he kissed me back."

"Nonsense," she dismissed, as traffic began to creep again. "That's natural reflex. You stick your tongue down any guy's mouth, he'll react—just from being a guy. Especially when it's someone you used to fuck with."

I grimaced. "That's a crass way to put it."

Charlotte smiled. "Sorry. Someone you used to be with," she ameliorated..

A moment passed as traffic crawled to a stop again. We were near an exit for some street called La Tijera.

"Why do you want him so bad? Why after all this time?" Charlotte asked.

I zoned out, melding my mind with the uneven grooves of asphalt on the road. "Why are you here, Charlotte?"

"Excuse me?"

"Why are you out here in Cali with me? Why did you come?"

"Honestly, I'm here to show you support. That's the God's honest truth," she admitted. "I think it's great that you're out here, 3,000 miles away, following your passion. That kinda shit inspires me. So I decided to follow my passion."

"Acting?"

"Yeah," she nodded. "I mean, really. We all know that there's only but so much acting you can do in Atlanta, and it's mostly just for the stage. I don't care if Tyler Perry's building a studio. If I'm gonna be real about this, if I'm gonna be true to myself and my soul and pursue my dream of being a film actress, I'm gonna have to find out if I was really meant to do this. And the only way I can find out is by coming out here. Just like you, I've gotta find out. I've gotta take a chance."

That last part really resonated with me. Traffic began to move more freely.

"You know why I want him so bad, after all this time? Because I still love him, and I know that love was once mutual. But if there's any way we can revive that love, I've gotta find out. I've gotta take a chance."

*

Angie made a nice little addition to our growing girl group. When we hit the LA nightlife scene, we looked like the second coming of Destiny's Child. We all bared a little something: Charlotte—legs, Angie—cleavage, and myself—

midriff. Showing up at the door to the party back room of the hip Beverly Hills restaurant called Spark (formerly known as Reign, and once owned by pro football player Keyshawn Johnson) looking the way we did assured us of getting in for free.

Once inside, I was severely disappointed. The room was full of me's. Everywhere I looked there were tall, impossibly beautiful women who had bodies as good as mine with better hair. I was humbled instantly. And there were just entirely too many of them in the room. I counted only ten men in a room full of at least forty women.

Charlotte and Angie didn't seem as intimidated, however, as they made a beeline for the bar. Accustomed to always being one of the finest women in the room, I painfully accepted the fact that I might actually have to pay for my own drink in this place. After Charlotte spent ten dollars for a drink, with tip, I decided that I would never be that thirsty.

Within a few minutes, they both struck up conversations with attractive, if not vapid-looking men. I enjoyed the loud hip hop music and impressively smoke-free, chatty atmosphere of the pseudo-club. No smoking in a club? Gotta love LA.

Try as I might, I still couldn't fend off the foolhardy from trying. Charlotte was fond of theorizing that there were eleven types of men. I think I met about four of them in the space of an hour.

"Hey, Pretty Lady. How are you doing tonight?" Mr. High Roller. He will give you money with no questions asked. He has a lot of style to him. He will show you the finer things in life. He will also overpay for everything, never return your pages, and feels he can come to your house at any time without calling.

After ten minutes of sustaining his very polished, thoroughly underwhelming game (I think he expected women to swoon at his feet just because he had a money grip the size of tropical eggplant), I dismissed him with an easy lie and unreceptive body posture. That did not stop him from foisting upon me his card, nevertheless. Real estate. Big deal.

"What's goin' on, Slim?" Mr. Playa. His game was real smooth. He will tell you that you're not the only one, because he keeps it real (and you in competition with low self-esteem chickenheads). He will tell you that you've changed him and that he's ready to settle down. Rarely will he ever mean it. He has a job and an apartment, and invites you to move in with him—but only to save money on rent. He is only sometimes decent in bed, expects you to believe all his lies, and generally won't stand up for anything. He won't acknowledge you in public. And don't let there be other women around, because I would lose my natural mind if I caught him peeping other chicks. And after you find out he's no good, he tells you that he was a playa in the beginning anyway.

No thanks. At one point in my life, I really went for that type of guy. You know, those guys who were sexy and a little dangerous, whom you knew weren't good for you but dated anyway. Jacque was one of those guys. Eventually, I grew up and deserved my Nick.

Hmph. My Nick. He will always be "my Nick."

I sent Mr. Playa along his way without even entertaining the idea of giving him my number. But, of course, he left his card. It was one of those photo business cards that had him shirtless, staring at the camera in a vain attempt to be sexy. What a waste of four and a half feet of bar space.

"How goes the evening, my sista?" Mr. Righteous Black Man! He will teach you black history. He fashions himself as a revolutionary. Inspiring and giving to you spiritually and emotionally, he wants a wife and family. However, he is counter-evolutionary (i.e. doesn't have a job), he's always wearing camouflage (like this joker here was), and he breaks up with you for a white piece of trash. Just like the rest of them, you find out he is just a trifling con artist.

Well, the revolution would not be televised—or at least not on WJAZ. I released him by turning into a conversation with Angie and Charlotte. Mr. Revolutionary did not have a business card, either. A business card represented yet another manifestation of the racist conformities of society at work in the representation of minority communities. Whatever.

"Hi. How're you doing?" When Mr. I'm in Entertainment stepped to me, I was so over men in this club I nearly dissed him out of hand. Good thing I didn't. Not only could this guy get us on the guest list at all the fly parties, but also he dressed nice and could hold a stimulating conversation. I still didn't know if he was homo- or heterosexual, but he seemed like a nice, if not flighty guy. And he just so turned out to be a talent agent.

"Ben," I lit up, moving aside, "meet my girl, Charlotte. She just so happens to be in town, looking for representation."

"Charlotte Royer," she introduced, flipping on the charm as she shook his hand.

Angie winked at me as I made room for them, removing myself from the bar. This tall, slim, tanned agent was good looking in his light Armani suit jacket.

With Charlotte charming the man while Angie drooled over him, I decided to explore a new area of the anteroom. As I wandered about, nursing my Amaretto Sour paid for by Mr. Playa, I saw a familiar face, surrounded by a gaggle of women.

Mark Dietz.

From out of his cloud of nubile LA fineness, Mark noticed me across the room. I didn't try to approach him, yet I didn't try to hide either. I just looked. He looked. Although ensconced by a posse of womanhood, Mark acknowledged my presence with a smile, then returned to his business of being a mid-level TV star.

As silly/shallow/ugly as it may have seemed, for an instant, I wanted him. And I was okay with that.

*

Suffice it to say, I called the number on his card. I found him to be pleasant, engaging, and accessible. It was primarily the latter part I was concerned about, as I had set up an interview for the next day. Angie and I set it up in one of the hotel's conference rooms, where Mark was gracious enough to meet us that afternoon. Charlotte was off meeting with Ben the agent, who wanted to audition her for the partners at the firm. My girl was off doing her job; it was time for me to do mine.

At times, it was hard being professional. When Mark swept in with his overwhelming sense of Hollywood actor cool, it was hard not to react. So Angie did.

Biting her lip, she murmured to me, "Dag, Miss Jasmine! He sho' is sexy up close!"

Now I firmly considered the black man to be God in the form of man. But the olive-skinned Filipino Mark gave me a moment of pause.

Shaking off my admiring camerawoman, I stepped over and

firmly shook his hand. "Mr. Dietz. Thank you for coming on such short notice."

Mark smiled warmly. "Not at all. I had the day off today anyway."

We both sat down. Somehow, Angie found her way behind the camera and began making her professional adjustments.

So did I. As I consulted my notes, I used my peripheral vision in the wonderfully subtle way us women did to check out a man without checking him out. I felt a little ashamed that I had briefly lusted for him the night before. Something about being in a room with a man that popular, and watching women react to that popularity, just did something to me. I'm not above admitting that I'm human. I just wouldn't admit to it too often. But that human weakness had served me well, by finally jumpstarting my excuse for being out here and calling the man for an interview.

The interview went well. As he had done at least a hundred times before, Mark handled the questions about the show, himself, and the Emmys with natural aplomb. It was a sit-down between two professionals being professional about their professions. Although a good interview, there wasn't enough here for me to win a HART. Mark was a good interview, but it wasn't sexy enough—not enough conflict, drama, or controversy going on in his life. I would need some more interviews with stars to make any kind of difference in my so-called Emmy Week special. I'm sure Beverly Bradley was crawling around on all fours through some crack flophouse about to expose the head of the Atlanta school board on drug possession charges or something. And look sexy while doing it.

At the end of the interview, Mark could sense something was not right. "Are you okay?"

"I'm fine" came my response.

"No, really. Was the interview what you were looking for?"

Mark was really intuitive—for a man. "Yes and no. There's just not enough controversy going on in your life, Mark," I chuckled genially.

He smiled. "I'll admit that. I'm living a bit of a charmed life right now. Well, save having a date for the Emmys."

I caught that, boy, I didn't say. Mark did earn a sly smile for his efforts.

"Well, while you're here, would you like me to set you up on an interview with some of my friends? They've got some drama going on."

My eyes perked up. "Like who?"

"Ananda Lewis, Charlie Sheen, maybe Robert Downey, Jr."

My mouth gaped open. Drama, drama, and mo' drama! "Are you kidding me?"

"Not at all. We meet over at my house for Scrabble on Thursday nights when we're not too busy. Ananda's a helluva Scrabble player."

Whatever. Just get me in! "Could I bring Angie with me and talk to your friends tomorrow night?"

"By all means."

I sighed. "Mark, that is incredibly generous of you. I don't know how to repay you. What would you like in return?"

"In return? For doing you this favor?" he clarified.

"Yes," I said, bracing for the inevitable. Whether I wanted to or not, it looked like I was going to the Emmys. Even Angie politely leaned an ear in anticipation.

Once again, Mark flashed a friendly, telegenic smile. "Nothing."

*

"For the record, I don't think this is a good idea."

"Duly noted," I told Charlotte. The three of us—Angie, Char, and myself—sat in the rented Benz, parked across the street from the Fox lot (I had decided to name my rental car "Connie," since she was a convertible. If you rented a car for three days or more, you had to name her, in my book.). Ostensibly, we were waiting on Nick.

"I think there are laws in California against stalking people, especially movie stars," Charlotte mentioned.

"I'm not stalking him, and he's not a movie star. Yet. He's my ex-boyfriend."

Angie and Charlotte glanced at each other. "Rrrrright," Angie said.

"Do you even know what kinda whip he's pushin'?" Charlotte asked. "Now that he got the big money and all, he might have a new ride."

"I don't think he's had the time," I assessed. "Back in San Diego, he was still rollin' in the 4Runner. Besides, I know for a fact that material things like a new car are not his focus right now."

"Paychecks can change people."

"But not my Nick."

It was nightfall, just a few hours after I had finished interviewing Mark. Charlotte's interview/audition for the agency had gone off well. They wanted her to come back in three weeks to audition for this big national L'Oreal commercial and ad campaign. If she was one of the three girls picked, the agency would sign and represent her. It was amazing what could come out of a few drinks in a Beverly Hills restaurant.

"I love you, J, but I ain't goin' to jail for you," Charlotte announced. Angie giggled.

"I thought you told me to follow my passion? I'm following my passion," I rationalized.

"I meant figuratively, not literally."

"Hey, look, y'all. A 4Runner!" Angie noticed.

It was Nick's. I recognized the license plates. As the sparkling forest green, chromed-out sports utility vehicle turned right on Pico and headed west, I had Connie bust a quick U-turn and followed him. Charlotte crossed her legs nervously and gripped the side of the car. Excited, Angie turned the camera on and began shooting some stock traveling footage of LA from the backseat.

We followed Nick for a good mile and a half. As it was eight o'clock, traffic was lighter, but not nonexistent. The warm, early fall breeze slapped us in the face as we pursued the 4Runner, the top down. Truly, I had no idea what I would say to him once I caught him. I just knew I had to do something, say something, having finally committed to getting him back and having flown across the continent in order to do so.

It was a mixture of anxiety and relief when Nick finally pulled into a Ralph's supermarket parking lot. I parked Connie several yards away and hopped out of the car. Vaguely aware

Angie was taping me all the way, I strode after Nick after he climbed out of his SUV. "Nick!"

Nick turned. His expression measured more anger than disbelief. "Go away, Jasmine."

"Nick, I need to talk to you!"

"What you need, Jasmine, is to go home," he retorted, not breaking stride.

My grabbing his arm ground him to a halt. He snatched his arm back. "What!" he snapped.

       "Five minutes," I huffed.

"You've got two." Coldly, Nick consulted his watch. "Go."

This wasn't quite as romantic as I had envisioned, but beggars can't be choosers.

"I love you," I said, as if that could solve our troubled, complex history.

Nick was not moved.

"And I know you love me, too."

Nick would not give me the satisfaction of a response.

"I'm ready to be with you. I want to give it a shot."

Nick was a sienna statue of silence.

"Please, Nick?" I begged. "Please?"

Nick checked his watch again. "Is that all?"

"Whaddaya mean 'Is that all?'"

"Are you finished? Have you said what you have to say?" he responded icily. "Because if you have nothing further, I have to get a few things before going home to my fiancée."

No, no, no, no, no! This was not how it was supposed to go down! "That's all you have to say for yourself? Don't you feel anything? Don't you have any kind of response?"

"Look, Jasmine," he growled, his patience growing thin, "I'm not even supposed to be talking to you. I promised my fiancée I wouldn't ever see you again. Now I can't help it if you want to stalk me—"

"I'm not stalking you," I interrupted.

"Whatever, Jasmine. I'm not a lawyer. But I don't want to see you come to my job. I don't want to see you following me around. I don't want to see you hounding me at the Emmys. I don't—"

"You're going to the Emmys?" That raised my antennae.

He seemed irritated by my question. "Yes. But the bottom line is I don't want to have this conversation. It's over. It's been over. We've been over."

"But our kiss..."

"You mean your kiss. You kissed me, twice. That proved nothing." Nick turned to leave. "Go home, Jasmine. Find a man who loves you and get on with the rest of your life. Because I have. And I simply don't love you anymore."

Nick left me standing there, in the parking lot, slumped shoulders and all.

*

With the ignominy of last night behind me, I piloted the girls and Connie up some treacherous curves of picturesque Laurel Canyon in the Hollywood Hills. We were en route to Mark's house, a two level, four thousand square foot home that rested atop one of the many wooded peaks that afforded a spectacular view of LA and the San Fernando Valley. I parked Connie next to a shiny black Jaguar coupe in the rotunda style driveway to Mark's large, beautifully landscaped home. We admired every detail life of the rich and famous afforded us. It had been a few years since she had dated a professional athlete so Charlotte re-accustomed her eyes to such a display of wealth. Angie had never seen such personal largess, greedily capturing what she could on tape with the shoulder-mounted camera.

Mark greeted us at the door. Once inside, I had to take inventory of the place. His was a tastefully done, modern style home, characterized by an eclectic mixture of Asian, European, and American art with high vaulted ceilings. The decor was simple yet expensive, a hallmark of the rich who liked to keep life uncluttered. Just the fact that I had noticed all this bothered me. It had been Nick who had solidified my love for houses and interior design.

In the nicely decked out game room, the gang was all there. Ananda wore a furry, skimpy, dressy casual top with a pair of leather pants as easily as if she were wearing a tank top and sweats. Charlie Sheen smoked a cigarette out on the patio that

80

shot off of the game room, while a not-quite-so-sober looking Robert Downey, Jr. set up the board and the word pieces. Even when he was allegedly, publicly "sober," he looked like something the wagon had tossed off. Introductions were made and drinks were offered as Charlotte helped Angie set up to tape.

As promised, each of Mark's friends were interesting, with drama to spare. Sistagurl Ananda, whose dead talk show had once been groomed as a younger, hipper Oprah, entertained me with tales of professional obstacles on the comeback trail (she had starred in several cheesy reality shows—clear cut signs of the C-List TV personality; plus doing—gasp!—morning radio) and personal male conquests off camera. Charlie Sheen would only talk about his TV show, which still opened itself up to reports of personality clashes on the set, as well as about the Emmy he was up for as Outstanding Lead Actor in a Comedy Series. Robert Downey, Jr. was sullen and withdrawn, barely answering my questions and opening speculation up to if he was back on drugs again. Regardless, I had three priceless interviews in the space of an hour, something that could be spliced together into an excellent special report. Angie and I would go over to our Los Angeles Fox affiliate back on the infamous Fox lot to cut the video and send it over to Nadine in Atlanta.

A fierce game of Scrabble ensued. "Minorities" versus "The Man," as they called themselves—Ananda and Mark versus Charlie and Robert—went at it for a good two and a half hours. One thing I learned real quick was that Ananda could manufacture a triple word score out of five consonants and no vowels.

After the Minorities won for the third time in five games, everyone decided to call it a night. Charlotte, aglow that she had met one of her fashion inspirations, gave Ananda a hug before the talk show host left. Angie dismantled her camera set-up and headed toward the car. Charlie walked Robert out to their cars. As I helped put away the Scrabble pieces, Mark and I had a moment alone.

"Thanks for coming," Mark actually said. "You added a real cool vibe. They all like you, and trust you."

"Pretty rare for a journalist, huh?" I grinned. That was why I was going to win the HART, dang it!

The Scrabble game was all boxed up. It was time for me to go. Mark walked me to the door. No kiss, just a very tight hug.

"Yes," I said.

"Pardon?"

"Yes, I will be your date to the Emmys on Sunday."

*

Friday was pretty straightforward. Char dropped us off at the Fox lot that afternoon to go drive around to modeling and talent agencies to submit headshot resumés. Angie and I breezed by Security Guard with a smile, as this time we were on the list (thank you, Nadine). I resisted the temptation to go over to Stage 19, the big studio where they were filming Sand Adventures. To see Nick so soon would only anger him more. We spent about three hours in one of the editing suites cutting footage into a nice little thirty-minute package to send to Nadine to cut even more. I took a good look at the surroundings in the Fox national headquarters. Winning the HART would yield me all this, the brass ring, a shot at a national anchor desk position.

When Char scooped us up, we headed straight to the bars of Sunset Boulevard, where we easily passed the time until the clubs opened. The three of us settled on the Goodbar, a small, trendy, packed place at the western end of the Sunset Strip that featured more nationalities than the United Nations, all dancing under the universally cool hip hop beat. Once again, when faced with stiff beauty competition inside the club, I realized that I was just a blip on the radar in this strange land of similarly long-legged creatures. I think we stumbled back to the hotel about three in the morning.

Saturday was different. We had a day to prepare for tomorrow evening's Emmy awards show. I kept that in mind as we cruised through the upscale outdoor mall of Century City under cloudless skies. I was nervous. I had never been to a major, internationally televised Hollywood awards show. The dress had to be just right. And with Mark footing the bill, it would be.

To hear Char tell it, the dress had to be something more. "Yo, ma. Put that one back."

"What's wrong with this one?" I asked, holding up the elegant, long, simply red Donna Karan spaghetti strapped dress.

"It's nice but this store ain't for you," Charlotte decided, steering me toward the exit. She snatched a Calvin Klein dress out of Angie's hands and tossed it in the general direction of the rack on our way out the store. Diva Fashionista was on the case.

DF wouldn't let me go into my favorite store of all time, Ann Taylor, so I gave myself entirely to her fashionably informed hands. We roamed from boutique to boutique rejecting more than accepting. Diva Fashionista spurned elegant trifles from Carolina Herrera, Vera Wang, and Oscar de la Renta. Charlotte was clearly the Beyoncé to our Destiny's Child.

And then she found it. Holding it up with fragile hands as if it were the Miss Universe tiara, Charlotte revealed the fruits of our labor. It was stunning. It was backless. It was a blue Badgeley Mischka.

Allowing Angie to hold the gown ever so gingerly, Charlotte twirled me around slowly, reinforcing her vision. Her lips formed into a smile.

"Oh yeah, ma. We gonna make you look hot!"

*

I don't know why I was watching it, but I was. Funny how I had seen myself on TV or tape hundreds of times now, yet watching Angie's taping of my parking lot defeat with Nick was brutal. Almost unwatchable.

I studied my body language. I didn't seem confident at all. Not at all of singular purpose and mission. Kinda like I was half-assing the entire venture. Shoot, I would've rejected me, too. Rarely had I ever looked so unconfident on tape. What made it even worse was the fact you could tell all this in the poorly lit footage taken in a Ralph's parking lot from a distance. Maybe the uncertainty came from not knowing what to say and how to say it. Maybe the uncertainty came from having to say anything at all.

Angie shook her head as she twisted my hair with a curling iron. She was already in a simple working dress that was classy enough for the affair tonight yet still free enough to allow her to carry her camera. Charlotte buzzed around my dress in the bathroom, gently steaming free any wrinkles with her portable mini-iron. I sat on the edge of the hotel room bed, knock-kneed in my slip, pressing rewind on the large shoulder camera Angie had hooked up to the TV. "You sho' is a glutton fo' punishment, Miss Jasmine," Angie commented with a gentle suck of her teeth.

I blocked her out, focusing on my performance.

The phone rang, and I leaned over to get it. "Hello?"

"Jasmine, honey. It's Nadine."

"Whassup, girl."

"If I've said it once, I'll say it again—great piece for the pre-Emmys awards show," Nadine gushed. "We just ran the four interview story for our in-house staff and they flipped. I'm putting it on in an hour, right before the telecast."

"Thanks, Nadine."

"Is this HART worthy? Probably not," she admitted. "But you've been building quite a nice little résumé for yourself this past week."

"How's Polly doing?" I asked, eager to deflect the attention.

"Struggling," snorted my boss. "Just do a good job tonight, hurry up, and head home soon, okay?"

"Yes, ma'am."

"Shush, honey."

I smiled. I loved it when Nadine "shushed" me. So Southern, so old school.

"You have a great time tonight," she wished. "Have fun."

"Go home, Nadine. Go home to your fiancé."

I could almost hear her smile. "Will do. Bye."

"Bye." I hung up and rewound the tape. Angie finished doing my hair and began to start on my makeup.

Eventually I spoke, as the tape ran again. "Char?"

"Yeah, ma."

"What's the best way to get an ex-boyfriend to notice you?"

Charlotte stopped steaming long enough to consider the question. Then she smiled. "To look better than his new girl."

"Right."

"To show up looking devastatingly better than his new girl."

I stopped the tape, right at the part where Nick entered the supermarket and my shoulders slumped. Sometimes the best offense was no offense at all. I glared steely determination at the image frozen on the screen.

"Do it," I authorized. "Let's devastate."

*

The Shrine Auditorium was a classically built structure, a Spanish Colonial Revival style building with shining white domed cupolas on opposing ends. The building was impressive in its Moorish detail, capable of holding 6700 people, according to the press kit. The very informative press kit also notified me that the Grammys, the American Music Awards, and occasionally the Academy Awards were also hosted in this building. Not bad for a building located just north of the infamous South Central Los Angeles area, right across the street from the University of Southern California. I clearly hid behind my press kit when the conversation faltered inside the limousine.

Angie had gone ahead of me by half an hour to set up outside the red carpet with the rest of the press corps. Charlotte, who was without an invite or a press pass, was chillin' back in the room, watching the events on TV. And here I sat in a limo with my Emmy-nominated TV star date, a man I had known for all of one week.

I did give Mark his props. He had been a perfect gentleman so far to this point. He showed up with a modest arrangement of flowers as a thank you for the date. The limo was a nice touch, however standard it may be for these types of events. And, most importantly, he appropriately complimented me on my beauty.

I have to say that I looked ravishing tonight. With few alterations, the Badgeley Mischka hung off my peanut butter body like it was made for me. My hair was curled and swept up, caught by two black chopsticks in the back. One scintillating curl dangled down the left side of my face. My light brown, pecan flavored skin was exposed from the neck down to my shoulders, as the shiny blue dress cupped my breasts in the front, swooped down my sides to my butt, exposing my elegant, if not bony, back and shoulderblades. The gown flowed down to my knees, where it flared out into an ecstasy of blue ruffles just above my matching Prada shoes. I even smelled good, wearing my new favorite fragrance, Shisheido. Topping off my outfit was a simple, sparkling Tiffany diamond necklace Mark had surprised me with when he had picked me up at the hotel. Over my protestations, I ended up wearing it because it really set the whole dress off, if not for his overwhelming generosity. I had no intentions of keeping the necklace, especially since Mark told me it was on loan. I was not that type of woman.

So when the limo pulled up to the red carpet just as another one had pulled off after dumping out the Will and Grace co-stars, we stepped out into a chorus of snapping shutters and hailstorm of flashing bulbs, the picture of Hollywood perfection. Mark strayed a bit from a traditional tuxedo, opting for a tieless, collarless Versace dress shirt underneath a custom made black Hugo Boss suit. In his only homage to Hollywood star life, Mark, regrettably, wore sunglasses. It made him look too-cool and very Hollywood. But who was I to judge? I was in a bright blue, fitted, six thousand dollar concession to his world.

Mark had been to a few of these so he knew how to vamp appropriately for the press. I copied him. Hell, just fifteen months ago I was just another mid-level production assistant at the TV station. My local mini-celebrity status as a broadcaster the past year had not adequately prepared me for global functions like this.

Just when it occurred to me that millions of people around the world were watching my entrance with one of the finest men in Hollywood, and that old, jealous windbag Joan Rivers might be inventing some disparaging remarks about my dress for cable television, I sought out Angie, who was sandwiched in the midst of the press corps halfway up the red carpet, pressed against the velvet rope restraint. I led Mark over there and stood directly in front of Angie to give her the brief exclusive. She thrust a WAGA emblazoned microphone into my hand and we were on our way. We were going live back home.

"In three…two…"

"Thanks, Polly. Good evening, Atlanta. This is Jasmine Selene, live from the red carpet in front of the Shrine Auditorium in Los Angeles, California for the 58th Annual Primetime Emmy Awards. As you can see, this is a star-studded affair complete with actors, producers, and directors from the small screen, as well as the requisite California sunshine. So why should my date be any different?"

I saw Angie zoom out to include Mark in the shot.

"My sponsor for this evening, my guest pass to the Hollywood glitterati, is TV star and Emmy nominee for Outstanding Supporting Actor in a Drama Series, Mark Dietz. Say hello to the folks back in Atlanta, Georgia for us, Mark."

I handed the mike over to Mark, who smoothly said, "Good evening, Atlanta. You all have a wonderful anchorwoman here. I have to say I'm jealous. You all get to enjoy her every week on TV while I just get to enjoy her for the evening. I'll make sure she has a good time."

I couldn't help it—the man made me blush. My professional playfulness saved me. "Hear that, folks? Even on their night off, they're still acting out here in LA!"

Angie grinned wildly, giving me a thumbs-up from behind the camera. Mark laughed good-naturedly. Cedric the Entertainer, Jennifer Aniston sans the latest boyfriend, and Martin Sheen rolled past me in the background.

"Well as the stars continue to shine, Atlanta, I'm afraid I have to go. I hear they only serve the rubber chicken to the first fifteen hundred inside while the rest have to get by on breadsticks. Stay tuned to Fox 5 for all of your Emmy awards coverage, including the ceremony televised live in an hour, a repeat of my interviews with Mark Dietz, Ananda Lewis, Emmy-nominated Charlie Sheen, and former Emmy award winner Robert Downey, Jr., and for our post-Emmys report, live from one of the many Emmy parties sure to be happening after the show. In the meantime—"

I grabbed onto Mark's arm, linking his with mine.

"—I'm going inside to have a good time." Inexplicably, I winked at the camera. I was such an actress when the cameras rolled, I swear. "Have a good night, Atlanta! Back to you, Polly."

Angie switched off the camera, lowering it. "That was it, Miss

Jasmine. That was it!"

I scrunched my nose knowingly at her. "I'll see you later, Ang." Arm still linked with Mark's, I said to him, "Shall we?"

Mark grinned at his newly and professionally validated arm-charm for the evening. If I had cared, I think my stock just shot through the roof with this guy. "We shall."

As we strolled up the red carpet arm in arm, radiating sparkling glam Hollywood multiculturalism, I barely noticed a stunned looking tuxedoed man and his earthily/eclectically dressed woman gawk at our passing. The moment was brief and instantaneous. With his woman on his arm, he noticed me. I noticed him notice me. His eyes were pure shock, if not tempered with a twinge of admiration. A thin smile formed on my full lips as I turned my head back to the front. It was Nick with Tabitha.

Char would be proud. I devastated.

*

Sometimes I would like to be wrong about things. The chicken was rubbery and a no-holds barred disappointment. The star atmosphere, however, made up for it. While maintaining a faux-aura of belonging, I delighted in seeing all my favorite TV actors in the same very large room.

Once we were settled into our seats for the ceremony, I could see Nick about three rows away, two in front of me, one over. I didn't stare him down but I would sneak occasional peeks at him, just to see if he was still "devastated" by my appearance here. When I caught him flit his eyes in my direction once, I knew that he was. Told y'all I looked good.

As they rolled through award after award, stopping for the requisite commercial breaks, they finally got to Mark's award.

"The nominees for Outstanding Supporting Actor in a Drama Series are…"

They announced the nominees and everything. I clapped after Mark's name, the last listed, was called. That's when I noticed Nick cut his eyes at me again! This time he wasn't even slick about it—he dared to check me out with his woman right

88

next to him. Just the fact that he looked a second time, corroboration of the facts of his interest if you asked me, made me happier than Tabitha's quietly panicked reaction of giving him a weak kiss on the cheek. I smirked in victory.

"And the winner is…"

I already knew. Me.

This was the dirty work you would never hear about. The on your belly, crawling through the dusty, rat-inhabited crawlspace that made actual knowledge of their jobs thoroughly unglamorous, yet wholly necessary nonetheless dirty work. Six members of the Atlanta Police Department's elite, special forces Red Dog unit inched along the ground on their bellies—plus two.

Their two hangers-on were annoyances, but annoyances whose presence was beyond their control. They would tolerate them, so long as they still made the bust.

One of the additions had her bright red hair pulled back into an unusually ordinary ponytail that stuck out the back of her police issue baseball cap. She crawled on her belly through the crawlspace right behind the Red Dog, her cameraman two steps behind her. Her name was Beverly Bradley.

The captain of this squad stopped crawling. He indicated for everyone to stop with a clenched fist. They all stopped. He watched the floorboards of the crawlspace ceiling creak under the weight of human pressure. The distinctive stench of pig's feet was so strong it managed to filter into the crawlspace. Beverly considered holding her breath.

Snapping his fingers two times brought a micro-sized one-eyed surveillance kit, complete with a long, pencil thin surveillance stick. The captain filtered the device through the vent directly above him and into the room. The device was so small, one would have to be looking for it to find it. And no one in the room full of people who sat around cutting vast amounts of cocaine into nickel and dime bags knew that Red Dog was coming for them.

After seeing what needed to be seen, the captain led the retreat from under the crawlspace and into the backyard of the place. With everyone dressed in black SWAT-stealth approved gear, they meshed with the darkness of the night. Following the captain's lead, the six-member detachment, plus two, scurried silently around to the back door, save the cameraman tripping over a dog chain, but not falling.

The captain took a visual assessment of the five others to see if they were ready. He could've given two craps about the representatives of the free press. They were Red Dog, not Cops. A portable battering ram was passed to the man right next to the captain. Third man down the line adjusted the Velcro to his bulletproof vest. Then a thumbs-high. His men were ready.

Counting silently with his fingers, the captain showed... One...Two...Three!

The battering ram busted down the door with one, shattering swing.

"Red Dog, Red Dog! Atlanta Police! Red Dog!"

Red Dog members rushed inside the house, weapons drawn, barking and screaming, flowing off the adrenaline rush of doing their job. They really were barking like dogs while a couple others kept screaming out their identity. "Red Dog! Atlanta Police! Red Dog!"

The drug dealers scrambled. One darted out of the kitchen they raided, presumably toward the front door. Another dealer rushed toward the bathroom, only to be tackled by a Red Dog who seemed to know his instincts before he did. The other dealer overturned the table stacked with cocaine and threw himself behind it. The entire scene was fast, thrilling, and exciting—and it was all caught on tape.

Beverly entered the kitchen less than half a step behind the Red Dog, her cameraman by her side. The dealer behind the table popped up with a Magnum and began firing. Before catching a bullet right in the thigh and falling, the dealer fired, with Beverly catching one square in the chest! She fell right on her back.

"God-fucking-Damnit!" cursed the captain, attending to his civilian. From his kneeled position, he barked the order, "Nelson, make sure Jefferson gives up that fucking piece!"

The captain turned back to the fallen Beverly Bradley. "Fuck!"

Red Dog Nelson calmly placed a gun to the temple of the fallen drug dealer Raytonio Jefferson. Although there was a pool of blood beneath his thigh, he would be all right. Without a fight,

Raytonio gave up the gun.

Fluttering her eyes after a moment, Beverly opened them wide. "Am I...?"

"Jesus, Bradley!" The captain yanked her up to her feet. "You caught a bullet in the vest. Scared the shit out of us!"

Numbly, Beverly nodded. The wind was knocked out of her, so she took the opportunity to rest by hunching over, catching her breath.

"You could've gotten fucking killed tonight! This is the exact fucking reason why I don't want you fucking civilians trying to turn our special action unit into fucking Cops!"

Regaining her acid civility, Beverly brushed herself off as she said, "Thank you. I'm alright. How're you doin'?"

"Ahh!" The captain stalked off in disgust while Nelson worked on cuffing Jefferson.

Beverly unVelcroed the straps to her bulletproof vest so she could breathe a little. Pulled out the bullet—which was still hot— from her vest. She turned to her cameraman, whose light was on with the camera. "Did you get all that?" Beverly wheezed.

"Did I!"

Beverly smiled, patting her cameraman on the back. "I mean you got all of that? The part where he shot me in the chest?"

"All of it, Bev."

"Great job, Ernie."

The anchorwoman for WXIA glanced sadly at the bleeding Raytonio Jefferson, lying on the floor, being cuffed in a pool of his own blood. Briefly, Raytonio glanced back. Beverly turned away, awash in a small smile of ultimate satisfaction.

It was sad when the media did a better job tracking down criminals than the authorities did. That was the only way Beverly had bargained her way—and her cameraman's—onto this highly dangerous ride-along with the APD's specialized crime task force. She had done their work for them.

When she had approached Raytonio Jefferson, he knew he was going down. If a friggin' white newscaster could find his black ass in the midst of Atlanta's all-black SWATs by herself, there was no way to keep the cops off of him. So Beverly had given him a heads-up. Raytonio had hidden most of his assets in laundered accounts that would be waiting for him when he got out of jail, plus interest. His family (four kids by three different mothers) was quietly provided for before tonight. And he had turned in an excellent performance by shooting Beverly in the chest, right on cue.

The exchange was mutual. It was the best two grand Beverly Bradley had spent in her career

5

"I CAN'T ACCEPT THIS, MARK."

"Yes you can." Mark leaned suggestively toward me in the limo. We were parked outside the Westin early the next morning, around 5AM. We were drunk off the air of celebration following the Emmys that night. The parties had been off the hook. "It's not like I'm doing a Ving Rhames and giving you my Emmy."

I was so proud of the fact that he had won the darn thing. When it had happened, when Bette Midler had said, "Mark Dietz" as the winner of Outstanding Supporting Actor in a Drama Series, the cameras had instantly zoomed in our direction. Mark had emitted genuine surprise, and I had looked like the pimpstress of the evening. Although I had not checked at the time, I'm sure Nick must have felt something to see his ex-girlfriend carrying on with an Emmy-award winning actor.

With childlike eyes, I gazed at the gold plated, atom-toting, angelically structured statuette for the umpteenth time that evening. They were pretty, they were heavy, they were sharp. The angel's pointed wings could've taken someone's eye out if the limo had hit a pothole.

But we were talking about something altogether different. "Still, I can't accept this."

"It's just a necklace. It's a gift."

"Mark…this is a twenty thousand dollar gift," I pointed out. "I thought you said it was on loan."

"It was. It's not anymore."

I sighed. "Why would you want to buy this for me? You hardly even know me." And don't you dare think this sparkly piece of diamond delight is gonna get you upstairs, either.

"I like you, Jasmine. Can I say that?" A charming smile.

"You just did."

"I like you, it's beautiful, and it looks great on you. You should wear it. You should have it," he said.

I ran my fingers over the smoothly polished stones that lounged around my neck. They didn't make the protest any easier.

"Don't think you can curry favor with me by buying me things." I stopped my fingers from running over the South African diamond hills on my chest. "Even expensive things."

"Like I said, Jasmine, consider it a gift. From one friend to another," Mark offered innocently.

Yeah, right. "Friends?"

"Friends," he affirmed. "On one condition."

I sighed again. Here we go… "Which is?"

"That you come and play Scrabble with us next time. Bring your friend Charlotte, too, if she's in town."

I gave the Emmy award-winning Supporting Actor in a Drama Series a peck on his cheek. I beamed. "Deal."

*

When I returned to the room, it was dark. Charlotte was already asleep on her side of the bed while Angie was knocked out in her room down the hall. I always thought it funny that a woman as pretty and feminine as Char could snore chainsaws with the best of them. I tried not to wake her as I shuffled around in the dark, but the bathroom light awakened her.

"That you, J?"

"Go back to sleep, Char. We'll talk in the morning."

"No, I'm up," she struggled, turning on the dresser light and propping herself up on her elbows. "How was it?"

I emerged from the bathroom, my hair now let down. "It was cool."

"I bet. I saw you on—Holy shit!" Charlotte had just noticed the Tiffany necklace still around my neck. "Damn, ma! I saw you on TV with it on, but he let you keep it!"

I kicked off my shoes. "He insisted. He's a real sweet guy."

"And you're a sucker! You really think he's gonna give you

some eleven thousand dollar necklace without expecting somethin' in return?"

"It's twenty," I corrected, cracking open a bottle of water and taking a sip. "And he's going to have to. Because you know I don't play that. He said it was a gift."

Charlotte shook her head in obvious disbelief. "Hollywood, ma. Nobody gives gifts like that but Hollywood. That's wild."

"He did give it to me on one condition." I sipped. "He said that the next time we're back in town, we have to go over and play Scrabble with them."

Charlotte snorted. "I ain't playin' Scrabble with Ananda! That girl can win a game with nine vowels and a dictionary."

"So did you watch the show?" I asked, slipping out of my dress.

"Yeah. It was aw'ight, I guess," Charlotte grumbled. "Once again, not enough black representation among the nominees or the winners. Typical Hollyhood."

"Yet you want in on this lifestyle?" I critiqued.

"Desperately," Charlotte breathed. Switching gears, she asked, "So when do we go home?"

"You can go home anytime you like," I invited. "I want at least one more full day here to get at Nick."

"Slow your roll, Beyoncé. We're a team now. I go when you go."

That was touching. Char really was my girl. In a lot of respects, she reminded me of Mia, when things had still been good between us. "Thanks, Char. But don't you have a job?"

"It's temping, girl. They ain't missin' me," Charlotte said. "So what're we doing tomorrow?"

Standing there in my slip, I fingered the necklace for the sixth time since it officially became mine. "I've got an idea."

*

Late next morning, I marched with a full head of steam into the offices of Townsend Talent Agency. I had learned that Shelby Townsend was Nick's agent from a quick call to the Screen Actors Guild. I was dressed conservatively professional in a sexy little gray business suit. Charlotte accompanied me, dressed similarly in a navy business suit. We wore austere, serious looking faces, even though we were on a mission full of crap.

A strapping, young blond guy tanned within an inch of his life greeted us at the receptionist desk. "May I help you?"

"Yes," I said tightly. "May I speak with Shelby Townsend, please."

"Do you have an appointment, ma'am?"

"No."

He picked up the phone. "And you are?"

"Ana Roulet and Marielle Rodriguez with Tiffany & Company."

Tan Man relayed the curious message to his boss. After her response, he asked me, "And this is concerning?"

"A private matter with one of her clients—Nick."

"Oh, okay." Into the phone: "No, it's not about Fredo this time. Nick. Okay."

Tan Man hung up. "She'll be with you shortly."

"Thank you."

Noticing us not move, Tan Man said, "You can have a seat."

"No thank you. We prefer to stand," I squashed in a clipped tone. Charlotte/Marielle sneaked a glance at me. I think she was surprised at how far I was taking this. You ain't the only actress, baby.

Shelby Townsend appeared in all her red-haired, pale-skinned glory. For a woman who lived in the perpetual sunshine of LA, I expected her to be a little darker. Guess she spent a lot of time inside, hammering out deals. "Yes? I'm Shelby Townsend."

"Ms. Townsend, my name is Ana Roulet, and this is my associate Marielle Rodriguez," I faux-introduced. "We are with Tiffany & Company fine jewelers."

"Yes. How may I help you?"

"It was brought to our attention last night that your client, an actor who goes by the single-named moniker of 'Nick,' lost a very valuable item at a post-Emmys party at the Goodbar," I fabricated.

"Really? What was it?"

96

"It's a very expensive diamond encrusted necklace," I announced. Charlotte nodded in agreement. "It was returned to us this morning by the Goodbar janitorial staff."

"Okay. I'll be sure that he gets it," Shelby said, hand outstretched.

"I'm sorry, Ms. Townsend, but my orders were specifically to deliver the necklace to Nick himself."

"I'm sorry, Ms. Roulet, but that will not be possible," denied Shelby. "I am Nick's agent. I am his official and professional intermediary. To get to Nick, you have to go through me."

"Oh, that's perfectly understandable. My job is somewhat like yours, too. I am the VP of Secured Transaction Sales," I flat-out lied, "and I am the official intermediary of my company, as well. I assure that custom ordered jewelry for our customers reaches our customers. Especially when we are talking about a necklace of such considerable value. The only way—and I do mean the only way—we are to relinquish the necklace is to hand it to Nick in person. That is why Ms. Rodriguez is accompanying me. She will witness and verify the official receipt of the necklace to the customer."

Shelby looked at me skeptically. I held firm. "What kind of a necklace are we talking about here?"

Wordlessly, I removed a velvet black Tiffany box from my purse. Then gently, I opened the box to reveal a sparkling, twenty thousand dollar universe of diamonds.

There was so much ice in that box, Shelby caught a chill. "Wow," she gasped, eyes never straying from the jewelry.

Heartlessly, I snapped the box shut. "It's a fifty thousand dollar kind of necklace we're talking about here," I stated. "And I can assure you that there is nothing more important to our company than the safe and secure delivery of our customers' most privileged purchases."

I could see the internal shrug in Shelby's eyes. Must be important if Tiffany sent two representatives. "Tad, look up Nick's home address for the ladies." She turned to me. "And give him a call for me. Tell him representatives from the Tiffany Company are coming with his necklace."

Damn. I hadn't expected her to call him. My plan was beginning to show more holes than a hooker's fishnet stockings.

"You can find him at home today," Shelby assured.

"Thank you," I managed. Still, I had gotten Nick's home address. Not bad for five minutes of fabrication.

The second Shelby turned her back again, I stole a look over at Charlotte. Her eyes shimmered with respectful admiration. You the shit, ma!

*

My journey for Nick would take me to Playa del Rey, a high-priced beachside residential area of LA nestled between Marina del Rey, LAX, and the ocean. For our purposes, it was pretty convenient, too. I was able to drop off Angie at the airport to send her back to Atlanta, and Charlotte at the Cheesecake Factory in Marina del Rey, where she met Ben the Agent for lunch.

Emboldened by my own shrewdness, I parked Connie on the downward sloping street right in front of Nick's house. The house was a modern, angular, white painted house with bay windows that faced the ocean. I was impressed. In a strange sort of way, I was proud of him. He'd earned this.

Taking the necklace box with me, I marched up to the front door and rang the bell. This time, I was confident, full of purpose and on a singular mission. Rejection was an impossibility. If it's Tiffany's he was expecting, it's Tiffany's he would get.

Until Tabitha answered the door. She had answered the door with such gleeful expectation. No doubt she had been expecting something to arrive in a velvet black box. I don't think she expected it to come with me.

Instantaneously, her face morphed into an altogether different animal. Quite honestly, from the look on her face, I thought the woman would hit me. If rage could speak, it would be her. "What the fuck are you doing here?"

I wasn't the smartest girl in the world, but even I knew when to shut up and take The Fifth.

"Nick isn't here. And even if he were here, he wouldn't be talking to you," she seethed.

"I made a mistake," I mumbled, turning to leave.

"You damn right you made a mistake you trifling-ass bitch!" she hollered, stopping me in my tracks. "There's only so much I'm gonna put up with! First you wreck my wedding and then you show up at our home! When will you get the hint? He doesn't want you."

Tabitha sucked her teeth with ultimate disdain. "You know what? You lucky my man doesn't believe in putting his hands on women, because I'd hold you while he hit you."

Dangerously, Tabitha sidled up to me, invading my personal space, her fists balled up at her side. I gritted my teeth, ready to fight—or, more accurately, to defend myself. I've never been in a real fight in my life. But from what I had heard about and seen from this girl…Well, she was no stranger to whuppin' ass.

Using the control of a third world dictator, Tabitha simmered out this very real threat: "If I ever see you again, I am going to beat your curly head straight. Stay the hell away from my man."

I turned and left. I wouldn't give her the satisfaction of showing it, but I was shaken. Connie could not peel away fast enough.

*

I grunted and sweated my way to an ass-whuppin'. Every kick and punch was a manifestation of my anger. The punching bag rattled from fury.

Soaking through my sportsbra, I was at a Bally's, kickboxing. I hated the fact that bitch had intimidated me. Punch! I hated the fact that I didn't say something back to that bitch. Kick! And I hated the fact that that bitch was marrying Nick! Punch, kick, punch-punch!

"Arrrrgghhhh!" I screamed, unleashing a hailstorm of punches and kicks until I couldn't punch or kick anymore. I threw down my gloves in exasperation. I wanted to be strong. I wanted to know how to defend myself. I wanted to kick…her…ass! As I changed after my shower, I made a mental note to join a kickboxing class at Run 'N Shoot when I got back home.

Half an hour later, I scooped Charlotte up from the Tower

Records in Marina del Rey and we headed back to the hotel. She could tell something was up by how quiet I was.

"What up, J?"

"We're going home."

"When?"

"Tomorrow morning, if I can swing it."

"Well, what happened?" she prompted. "Did you see Nick?"

"His fiancée answered the door."

"Dag, ma." Charlotte let a respectful silence pass before she asked the question she really wanted to ask. "So what happened?"

"She threatened me, and I didn't say a word." I gripped Connie's wheel as if I could wring blood from it. "I just turned and left. I felt like such a coward."

"Why didn't you do anything? Why didn't you at least say something?" the Flatbush native challenged.

I ground my teeth like coffee beans. "I don't know. Well, actually, I do. I was scared. No two ways about it. From what I heard about her...If she says she'll beat your ass...she will beat. Your. Ass."

Charlotte shook her head. "Didn't nobody teach you how to fight, growin' up?"

"If it wasn't ladylike, Winnie wasn't havin' it."

"Your sister?"

"Nia's a bigger priss than I am," I demurred. "How'd you learn?"

"Please, ma. I got three brothers. I came out the womb fightin'!"

"Well, I went to Bally's and did some kickboxing. If the road to Nick is through that trick, I'm gonna be ready," I vowed.

Charlotte rolled her eyes at me, her bougie, self-defenseless friend. "Rrrrright."

*

When we got back to the hotel room, I received another shock. Roses filled the room. Everywhere. A dozen dozens of roses adorned the dresser, desk, TV stand, etc. I was overwhelmed.

Mockingly, Charlotte sighed dramatically. "For me?"

I smiled as I sniffed the rosy floral scent from individual flowers themselves. I couldn't find a card, but enjoyed smelling and looking. Maybe they were for Charlotte.

"Aha. Found a card." Charlotte snatched up a card that rested against the telephone. She checked it real quick. "Guess who they're from?"

"Mark," I grinned.

"Nope."

"Nick?"

Charlotte laughed. "Yeah, right."

"Well then who?"

"Are you ready for this?"

"Just spit it out, bitch!"

With all the drama she could afford, Charlotte dropped the bomb: "Jacque."

*

I had been able to get us on a flight leaving LAX at 12:30 the next day. Around 11:00, we busied ourselves with checking out down in the lobby, sans flowers.

My mood was a bit onry. The flowers didn't put me in a great mood, nor did my failing to connect with Nick. Alright, I'll admit it: I was pissed off. Technically, this hadn't been a wasted trip, but emotionally, it sure felt like it. And fucking Jacque would just not go a—

"Hey, Pretty."

God! I whipped my unbelieving eyes around with a furious face.

Jacque quickly made amends. "Sorry. Hello, Ms. Selene."

Charlotte, sensing the tension even a Republican (blind man) could see, quickly excused herself. "I'm gonna go…uh…check on the…concierge. Or something."

"This isn't funny, Jacque. What the hell are you doing here?" I demanded. Ever since I've known him, Jacque had the most infuriating habit of popping up unannounced. "How'd you get those flowers into my room?"

"You'd be amazed what a C-note gets you with Housekeeping," Jacque smirked. "Did you like them?"

"Yeah. I liked them so much I left them in the room," I spat. "How the hell did you know I was in LA?"

"Nadine."

I could go Hannibal Lecter on her ass. I mean I really could eat her alive, I was just that mad. Who the hell was she to be doling out my whereabouts to my ex? Just exactly whose team was she on? "I'll deal with her later. But you, you have no right to be out here, putting roses in my room, just popping up at my hotel! What're you doing here!"

"Well we did have a little business to do out here. But after I saw you on TV at the Emmys with that Asian guy, I decided to handle it myself," Jacque confessed.

"And you called Nadine."

"And I called Nadine." Jacque affected a sincere, goofy smile. "I haven't stopped thinking about you since the interview. I love you, Jasmine."

I tried to keep my disgust to a manageable minimum. I signed the bill for the hotel room so hard, the pen ripped through the paper. I was extremely not interested in buying anything this snake oil salesman of sincerity was selling.

Jacque was relentless. "Did you give any thought to my proposal?"

"Jacque," I huffed, "the answer is—"

"No," he stopped me. "That's my fault. I won't rush you. I did say I'd give you three weeks to think it over."

"Jacque, I still—"

This time he stopped me with a kiss. Before I could fight him off, Nature took over. His tongue merged with mine. My mouth slackened to his will. The unthinkable happened. I responded. I kissed Jacque back.

When Jacque ended the kiss—yes, Jacque—I had to blink twice. What the hell just happened?

His earnest eyes sought out mine. I was confused. Why did that feel so good? Moreover, why the hell did I kiss him back? I loved Nick, not Jacque. I was confused. I had to flee the scene.

"I've gotta go."

Jacque held me by the elbow. "Stay."

I wriggled free easily. "No...I, uh...have to go."

I stumbled my way to the door, outside of which sat Charlotte in the Benz with the motor running. To my own surprise I said, "Bye, Jacque."

Jacque smiled hopefully. Progress. "Bye, Pretty."

*

Nothing helped clean out your psyche like deep conversations about life at 36,000 feet. Charlotte and I sat in first class, courtesy of WAGA. I think we were somewhere over Texas. Char accommodated me by listening to my pathetically confused rambling. She was pretty good at putting it all into perspective, too.

"So let me get this straight, J: You're in love with your ex, who is in love with another woman, while your other ex is in love with you."

"Yes."

"And, put another way, you're in love with a man who is engaged to be married while a man who loves you wants to engage you to be married."

"Yes."

"This man you are in love with may still have feelings for you, even though he's set to marry someone else, while the man who loves you, whom you may still have feelings for, wants to marry you."

"Yes."

"We also have a TV actor—whom you don't love at all—who buys you twenty thousand dollar necklaces and six thousand dollar dresses, while an ex-boyfriend whom you did love buys you four carat diamond rings. Right?"

"Yes."

"Wow, Jasmine. I wish I had those kinda problems," she kidded. "It would vastly improve my wardrobe."

I sighed. "I'm pretty messed up, huh?"

"What did you feel when Jacque kissed you?" Charlotte tactfully sidestepped.

"Familiarity. Warmth. Comfort" was my answer.

"And what did you feel when you kissed Nick in the church?"

"Everything. Like I was made to love him."

Charlotte could've melted. "Aww…That's sweet, ma."

"It's true. We used to say that to each other on a few occasions." I shifted in my seat, embracing the memory. "It would always be at the quietest moments of our relationship, during the most ordinary, routine, mundane part of our day. We could be laid up against each other in my apartment watching the news, or up in his apartment playing that damn PlayStation, or watching SportsCenter from the bed…And he would just say it. Like a whisper. Like a kiss sent down from Heaven."

Char was about to climb out of her seat, she was so taken with my memory.

"'I was made to love you,'" I stage-whispered, just as Nick would say to me. A tear welled up in my eye. It took all of my resolve to keep it from leaking out from my past and into my present. "I was made to love you."

I could see Charlotte bow and shake her head, perhaps fighting a tear herself. Naw. She was way too much of a "dating realist" for that. Charlotte just didn't want to broadcast her pity.

"You just don't say things like that to anyone else but your soulmate," I reasoned, when I knew full well that reason was contrary to love. "He's the only true love I've ever known. Every sappy, cheesy, syrupy sweet love song ever made was a mere attempt to describe what we experienced on a daily basis. We were love."

Were. Just the use of that past tense leveled me. "How do you forget that kind of love, Charlotte? How do you get over that kind of living fantasy that was once your reality? How do you stop loving someone like that?"

"I don't know," Charlotte said quietly, awestruck and confused. "I've never been in love like that."

"And I may never be again," I moaned. My voice turned small, squeaky. "Because I was made to love him. Only him."

I lost my fight with the tear. It escaped out of the corner of my eye, dragged itself down the side of my face. I collapsed my face upon itself, trying to control my emotions, trying to master the ultimate contradiction.

A woman is not weakened by crying. But a woman is perceived as weak when she cried. Although I knew it was silly to even care, when we were all capable of the same emotions, I still had to appear strong. So I got myself together, gathered my emotions, and limited it to a single tear. Remarkably, I was able to master the ultimate contradiction.

Charlotte, however, was merely trying to understand. Even with Janaya's father, I don't think she had experienced true love yet. The idea of it scared her so much, she was sometimes unsympathetic and standoffish about it. If it was in her, that kind of all-encompassing love, Charlotte didn't readily have access to it, nor knew where to find it. "Is that what makes you want him back so badly?"

"I want us to go back to that feeling we had, when we used to love each other completely."

"You can't go back to the past, Jasmine," said Charlotte softly.

"I know," I agreed, beginning to get myself back together. "I just want to reclaim our past. I want to recreate that feeling in the future."

Charlotte sighed a motherly sigh. You know, the kind of sigh mothers gave children when they knew that their children should know better. "Okay, Jasmine. Okay. You've chased him all around LA, confronted him several times, just for him to deny you repeatedly. Just be prepared for the possibility that he may go ahead with the wedding and not love you back. And what happens then?"

I had no answer for that. It wasn't a possibility. I just knew in my heart that Nick still loved me. He had to. Because I was made to love him.

For the first time all flight, I was able to focus on the in-flight movie. It was almost over. When I saw Eddie kissing Halle, completing their comeback, their romantic reconciliation, I knew what movie it was. This movie gave me hope. This movie gave me encouragement. This movie brought me back to the beginning—of my trip, of my love, of everything. This movie was Boomerang. Of course.

From Humble Beginnings

I can admit when I'm playing Wendy Wallflower. Some

105

nights, I simply did not want to be bothered. But tonight, I had reason to be anti-social. Why then, of course, was I at this house party in Queens?

Mia. It was all her fault. "Yo, you need to get your flat, yella ass outta the crib and go kick it with your girl one time."

I sought her out on the converted living room/dance floor. She was one of three women freaking this darkskin dude who seemed to have energy for days. I watched Mia dance the poor boy down to the floor, even when the other two girls couldn't dance that low. I snorted. God bless you, Mi. Do your thang, girl.

Forgive my high post attitude tonight but the wounds were still fresh. Three months ago, I had caught my boyfriend— ex-boyfriend—Jacque cheating on me.

How did I find out? Of course, it would have to be painfully obvious, because I was so naïve and stupid and in love, I never thought to check after him. Of course, it would have to be when I was doing something nice for him, like changing the sheets to do the laundry for him before he got home from work one day. Of course, I noticed the semen stain on the sheets—hell, that's why I was changing them. I could've sworn he had come inside me the last time we had made love, but I suppose there had been spillage. Of course, I was only on the pill because Jacque liked feeling me, all of me. Of course, it never occurred to me that he could be fucking some other chick and mixing her sexual history with mine every time he penetrated me. So, of course, I would notice the size Small panties caught under the bedsheet when I wear a size Medium.

Well that explained the cum stain.

That fucking bastard. Literally.

I tempered my anger with a drink. Two guys tried to holla at me, separately. I dismissed them both. Another brave soul tried. He was too friggin' smooth for me not to take his number. Memo to Self: Do not wear a midriff-bearing halter top to a party if you want to be left alone.

After I sent away the smooth guy, Mikal, I wasn't bothered for a bit. I absently bobbed my head to the reggae beat and finished my drink, the last of the night for me. I'd be damned if I let the memory of Jacque get me blazed tonight.

106

"Hello."

I hadn't even noticed him step up, I had my head in such another place. Offering nothing but decorum, I responded with, "Hi."

A brief, potentially awkward pause followed. I took the opportunity to size up this stranger. Well, he was tall enough, but just barely. I estimated about six feet tall, maybe six-one. At five-nine, a girl like myself had to make sure I could wear heels with a brotha and not make him feel self-conscious. He was darkskin, low haircut, faded on the sides, pretty good looking, I guess. The boy wasn't the finest thing in the room, but he wasn't ugly either. Guess that had to count for something.

But one thing seemed to stand out about this one— the lack of pretense and game. Between him and the last guy who stepped to me, Mikal, it was almost a study in contrasts. Whereas Mikal had oozed charm and game (and I was a sucker for both) from the opening line of his approach, this tall, slightly broad-shouldered stranger didn't "ooze" anything. As far as I could tell, he just "was."

"My name's Nick. What's your name?" He extended his hand.

Well, at least he's polite—if not boring. I shook it gently. "Jasmine."

I noticed a subtle, ever so slight brightening in his demeanor once he shook my hand. I grinned inwardly. My lotion. Honeysuckle from Victoria's Secret. Kills 'em every time.

"So how do you know Cheri?" Nick asked timidly.

"I work with her."

"So you're a lawyer?" he assumed.

I smiled coyly. What was it they said about when we "assume?" "No, I'm an administrative assistant through a temp agency."

I guess his assumption caught him short, too. "Oh."

He was desperate to generate conversation, I could tell—he turned his attention back to the dance floor. We both seemed to notice the same thing: the guy that Mia was dancing with, who also danced with a few other women simultaneously.

"Have you met Cheri's cousin before? Malloy?"

"No, I haven't," I said. I squinted toward the grinding, winding bodies that grooved to the reggae beat. "Is that him, the

107

one in the middle?"

"You mean the one gettin' freaked from all sides? Yeah, that's him," Nick affirmed, smiling.

"That's your boy?" I questioned. Just what kind of crowd did this guy hang out with?

"For better or worse," quipped Nick a little easier. Despite my best efforts, I had thrown him a bone. We were officially having a conversation. Ack. "Do you live in Queens?"

"No, Brooklyn."

"What part? I'm stayin' with my boy out in Crown Heights."

"Bay Ridge."

I could tell he didn't know where that was. And I would not help him.

Well, I guess Nick was ready to move on because he said, "Look, I'm gonna go get something to eat in the kitchen. I don't want to spoil your game none, so I'll leave you alone. I just wanted to know if I could get your number."

I didn't smile and I didn't encourage him none. I gave him nothing to work with. Yet still, he had gotten this far with me, and knew when to cut his losses and dip. This Nick guy had done a good job.

Still, I couldn't let him off easy. I was distrustful of men right now. That fucking bastard didn't let me off easy, so why should I let Nick? "I don't have any 'game' for you to spoil. And I don't give out my number."

Nick took rejection well.

Inside of me, something relented, and melted my cold, frosted-over heart. I gave him a chance. "But I will take yours."

He probably thought this was a brush-off, but I didn't care. Maybe it was. I hadn't decided on the matter yet.

Nick produced a pen and what looked like a receipt. He scribbled his name and number on the back of it. When he finished, he held the receipt away from me between his index and middle fingers. "Now I'm only gonna to give this to you if you're gonna call."

Who does this Negro think he is? My face served up more indifference.

"I'll call," I lied. Once again, that decision had yet to be made.

"Alright." Nick extended his hand. I liked that. He was very polite. I guess that had to count for something. "Nice to meet you, Jasmine."

"You, too," I responded in kind.

He gave me a nod as he backed away, heading toward the dance floor. "You take care now."

Then, Nick tripped over the oblivious, outstretched leg of a dancer gyrating to the music with the lower body, soca style. Nick tried to play it off but he had to have known I saw that! Still, I tried to be discreet, hiding a smile with my hand. By the time I recovered, Nick had disappeared, to the greater benefit of the universe. I probably would've kept laughing had he hung around.

I tucked the receipt into my bra, along with the other number. My mini-skirt had no pockets.

There was no way I could tell then the magnitude of that generic little first meeting. There was no way I could tell then that I was made to love him.

But I was.

6

MY ATTITUDE ON THE AIRPLANE trip bothered me. It bothered Charlotte, too. Shortly after we touched down, she decided to save my soul. She did what she would do to make herself happy. Charlotte took me to the theater.

We were barely in time to make the opening curtain for a play at Atlanta's 7 Stages Theater. I had seen Charlotte perform there twice in For Colored Girls and Fences. She played a helluva Rose Maxson. After that performance, I have never questioned her passion for theater. It was such a subtly heartbreaking performance that she made look so easy, I questioned why we all didn't have that same passion. As a television personality, I could appreciate the actor inside all of us.

Tonight's play was a new original work by a local Atlanta playwright. Charlotte knew the playwright and respected her work. She had promised me that this would renew my soul, invigorate my spirit. I thought my Oprah magazine on the way out to Cali was supposed to have done that.

When she's right, she's right. The play was fantastic. It was about a woman with a crazy, non-supportive family who doggedly pursued her dream of being a singer. I mean this woman lost everything—her job, her baby, her man—yet she still pressed on. She would say this over and over to herself, when times got their darkest: "Define life; don't let life define you." Everyone thought she was crazy. No one could see the light at the end of her tunnel. She did not waver in her purpose.

Eventually, it was that singularity of purpose that earned her a tryout for a label exec. Before she had her audition, her man, five years after he had left her, came back to her, strictly because she had held onto her vision, her dream. She had defined life, life did not define her. She blew the audition out of the water and

110

won a recording contract. The dialogue was astounding; the message truly did uplift my spirit.

As we filtered out of the theater, I pulled Char's coat. "You knew what you were doing tonight."

Charlotte hid a smile. "Why you say that, ma?"

"'Define life; don't let life define you?'" I quoted. "You knew I needed encouragement, even if you don't agree with what I'm doing."

"It's not that I don't agree with what you're doing. I just don't understand it," Charlotte adjusted. "But I do know about struggle. Hardship. Triumphing over adversity. Going for what you want at all costs. Making the sacrifices necessary to pursue your passion, to pursue your dream."

We stopped walking there on that sidewalk in Midtown Atlanta in the lamppost-illuminated night.

"Whether I think the love of an unavailable man is a worthy goal is not for me to say," Charlotte said. "But I did see in your eyes how committed you are to loving him. And I do know something about being committed to a goal."

I hugged her. I was so fortunate to have her. "Thank you, Char. I needed that."

"So do what you gotta do, J," she authorized. "Just don't let that bitch kill you."

I smiled. I knew what I had to do, and I only had eighteen days to do it. I had to call upon "my friend."

*

I was never too keen about coming into work too early, seeing how I went on the air at 6AM anyway, but I had a bone to pick. Once I was already in wardrobe and had Tyrone do my makeup, I marched over to Nadine Montgomery's office. At this hour, no secretary was present yet and I was free to come in unannounced.

Nadine, as usual, was already there, working. Well, usually she was working. When I entered, she had her feet up on her desk, watching something on her elevated TV/VCR combo. "Nadine," I said sternly.

"Hey, Jasmine, honey. Sit down," she invited, not taking her eyes off the screen. "Take a look at this."

"Nadine, I wanted to talk—"

"Shush, honey! Come take a look at this!"

Reluctantly, I angled my chair to take a better look. Dominating the screen was Beverly Bradley, decked out in SWAT team-like gear. She announced the severity of the undertaking they were about to embark upon as guests of the Red Dog special crime-fighting unit of the APD. Next thing I know, I saw wobbly images of running behind Red Dog members, à là Cops. I really couldn't hate on Cops, seeing how it was originally a Fox network show. What I saw next shocked the hell out of me.

"Red Dog, Red Dog! Atlanta Police! Red Dog!" A door flew off its hinges, aided by a police battering ram. Drug dealers scurried. A table was overturned. Beverly Bradley thrust herself into the midst of danger, amid shouts of police identifying themselves and strange barking noises. And then I saw Beverly Bradley get shot.

I saw Beverly Bradley get shot.

"Shit!" I exclaimed. I didn't know whether to be happy or sad. I know this was a cruel thing to think but did that mean the HART was practically mine?

Nadine didn't even bother to chastise me for cursing, she was so engrossed by the footage. "Watch."

The footage cut to Beverly fluttering her eyelids and being yanked up by a Red Dog officer. Cut to Beverly painfully opening up the Velcro straps to her bulletproof vest. Zoom in on the vest, to where the bullet was stopped. Nadine stopped the tape.

Damn. That answered my question.

So did Nadine. "Well, Jasmine…I think we can just gift wrap the HART to Beverly Bradley right now. That's just some amazing, fearless journalism!"

And my interviews with TV stars before the Emmys weren't? "Look, Nadine, I have a bone to pick with you."

"Look—he asked, I told," she headed me off. "That's it."

"It was unprofessional, an infringement of my personal privacy, and just flat-out wrong, Nadine!"

"Oh, shush, honey. The man loves you! I think you need to give him a chance."

"That man fucked some trick behind my back!" I retorted. "He hurt me so bad that I couldn't marry the man I wanted to marry when he wanted to marry me! I don't need to give Jacque Anthony Daniels a muthafuckin' thing!" And don't "shush" me!

Nadine simmered. "As your boss, I respectfully ask you to lower your voice. As your friend, I would appreciate it if you didn't curse at me. That being said, I admit that I may have overstepped my—"

"May have?"

"Let me finish. But first and foremost, I am your friend. I care about you, Jasmine," she declared. "I want to see you happy. I kinda feel like…well…in a small way, like I owe you."

I shook my head, looking down at my lap. "You don't owe me anything for Rodney."

"I know. I know that. That's what my head tells me, and that's what you tell me, and you're right," Nadine acknowledged. Her dark face turned dour. "But sometimes I just feel like…like if I can get married, you can, too."

"Thank you very much for being concerned about me. I really mean that," I responded honestly, deliberately. "But I don't need or want you to fix me up, or to mess with my love life, Nadine!" Any more than you already have, I did not add.

Nadine's eyes wandered away from mine. "Jasmine…you're in love with somebody else's man. Can't you let him go and let Jacque love you?"

"Jacque doesn't know how to love me" came my immediate, reflex response. If he fumbled once, he will fumble again. "Look, all I'm saying, Nadine, is to please try and restrain your guilt-ridden, maternal tendencies. That's all. I advise you on your love life, but I don't meddle in it. Just like I didn't stop you from dating Rodney; just like I didn't try and hate on your happiness. You don't know the history with Jacque and me. I know you mean well, but just leave this alone, okay?"

Nadine wasn't very forthcoming.

"Okay?" I prompted again, expectantly.

In defeat, Nadine sighed. "Okay."

*

At lunchtime, I made the call to my "friend." He was a private investigator, the same one who had helped me find out about Nick and his mom's situations that allowed me to crash the wedding. He also had an interesting bead on Tabitha's past.

"Aaron Moore, Private Investigations."

"Aaron! How're you doing? It's Jasmine Selene."

"Ah, my favorite, bodacious broadcaster," he flattered. "What's going on?"

I smiled at my desk at work. Aaron was sweet. "Remember that stuff you heard about Tabitha Washington? My ex-boyfriend's fiancée?"

"You mean something about the ju—"

"Yes, that." I didn't want to hear any more about it. Saying it just indicted me more. I felt bad about what I was doing but all was fair in love and war. I was defining my life, Damnit. "Can you get proof?"

"Like tangible documents?"

"Yes. Those."

"Sure. I'm a private dick," Aaron enunciated leeringly. "I can get anything."

I bet you can, you crazy ass white boy, I grinned. "Great. Get on the case for me. I'll make it worth your while."

"Anything for you, Ms. Selene," he sang out.

"Happy hunting, Aaron." I hung up. A tremor ran through me. I just did a very bad thing.

*

Planning for Nadine's wedding drove me crazy. As her dual maids of honor and two-thirds of the bridesmaid crew, it was up to Charlotte and I to plan out the details of the bachelorette party and wedding shower. The wedding was in eleven days.

Call me a Grinch, but I was so not interested. While I was happy for my girl Nadine, I still wasn't excited over the details of the thing. I just wanted the wedding to get here. For the most part, I sloughed all the heavy lifting on the matter over to

Charlotte, choosing to ignore it all until I absolutely had to. Tonight, I absolutely had to.

Call it research. Call it entertainment. Call it what you will. But whatever you do, don't call it a strip club. Please. Because I couldn't even believe I was here.

Charlotte had dragged (okay, not exactly dragged) me to this co-ed strip club in the Buckhead section of Atlanta called the Coronet Club. We were there under the guise of scouting out the place for Nadine's bachelorette party. They had men on one side of the club and ladies on the other. I have done a lot of things in life but I cannot say that I had ever been to a male strip club before. Charlotte, on the other hand, Body Tap alumna, felt right at home. As she should, I thought, while a brotha wearing only a bulbous looking pouch over his dick pulsed his pouch in Charlotte's face at our stage-side table.

I can't say that I was disgusted, or shocked. I was mildly entertained. If only Winnie could see me now…

"Charlotte, darling."

Char's head danced back and forth to the swing of her man's bulbous pouch in her face.

I tried snapping my fingers, to no avail. Charlotte waved me off. When he guided her hands to grip the sides of his ass, I had had enough.

I grabbed Ol' Boy by the 'nads and pulled him over to me. He wasn't even in pain. In fact, I felt his pouch…um…grow. Quickly, I freed Willy, stifling my inner schoolgirl. Damn he was hung! "Um, excuse me, Mr. Stripper Man? May I speak to my girl here right quick?"

"The name's Baby Boy," he smirked huskily, continuing that annoyingly sexy pelvic gyration of his. "Baby Boy" had talent. A prodigious talent. "You sure you don't want you a dance, Fineness?"

"I'll take a raincheck, Mr. Boy," I declined, stealing a glance at the pouch one last time. Baby Boy shrugged and gyrated off.

"Daaaaaayum, ma! I coulda hung clothes off that boy's stick!" hummed Charlotte.

"Charlotte—"

"I wonder what it'd cost to take it all off."

"Charlotte…" I said, more alarmed.

"I mean, really. I wanna see what kinda pole he's packin' in his tent!"

"Charlotte!" I grabbed her by the sides of her face. "Stay. Focused! Act like you've seen a dick before."

"Mm! That's not a dick. That's a foot-long reason to sin!"

I tried not to roll my eyes. "We're here for Nadine, remember? We did not come here for you to get some!" Besides, I wasn't walking home if Char ended up being Baby Boy's new toy.

Charlotte shook off the memory. "I'm straight, ma. I'm straight."

A statuesque, jet-black brotha with arms the size of my neck and a chest the size of a billboard, strolled on up to the table. His pouch was twice the size of Baby Boy's, if possible. He grinned. "Y'all ladies want a dance?"

Charlotte's eyes glazed over. "And why're we here again?"

I shook my head, placing it in my hands.

*

The next day after work, I had lunch with Rodney. I treated the groom to the Sports Zone. I wanted to do something nice for him in a space where if the conversation ever became too tight, we could be amply distracted by the dozens of TVs broadcasting SportsCenter or sporting events. As the salad came, I realized that this was the first time we had been alone together since the announcement of Nadine's engagement six months ago.

Rodney looked good. He was a solidly built, six foot two inch, cocoa brown black man. He was thirty-three years old, originally from Memphis. Had a good, stable, boring job as a tax attorney for Troutman Sanders law firm in Midtown. His father was dead, he loved and supported his mama, and he had one younger brother in jail for statutory rape that he visited when he could. Even though his brother's sentence was only sixteen months and he was due to be out next month (his brother was twenty-two when he messed with a sixteen year old girl who'd lied and said she was seventeen, the legal age of consent in Georgia), Rodney made the forty minute trip to the Gwinnett County Correctional Institution every three weeks to see him.

His brother was a perpetual screw-up, yet Rodney still supported and loved him. Rodney was a good man. That's why he used to be my man.

We danced around small talk through the course of lunch itself. I ate my chicken pasta salad politely as I posed my fringe questions about his life. For the most part, Rodney did the same. Until dessert.

"I'm still surprised you're going to be Nadine's maid of honor," Rodney admitted.

"Why's that?"

"Well...I've always wondered what you thought about the fact that after we broke up, I started dating Nadine," he answered carefully. "I never really knew."

"Yes you did, Rodney," I said. "I told you that I didn't have a problem with it. Same as I told Nadine."

Rodney smiled genially before addressing his cheesecake. "Well, I've got to hand it to you, Jasmine. You're a better woman than I am. If my brother had dated you right after I did, I don't know if I would've been as understanding."

I smiled subtly as I began to eat my warm fudge brownie dessert. "You mean you would've gotten jealous?"

"Of course."

I knew I shouldn't have asked this question but I did. "Why?"

Rodney stopped his train of eating long enough to answer the question, no more. "You and Nadine and Charlotte are like sisters. Brothers don't go after their brother's ex-girlfriends. Shoot, neither do my friends. It just surprised me that you were cool with it."

Really, I wasn't. At the time they started dating, I thought it was tacky and insensitive and cheap. But because he had dumped me after I told him about The Phone Call I made to Nick over a year ago, The Phone Call that set my whole world on its ear, I really couldn't say anything about his new relationship with my friend two months later. Although Nadine had asked all the right questions and said all the right things ("If you don't want me to date him, honey, just let me know"), my damn foolish pride wouldn't let me be jealous. That same damn fool pride that kept me away from Nick for his four years in Chicago. That same damn fool pride that made me lose him in the first place.

So, of course, Damn Fool Pride wouldn't let me down. "I'm cool with it," I lied.

"That is such a relief. It means everything to receive your blessing for the wedding," Rodney exhaled, digging into his cheesecake with renewed fervor. He truly was relieved.

I, on the other hand, just sat there, letting my warm fudge brownie dessert go cold. Against my better judgment—and Damn Fool Pride—I had one question I needed to have answered, burned to have answered: "Why are you marrying Nadine?"

Rodney laughed—until he saw I was serious. "Why am I marrying Nadine? You're kidding, right?"

No, I wasn't. He had dated me for two years but proposed to her after only six months. I wanted to know. "Is it because she wouldn't kiss you for two months?"

"No, it's—"

"Is it because she won't give you none?"

"Jasmine, what're you—"

"Is it because you wanted to marry a virgin?"

"Jasmine, just stop it!" Rodney ended my badgering of the witness. "I'm marrying Nadine because I love her."

"What's the difference between me and Nadine?"

"Jasmine, don't do this…"

"No, I'm for real," I said, for once tossing DFP out the window. "I wanna know. What's the difference between Nadine and me? Why are you marrying her?"

Rodney gave me a serious, earnest look, a look I had seen before in the morning in bed, when we'd just lie there, and he would stare at me and tell me he loved me. It was the look of pure honesty and sincerity, a look I had a hard time imagining belonged in a man's repertoire.

"Because I love you…and you are in love with another man."

*

The truth sucked. I felt miserable for the rest of that afternoon. For some reason, I went back to work after that lunch, even though I didn't have to. I needed to be around people. I just didn't want to be holed up in my house, thinking about Rodney's all-too honest response.

But sometimes the truth was great. Waiting for me on my desk was a manila envelope from Aaron Moore Private Investigations. That crazy-ass white boy had done it again! I greedily opened up the envelope and found a five-page document with a Post-It stuck to the front page. Have fun with this, Ms. Selene! Your adoring fan, A. M.

I smirked. Proof. You better believe I'm gonna have fun with this...

Then it just hit me what I was doing. I was about to destroy a life. A marriage. How could I be so giddy about breaking up a happy home? Did this really have to be done?

I strolled over to my moral center, Nadine Montgomery's office. Even despite how I felt about what Rodney had told me, I put that on my mental back burner. I needed Nadine. I knocked. She was in. I shut the door behind me.

"What's up, honey?" Nadine mumbled, head over a stack of papers. "I think I'm gonna pull you off weekend duty for good after this weekend. It'll give Polly a good training ground to get her act together. It did wonders for you."

I smiled at her smile, ignoring the kidding remark. My head was in a moral fog. "Nadine...I need to talk to you."

"I know, I know, I know. I have no idea what the heck we're going to do about that HART! Beverly Bradley's Red Dog tape has already been played five times just yesterday on WXIA. I don't know what we can do to counter that..."

"Nadine," I pressed a bit more firmly. "Screw the HART for a moment. I need to talk to you, not my boss for a minute."

Nadine removed her reading glasses and leaned back in her chair. "Sorry, honey. I'm listening."

"What if you knew someone who—"

"Stop right there. I'm bad with hypotheticals. Just give it to me straight."

I sighed. This was going to require me being more honest than I wanted to be. "I have some information on Tabitha, Nick's fiancée...Potentially damaging information that could change Nick's opinion of her. I've been thinking about telling him about it. What do you think I should do?"

"Information?" The newswoman in her leaned forward. "Do you have any proof?"

"Tangible proof."

"So we're back to Nick again, huh?" I could tell Nadine was not impressed with my pursuit of this man. Still, my motives and my heart have always been pure. Even if the means weren't.

"It's always been Nick."

I could see the gears turning in Nadine's head on whether she wanted to tread down that why-won't-you-let-him-go road. For the better benefit of both of us, she avoided it.

Leaning back, Nadine asked, "Now what do you think will happen if you told Nick this 'information'?"

"He would probably leave her."

"And she would be hurt, their wedding in two weeks would be off—again—and he would be hurt, too. Right?"

I felt small. "Right."

She let the idea ruminate in her head for a second. "And what do you hope to accomplish from all this?"

I sat there. Good question.

Lucky for me, Reverend Montgomery's daughter had more. "Do you want Nick to fall back in love with you? Do you think that by you uncovering this terrible, tangible information about his bride-to-be with just two weeks until their wedding would endear him any more to you? Don't you think that he would be hurt by learning all of this about his fiancée?"

This was exactly the reason why I came to Nadine, time and time again. My girl had a spiritually-backed, down-home sensibility that always brought my behind in check. I knew why I was doing what I was doing; I just needed her to keep it all in perspective for me.

She was right. She usually was. "Of course he would be hurt."

"Is it right to hurt the one you love? Maybe you should consider that before you go on and bust up his life."

My girl. I stood up and gave her a hug, patting her on the back. "Thanks so much, girl. I appreciate it."

"Anytime, Jasmine."

I left her office with a clearer head. Nadine never told me something I didn't already know; she merely reinforced it. Don't hurt him, hurt her. I sat down at my desk, took out a manila envelope with the station's logo on it, and addressed it to Tabitha Washington in Los Angeles, California. I replaced the Post-It on the document from Aaron Moore with a Post-It of my own: Don't you think he should know? That was all I wrote. I smacked that bad boy on the papers, stuffed it in the envelope, and sent it out Fed Ex, next day mail. That way I could track it.

I'm not saying that what I did was right. I would go as far as to say I wasn't even proud of it. But I had to let her know that I knew. If she truly loved him, she would tell him. And I truly loved him—because I didn't.

*

Charlotte and I worked away on Run 'N Shoot's StairMasters. In our Spandex and sportsbras, we looked pretty yet industrious. It was a lousy way to spend a Friday evening, but the night was young. I met her down there after she got off work, temping away at some computer software company. I could tell how utterly bored she was with the place by the way she chattered away eight hours of pent-up charisma and personality.

I let her, because I really had nothing to bring to table. Rodney's admission yesterday kind of floored me. I wasn't sure I wanted to open up that can of worms with Charlotte, even though she could keep a secret with the best of them.

After telling me what I'm sure would be a very funny story about a man, a woman, and a Donna Karan dress that the man would wear as a woman, Charlotte could tell something was up. "Hey, ma. Whassup?"

"Sorry, Char. I'm just a bit distracted, that's all."

"Bad day at work?" Charlotte offered. "You looked fine to me this morning."

"Thanks."

"Serious, J. Tell me what's goin' down."

I quickly weighed the pros and cons. With all the stuff floating in my head, I guess I didn't need to keep the Rodney thing inside my head making the waters even murkier.

"Rodney told me that he loved me."

"I know." Charlotte wasn't even fazed.

"No. I'm talking about that he still loves me," I clarified.

"I. Know." Charlotte continued pumping away on her machine, not engaging my eyes. "He's very subtle about it but I could tell he still has feelings for you."

"I couldn't tell."

"Even if I couldn't tell, he told me awhile ago."

"What! He told you he still loves me?" I was incredulous. Damn, Char, you really can keep a secret.

"Yeah, about a month ago. He called me up one night and just spilled his guts. It was sad, but kinda sweet," she reminisced.

"About me? Why didn't you tell me?"

"I figured it was nunya unless he decided to make it your business." "Nunya" meant "none of ya business." Charlotte finally looked at me. "I dismissed it as cold feet."

"Do you think he really loves me?"

"Sure. And why shouldn't he? The boy proposed to you. I swear, you get more proposals than J. Lo! And how did you respond? You haul off and call Nick, asking him to take you back. Then you tell him you called Nick, tell him the nature of your phone call to Nick, and then tell Rodney you can't marry him. That hurt him, Jasmine."

That sank in. "But if he still loves me, why is he marrying Nadine?"

"Because I think Nadine is ready. He's ready," she assessed. "Rodney is ready to begin that next phase of his life. He wanted to begin it with you. Luckily for him, he found someone who he could begin it with. And as far as women go, Nadine's a good woman."

"Doesn't it bother you that he's going to marry Nadine when he doesn't love her?"

"He does love her, ma. And he loves you. But he can't have you because you love another man," Charlotte pointed out. "And according to you…you always have."

*

I felt better at work today. I was back on set Saturday morning for the first of my last two weekend morning broadcasts. Nadine had me doing these as well as the weekday ones some weeks in order to accelerate my learning curve, she was just that confident in me. I felt pretty in an attractive blue and white suit top and a tasteful, gold necklace. I didn't care that nobody was watching at eight A.M. on a Saturday morning. It just felt good to be back at work, shoving the emotional complexities of my life aside.

My last story was a lighter one about a dog who would backflip every time he heard someone "whistling Dixie." As I professionally dispatched the story to greater Atlanta, mentally, I floated outside myself and made commentary. How country. Ain't that some redneck mess?

I was the only one doing the show this morning. I liked the autonomy and freedom of anchoring a show alone sometimes. As I signed off at the end of the broadcast, I began to mentally check out of the building. Within ten minutes, I'd be in Alexia, heading off to catch some movie. Mentally, I grumbled. Once again, Nick's influence on me. Before meeting him, I had always been too pretty to go to the movies by myself, let alone pay for one.

The bright lights above the set died, and I stepped down from the set. I breezed past several of the seldom-seen crew members who made our show hum. Detached my lapel mike and began to slip out of the suit jacket. As usual, I wore jeans underneath the set desk, despite my professional waist-up appearance. A quick stop by the bathroom and I wriggled into my more casual baby tee and light jacket, ready to hang up one of my spare outfits I kept at the office. A pit stop at the desk and I'd be on my way to the multiplex.

My jaw dropped as I rounded the corner to my cubicle. Sitting in the seat to my desk was…

Tabitha.

Nick returned home about eleven that night. He had had a long day on set, battling bad guys and jumping from set piece to set piece. He was looking forward to settling into their Jacuzzi master bath, getting a backrub from his darling fiancée, and making love in front of their master bedroom roaring fireplace.

When Nick traipsed up the stairs to the master bedroom, he found her packing. "Hey, precious. What're you doing?"

Not breaking stride, Tabitha said, "I've gotta go out of town and handle some business."

"Where are you going?"

"New York," she lied. "The publisher said there was a problem with my book."

"Do you have to be there for it?" Nick didn't have a clue about the book industry.

Tabitha grimly said, "Yes."

Nick frowned. There went his plans for a nice, relaxing evening with his fiancée. "When does your flight leave?"

"In an hour."

"Do you want a ride to the airport, Tab?"

"Publisher's paying for a cab."

Nick leaned against the wall to watch her throw together the smallest overnight bag in the history of overnight bags. Tabitha stuffed a manila envelope in it. She wasn't leaving-leaving him, because the bag was too small. But something was not right. "Are you okay, precious?"

There was a honk from outside. The cab.

Tabitha zipped up the bag and slung it over her shoulder. She headed for the door.

"Hey!" Nick grabbed her and kissed her softly. Searched her eyes for that peace and comfort for which he was marrying her. Found it. "I love you. Have a safe trip."

"Thanks."

"When will you be back, precious?"

"When the job is done."

7

I WASN'T THE MOST TIMID girl in the world, but even I knew when to shut up and take The Fifth. Tabitha—and her attitude—sitting in my chair. Like a bag of nickels ready to pelt me in the head. Subtly, I balled up my fists, ready for a throwdown. I'd been kickboxing. I knew what was what. If this bitch wanted to fight, we'd fight.

Since I wouldn't say anything, it was up to Tabitha. "What the hell is this?" She waved the manila envelope with the WAGA logo on it underneath my nose.

"What're you doing here?" I asked, vaguely remembering her threat.

Tabitha stood up, all in my face. "I'm here to make sure you leave us the hell alone."

I wasn't as scared as before, but I sure as hell didn't want to do this here. Not in my place of business. "Not here. Let's go somewhere else."

"Fuck that!" Tabitha snarled. "I flew three thousand miles for some goddamn satisfaction. We're gonna settle this now!"

"Are you hungry?"

The question caught her between the eyes. Quite honestly, it had nowhere else to go, she was so much in my face. "What?"

"Are you hungry?" I repeated calmly.

My calm defused her anger—and she hated it. To be in here this early, she must have caught a redeye flight, flown all night, and come straight to the station from the airport. Hell yeah, she was hungry.

Angrily, Tabitha spat, "Yes."

"You've come a long way. Let me take you to lunch." A little civility went a long way. Besides, ain't no way I was gonna fight this chick in my bebe baby tee.

"You're paying for it!" she snapped.

I tried a shaky smile. "Of course."

*

"Guess I wasn't too hard to find, huh?"

We were seated at an Original Pancake House in Decatur. There were enough people so that our conversation would be obscured, but not enough so that Tabitha could get away with a scene, if it came to that. And that was the point behind bringing the little piglet here: to avoid a scene. The girl presently gorged herself on a stack of pancakes, a grip of sausage, and three scrambled eggs. Souldance my ass.

"No," she said, bobbing for air. "I went to the station's website and checked your schedule. I knew you'd be there today."

"Right." Stalker. "Why'd you come all the way out here?"

"Look, Ex-Girlfriend," Tabitha sneered, "Nick is mine. He is my man. I came out here to reinforce that fact so you will leave us the fuck alone. We are engaged to be married, to create a spiritual, emotional, and legal union in the eyes of God. Forever. He will never be your man again. The sooner you realize that, the sooner you begin to live in reality."

I live in reality, baby. I'm the one who presents reality to people like you every day. I swallowed my sharp tongue and said, "I realize that."

"Then why did you go digging up this shit? That's really low, Jasmine."

I knew it was, but I didn't care. "Don't you think he has a right to know? How could you marry him without telling him everything he needs to know about you?"

"That's just it—he doesn't need to know!" she spat.

"How could you keep that from him? Omission is the same as lying," I reminded her.

Tabitha shoved aside her plate. I could tell she wanted to Riverdance on my eyeballs with the heel of her boot. "I don't need you to be my conscience."

"And I'm not. I wanted to give you the opportunity to do the right thing. If I really wanted to hurt you, if I really wanted to

126

hurt him, I would have sent it directly to him."

"Juvenile records, Jasmine!" Her eyes shot heavenward. "I swear, I am asking the Creator for all the strength of the living universe not to hurt you right now!"

"You mean like you did Natasha Mixon? You want to hurt me like you did her?" I challenged.

"You know nothing about that."

"I know you were charged with criminal assault on a minor," I continued.

"I was young."

"I know you ripped half the girl's hair out, sent her to the hospital for six stitches in her forehead, and kicked the living shit out of her," I countered. "She went into a coma for two weeks. Poor girl still has migraine headaches and only seventy percent of her hearing in her right ear."

"That's all behind me now," Tabitha said, feigning control.

"I know you still have anger management problems and have stopped seeing your therapist."

"I could fill a Bible with what you don't know about me," she hissed.

"Really? Like how you beat Natasha down while spending time in juvy on a drug charge?" That was my pièce de resistance.

Tabitha fell silent. As silent as a pot gets bubbling with steam.

"Look!" Tabitha exploded across the table, grabbed me by the ends of my jacket, pulling me close to her. Her eyes were livid and afire. For someone who prided herself on being this deep, earthy soulchild, she looked more like a rabid animal now. There was some fear, but I would never let her see it.

"Hit me. Go ahead – hit me," I provoked. "I know you want to hit me."

She did, she really did want to. I could see the debate raging in her eyes.

"C'mon and hit me. It'll make you feel better, I'm sure. You know you want to," I instigated.

Tabitha threw me back, settling into her chair again, almost against her will. "I'd never give you the satisfaction." She breathed. "Like I said, that's all behind me now."

"Is it? You're a loose cannon, 'Souldance.' I think Nick would be interested in knowing that his wife-to-be was convicted for drug trafficking and criminal assault, then stuck in juvy for eight months."

"I was fifteen!" she burst. "What do you want from me? I was young, I fell in love with a guy who used me. I was a mule, a fucking mule, Jasmine, and I didn't even know it. He was older, twenty-one, and I was so in love with him I didn't even realize he was hiding drugs in my bookbag. And when I found out how he used me...when I went to jail on a charge I knew absolutely nothing about...I was so angry, words weren't good enough.

"I had a rebellious, messed up, confused adolescence—like any other teenager—and I made a mistake. I also paid for it and learned my lesson. I took anger management classes. I started to deal with the anger inside me for not having had my father around. I learned to tap into my poetry inside juvy. It was a fucked up experience, living like that with so many badasses, but it ultimately made me stronger, a better person. I learned to love writing poetry and made something out of my life. I was a kid! Jesus!"

Tabitha was really upset, as she should be. I understood. What I was doing was really despicable, but I feared for Nick. I feared that he was marrying the wrong woman. "If all that made you a stronger person, why don't you share that with Nick?"

"Who's to say that I won't? But I would like to be able to tell him at my discretion, on my terms. It may have made me a better person but that's not a phase of my life that I'm particularly proud of. That's why they are considered juvenile records and expunged once you turn eighteen. They don't have anything to do with your being an adult."

"But this has everything to do with being an adult!" I fired back. "If you're willing to hide this from Nick, from your fiancé, what else are you hiding, will you be willing to hide? If you love Nick, you should tell him everything."

"What's the point, when you'll just do that for me." Tabitha turned her attention back to finishing off her pancakes.

She reached in her bag and thrust at me the manila envelope containing copies of her L.A. County Court juvenile records. "Here. Take them. I don't want them."

"I don't want them either."

"Yes you do. You want them so you can show Nick. You want

them so you can breed a seed of distrust between my man and me. You want them so you can make a pathetic little attempt to stop the universe from being the universe. He doesn't want you, he wants me. But if it'll make you happy to tell him all this, you go right ahead. You will hurt him, you will hurt me, you could possibly derail our wedding—again. But what you can't do is stop him from loving me. Only he can do that, and something like this won't do it. All it will do is cause him pain." She dropped the envelope in my lap. "I hope you sleep well at night."

The envelope sat in my lap like a Scarlet Letter of flesh-eating acid. I didn't want to pick it up. I felt like the lowest sort of life form on Earth.

Tabitha finished eating, and pushed away her plate. "I'm not perfect, Jasmine. I do not have the right to judge others. I am only as perfect as you are." She tossed down her napkin indignantly. "But because you seem to have the right to judge others, I am even less perfect."

*

I angled the TV/VCR combo so I could see it from the tub. The gentle bubbles and scent of Country Apple bubble bath from Bath and Body Works soothed me. As I had done time and time before, I hoped to glean some ray of light from the movie I firmly believe pertained to all aspects of life.

It was just starting to get good. This was the part where Marcus sat up in the bed, feeling like a hooker, after seeing the 200 dollars Robin Givens' Jacqueline had just left him on the nightstand after a passionate night of sex. The expression on Eddie's face was priceless: a wholly believable mixture of shock, sadness, and shame. Had I not been able to catch a glimpse of Robin's turquoise panties during one of their lovemaking scenes, I could've sworn they were really doing it, Eddie's painful face just looked that real in this scene. It did me good to see someone feel as bad as I did, even if it was just acting. Gotta love this movie.

Naturally, the second I started to feel better, the phone rang. I answered my cordless, which rested tubside. "Hello?"

"Hey, Pretty."

I wanted to sink my head into the water, taking the electrifying phone with me. This day—a freakin' Saturday, no less—had been classic. I had no doubt from whom Jacque had gotten my number, but I was too emotionally spent to care. "Jacque…what do you want?"

"How are you, Pretty?"

I was too exhausted to small talk this man, nor to enforce "Ms. Selene" today either. "Jacque, what is it that you want?"

"To tell you I love you."

"Duly noted."

"And I want you to check your front door."

"Huh?"

"Just go to your front door."

I groaned. "Jacque…not more flowers…"

My doorbell rang.

"I'll let you go, Pretty. I love you."

"Goodbye, Jacque."

I groaned, as I stepped out of the tub, slipped a towel around my body, and tittered up to the front door. I opened it to see three bouquets of a dozen roses. Freakin' Jacque. I can't say that I was surprised.

But this did. A hundred white doves and a hundred white balloons flew by the front yard of my house. My mouth gaped. After I saw the airplane with the sign trailing it that read, "Marry me, Jasmine!" you could've driven a semi through it.

Once the doves flew away and the airplane made its three passes, I sobered up. I dragged the dozens of roses into the house and put them in water. As I made my way back to the bathroom and eased my soft body into the tub, I allowed a little smile. While Marcus Graham told off Strangé and Jacqueline, that smile had grown. I needed that. I may have just been on the rebound but I needed that. I needed to have someone make me feel good. Strange (Strangé?) as it was to say it, I needed Jacque today.

*

130

After my broadcast on Sunday, I shredded Tabitha's juvenile records. I made out a check to Aaron Moore for three thousand dollars and dropped it in the mail. I can't say that I felt better, but at least I felt human. The realization was beginning to sink in that I would not be able to marry the man I love.

Just as I was getting ready to leave the station, about ten that morning, I returned from the mail chute. As I rounded the corner to my cubicle, once again, I was shocked as hell to see who sat in my seat.

"Nia! What're you doing here?"

I gave my sister a strange, yet sisterly embrace. She looked great, as usual. Like she was ripped from the pages of Ebony or Black Enterprise. Nia was a shade lighter than I and two inches shorter at five-seven. Yet what she lacked in height, she made up for in body. I used to kid her that when they were handing out butts, Nia went back for seconds. I felt like I should at least have half of what she had. And with her commitment to working out coming more from vanity than physical fitness, Nia would always look like a million bucks. Only now, in our adulthood, wearing a Ralph Lauren outfit armed with a Gucci purse, she literally did.

Niagara and I had a typically contentious big sister-little sister relationship. What made it worse was that not only was she older but she may have been, dare I say, prettier than me. Only in recent years have I come to terms with my jealousy of my big sister. But that was about the extent of my jealousy. She could be a cold, manipulative, self-serving bitch—but I loved her. Hell, she was family.

"Vince," Nia said simply. She disengaged from the hug. "What're you doing today?"

"Not a helluva lot," I admitted.

"Good. Come to the game with us. We'll have dinner afterwards."

"Sure."

*

Nia's husband, Vince, played for the Cleveland Browns, the

131

worst team in the National Football League. They were in town to play the Falcons. We had a prime seat, too, as guests in a luxury box at the Georgia Dome. I could have gotten into a luxury box through a friend of mine who worked at the Georgia World Congress Center, but one of Nia's classmates was an Atlanta printing company mini-mogul who had one of her own.

The game was exciting. Vince was an average player on a horrible team. Today, however, he had a breakout game as the linebacker sacked our aging white quarterback twice. Still didn't matter—Cleveland sucked. They lost 41-3.

It was interesting watching my now thirty-three year old sister sit there in the luxury box looking entirely bored with the whole proceedings. While the rush of professional football catered at the level of lavish expense afforded to guests in a luxury box still thrilled me, Nia was over it. This was simply what she did. With curiosity, I watched her down drink after drink, wondering why her whole attitude was more blasé than usual.

I found out over dinner. Surprisingly, it was just the two of us eating at the trendy, Euro-styled Café Intermezzo in upscale Buckhead. "Where's Vince?"

"He's flying back with the team tonight."

"He couldn't stay and have dinner with us?"

"He prefers flying with the team." Nia ordered a drink.

"How's my niece?" I asked, beaming like the moon. Victoria was five and uniformly wonderful.

"Hyperactive," Nia appraised. "I think we'll get her started on the clarinet or something."

I snorted. I was bougie, but I wasn't that bougie. "C'mon, Nia. Let the kid have some fun. Give her a basketball or something."

"Maybe I should have her take piano, like we did."

"Right. Only if you want a little person revolt."

There was a lull in the conversation. Sometimes that would happen with Nia if you didn't ply her with enough questions about her life.

"What about you, Jasmine? Who's in your picture now?"

"HART."

Nia's features wrinkled. "His name is Hart?"

"No, the HART Award. Heritage Atlanta Radio & Television

Award. It's this thing I'm up for at work."

Nia picked at her salad. "Bump work, Jasmine. Who are you with right now? You must have someone. You always have someone."

"No." I finished up my salad.

"Really?" she asked incredulously. "I thought I taught you better than that."

If you taught me anything at all, it was how to instigate, manipulate, and perpetrate. "Well…there is…Oh, never mind."

"No, tell me," Nia said, looking alive for the first time all evening.

I exhaled. Here we go…"Jacque."

Nia threw down her fork in triumph. "I knew it! I knew it! I knew you'd go back to him!"

I squinted at her like she done lost her mind. "You got that backwards, Sis. He came for me." Again and again and again.

"How long's it been? Four years?"

"Try six," I corrected.

"So what was he talking about? Is he still smooth as hell?" she grinned.

Was he ever. Nia had always liked Jacque. He was straight out of the Black Ken Doll mold Nia had always seen for herself until she had gotten involved with Vince. Nia had always been attracted to men of similar means as herself. So when Vince had established a pro football career, Nia had figured she would hold on for the ride. But that was back when he was playing for the Jets, having just been picked up as a free agent. By Nia's estimation, Vince had gotten lucky. Jacque, on the other hand, was a living, breathing CAD (Chocolate American Dream), with the requisite background. Just like my mother, Nia had approved wholeheartedly of the light brown, well-financed J. Anthony Daniels.

"Worse. He's so smooth, he's not even smooth anymore. He's just honest, I think," I replied. "I didn't think he could be serious but…Nia…He's asked me to marry him."

"Say what?" Her fork clattered to the plate again.

"I'm serious," I verified. "I was interviewing him for a piece at work. I didn't even know I was going to see him. He's this bigtime Internet exec now. Crazy paid. Anyway, we're in the middle of the interview, and he proposes to me. On camera."

"Can I see?"

"Hell no, woman! We stopped the tape," I denied. "I didn't think he was serious until he tracked me down out in Cali on business last week. He had my room filled with roses."

"How romantic!" she gushed.

"How annoying!" I squashed. "I don't trust him and I don't love him! I told him that, but he insists that his proposal stands, that he'll be back in a week for his answer. And I'll tell him now what I'll tell him then: No. Hell no. Four carat ring or no four carat ring."

My sister nearly choked on her drink. "Four carat ring?" Her husband played professional football and hers was only three carats.

"Carats don't move me."

"Hell, they move me, Bugs Bunny!" Nia drooled. "After all these years you two haven't talked and he proposes to you? Maybe he really does love you, Jasmine."

"If he loved me, he wouldn't have been stickin' some trick behind my back."

Nia grew quiet. "Do you think you'll ever get married?"

"Honestly? I don't know," I admitted. "I want to. Believe me I do. But…Dang. This is going to sound so ridiculous but…I'm still in love with Nick."

"Nick." Nia let that name settle. Like pesticide. She had never been a very big Nick fan. She didn't hate him, like Winnie did, but she tolerated him at best. For the most part, Nia limited her comments about Nick to herself. And I appreciated that. "That Anonymous guy?"

I smiled. That was him. Nick had spent a year in San Diego, looking for a wife so he could get married before his mother could die from breast cancer. He had secretly recorded the search for the San Diego Reader under the pseudonym "Anonymous," with the express purpose of proposing to someone in a year. Tabitha, I guess, had been the lucky winner. But not before "Anonymous" had become a media sensation, ending his wife-hunt with a nationally televised press conference outing himself. That this confession led to a slew of publicity and his current movie star gig, Nick earned brownie points in Nia's materially motivated mind.

"I thought he married someone already?" said Nia, puzzled.

"No, not yet. He's engaged, though." The disappointment clearly resonated in my voice.

"But you still love him." Nia regarded me with cool brown eyes. "Is he happy?"

"I don't know. I think so."

"Does he still love you?"

I engaged my sister's eyes. "I think he does. I really think he does. He just won't acknowledge it."

I bit my lip in frustration. "He gets married in thirteen days."

"Wow." Nia actually looked concerned. "What're you going to do?"

"What haven't I done?" I shrugged hopelessly. "He's the one true love of my life. Jacque couldn't hold a candle to him. I love what Nick and I had, and I firmly believe we can have that again. I was made to love him."

"Have you told him all of this?"

"He won't let me. He's so closed off and reserved and mad at me." In a small moment of levity, I giggled. "I guess I kinda crashed his wedding."

"You did what?" screeched Nia, aghast.

"Stomped right up to the altar and stopped the wedding." I was grinning sheepishly now.

Nia beamed at me with something like pride. "My lil' sis. Good job, Jasmine."

I was blown away. "Good job?"

"Hell yeah," Nia approved, chugging down a drink. "Do you have any idea how gutsy it was for you to go do that?"

"Gutsy? Some might call it stupid." Or arrogant. Or rude. Or mean.

Nia waved at the waiter for another drink. "It's so stupid it was smart. You followed your heart, Jasmine. Stupid people try to do smart things. Smart people just do what they do."

Accepting the drink, Nia lit into it. I was about to cut her off when she stopped guzzling long enough to speak. "Jasmine, look at me. I am not happy. I have a lot of money. I've moved twice since we've been married thanks to Vince being traded. I have an athlete husband who's cheating on me as we speak. I live in Cleveland. I married for money, I admit it. And I'm a stupid person."

I had never heard my sister be this honest. Probably because I had never seen her drunk before. She was a very controlled drunk—just extremely honest. Since adolescence, I had rarely known my big sister to be honest a day of her life. Self-pity just was not like her.

I didn't know what to say.

"Don't end up like me, Jasmine," she warned. "Vince cheated on me when we were dating, he cheated on me when I was pregnant, and he's cheating on me now. Right now. In the team hotel fucking the Falcons' head cheerleader.

"And I cheated myself. I cheated myself out of happiness, marrying someone I thought would be a good provider when all he was good at was being a selfish prick. Don't do what I did, Jasmine. Marry for love, don't marry for money. I'm not asking you this, I'm telling you this. As your big sister. Don't make my same mistake."

I was leveled at the staggering amount of honesty and emotion from a woman so prissy and cold in high school they called her the Canadian Front. "But why? Why are you still married to Vince if he cheats on you and you're unhappy?"

My sister sighed with the weight of the world clearly on her shoulders. "Because now this is more than just about me. This is about Victoria. This is about raising a life outside of my own, and making sure she has what we didn't: two parents there all the time. I love that little girl more than I love my cheating husband, and I will never, ever hurt her or let her down."

Amazing what growing up did to siblings. I had never known Nia to act so selflessly. Doing it for the kids. Guess it came with the territory of raising a child. Guess that was one of the reasons why I wanted one.

Instantly comparing Nia to Charlotte, I murmured softly, "You're a good mom."

"I love him."

Her statement caught me flat-footed. "Excuse me?"

"I love him." Nia sought solace in her empty drink glass. "God help me I do, but I love him. That's why I can't leave him. I love that pigheaded, bowlegged, two hundred and fifty pound of a man. I do. From the first time I saw him lifting weights at the gym that summer—when he dropped the barbell on his foot from staring at me—I knew I could love him. And I did. That was nine years ago. And I still do."

Nia motioned for another drink but I waved it off. She was done. She knew it, too. Her eyes sank to the bottom of the glass. "Loving someone is a thankless job, Jasmine. You will comfort them, you will counsel them, you will care for them. You will offer them your bleeding heart just so theirs can keep on beating. Most importantly, you will offer them yourself, and they will never realize how good they have it.

"If you are lucky enough to love someone, don't ever let that go. Even if they don't love you back. Because if you are lucky enough to have found someone you care that deeply about, to have ever felt that kind of unconditional love, that spirit of giving of yourself…When it's done right, there's not a better feeling in the world. If all I have left is to cling to the memory, then that's what I cling to."

This time, Nia met my eyes, leveling me with a simple look. "Don't be like me, Jasmine. Don't be stupid."

There you have it. For the first time in our lives, my big sister acted like a big sister.

Lavatory Occupied

He didn't notice the light go off at first, but I did. Nick was halfway asleep on the redeye flight, like everyone else in the cabin. I wasn't.

I was genuinely excited. This was our first vacation together—seven days, six nights in Maui. I had never been to Hawaii before. The thought of seven uninterrupted days in paradise with my man drove me batty with delight.

Which explained my restlessness. I couldn't go to sleep—didn't want to go to sleep—I had just that much energy to burn. I wanted to burn that energy with my man.

Mischievously, I popped my head above the seats and stole a look around. Only two lights tarried in the darkened airplane cabin. A Type A, white-knuckled businessman tapped away furiously on his laptop and an elderly Latina woman lost her battle to read a book to sleep. Even a flight attendant leaned against one of the cabinets way back in the galley, positively asleep on her feet. The opportunity would never be more ripe.

"Babyluv. Babyluv," I urged in a whisper. "Wake up, Babyluv."

Nick blinked twice. "Whassup, mami?"

"I'm going to the bathroom," I announced grandly, locking his eyes. Then I planted a kiss on Nick that rocked him into another dimension. "I suggest you use it, too."

I rose, leaving a slyly bewildered Nick damn near panting from our heat.

I entered the airplane restroom and began to have second thoughts. There was only just enough room to do your business, none for any risky business. What if one of the flight attendants needed to use it before Nick got here? What if someone could hear us? I've had better ideas.

But not in a while. When Nick showed up, opening the door and invading my personal space in that coffin of a room, armed with his patented, sexy little smirk, my freaky little idea gained instant validity.

I stepped out of my wet panties the moment he shut that door. Under the authority of a kiss, Nick propped me up on the sink. My tight, round ass filled the narrow little space. I pulled up my skirt a little so Nick could work more freely. I bit my lip in anticipation as I saw him reach for the button on his jeans. Eyelids closed as I heard the distinctive sound of a zipper unzipping. As that little sigh escaped my lips to the arching of my back when Nick did that thing the way he always did to make me do that thing I always do, I privately congratulated myself. Go Jasmine, it's your birthday!

As I could feel the length of him fill the whole of me, I breathed into his ear, "I love you."

Nick countered with, "I was made to love you."

In the middle of jousting and retreating, I murmured, "Lock the door, papi."

Our bodies vibrated in unison, symbiotically. Never breaking his stride, nor the feverish, desperate, hungry look we shared, Nick reached back to lock the door. I smiled, and then hummed.

Outside the restroom door, somewhere in the airplane

cabin, the light went on.
Lavatory Occupied.

8

I DON'T KNOW WHY I did it, but I did it. My body needed it. My body didn't need him, but it needed "it."

I slept with Jacque.

How the hell did I end up here? That was the question I asked myself repeatedly as I drove home from the Ritz Carlton where Jacque was holed up in a luxurious suite. Was it desperation? Was it the final act in a crescendo of loneliness? Was it pure and simple lust?

When I had left the restaurant, I dropped Nia's drunk ass off at her hotel room. As luck would have it, she had a room at the Ritz Carlton. I had Alexia valeted while I had escorted my sister upstairs, to make sure she would at least change into her PJs before blacking out. Mission accomplished, I had bumped into Jacque as I was passing through the lobby. He was in Atlanta only for a night, on business. Of course, he had stopped me. Of course we had sat down for a couple of drinks in the hotel bar. And, of course, I had slept with him.

I shivered as I gripped the steering wheel. I could still feel his warm breath on my neck. His scent of Paco Rabanne in my nose. The nimble hands at my thighs. His tongue and mouth on my chest. I shivered from pleasure, staring out at the darkened highway at four in the morning.

I don't love him. I told myself that gentle refrain over and over again once the act was done. While we were doing it, I didn't think anything at all. I just reacted. And felt. And gave in. I was angry with myself for him making me come.

How did I let myself get so weak? I couldn't even say it was the flowers and the doves and the aero-sign that did it. It wasn't that I suddenly realized that I loved Jacque all along because I didn't. Sometimes there are things that we do that simply are unexplainable. This was one of them.

As I bypassed home for the station, as I was due in somebody's makeup chair in a half an hour anyway, I decided that this weakness would die right here, right now. No one would ever know I had slept with Jacque. If Charlotte found out, she would congratulate me for pimping the man; if Nadine found out, she would congratulate me for falling in love with the man. Neither was right. Jacque wasn't the answer. If Jacque was the answer, I needed to change the fucking question. I had made a mistake, a momentary capitulation to weakness. At a time in my life when the forces of emotion were slowly circling my heart like buzzards ready to feed, the last thing I needed was my weakness on display. Whether I liked to embrace it or not, my weaknesses, momentary or not, made me human. And for these next twelve days, where I would have to potentially endure two weddings and a broken heart, I would have to be superhuman. I would have to be Jasmine Selene.

*

After work, I paid a visit to Aaron Moore. His office was stashed away in the holds of the fifth floor of a medical-dental building in Little Five Points. Unlike those seedy, dimly lit P.I. offices you saw in movies, Aaron Moore Private Investigations was held in a small, neat-looking one-room office that easily could have been the home to a CPA or a working professional.

As usual, I found him working hard at hardly working. His Nerf-hoop mini-basketball shot had improved dramatically since I last saw him. I guess that last check I sent him had him straight on his overhead for the month. He lit up when he saw me enter. "Jasmine Selene! My favorite TV hostess with the mostest! Have a seat!"

I allowed my grim demeanor a smile as I sat down. The blond Georgian always had a way of making me smile with his corny, half-assed attempts at flirting. He and I both knew I would have to be blinded with the heat of a thousand suns to ever consider sleeping with him. "How're you doing, Aaron?"

"Mighty fine, Ms. Selene," he sang. "Not too busy around

here, as you can see. Just one little surveillance job that I'm almost through with. I swear, darlin', if it weren't for cheating husbands, I'd probably be off selling cream-colored sweatshirts at The Gap."

"The Gap doesn't make cream-colored sweatshirts," I teased him.

"They would be if I worked there." He leaned forward with interest. "Hope you've got somethin' to put off my retail career."

I sighed. Last night's shameful submission still did not deter my purpose. If anything, last night's talk with Nia over dinner stayed with me more than the taste of Jacque's familiar tongue in my mouth. Don't be like me. Don't be stupid, Jasmine. I knew that I was wavering in my quest for Nick. But even in my uncertainty, I had to pull out all the stops. I had just twelve days until his wedding.

"I have another mission for you, Mr. Moore," I prefaced. "And time is of the essence."

*

That evening, Charlotte and I worked it out on the StairMasters at Run 'N Shoot. For some reason, I noticed all the leering eyes more this evening than I normally did. Run 'N Shoot had always been a meat market of young, toned, firm brown flesh, but I usually was oblivious to it in my own quest for physical perfection. Tonight, I felt as though these physically superior specimens could see right through my Nike sportsbra and Spandex shorts. Something about breaking the two month hiatus from sex that made me glow like Hester Prynne with a scarlet letter. Letters: S-E-X.

Good for me Charlotte was her normally talkative, engaging self. I don't know if what she had to tell me was something I needed to hear tonight, though.

"I am so sick and tired of people using love as an excuse," she fumed.

"What do you mean?" I asked. Char sounded like Halle in Boomerang, right before my favorite part where she slaps the shit out of Eddie.

"Remember Mr. Issues?"

Vaguely. Mr. Issues was this guy who was an emotional time bomb, still ticking from his messy separation from his wife six months ago and just waiting to explode with commitment for whomever was around him. That commitment-phobic woman, however, just so happened to be Charlotte—and she wasn't having it. "Sometimes I need a scorecard with you, Char."

"This is true—but beside the point," she dismissed. "Well, I'm fuckin' him the other night—"

"Must you be so crass, Char?"

She turned to look at me, sweat pouring down her face as we both stepped away. "Well I wasn't making love to the nigga. Dayum."

I cringed again. She knew I was also trying to wean myself off of the "N-word," too, another by-product of my youth.

"So, I was fucking this nigga the other night," Charlotte continued undaunted, "and he stops right before I'm about to come, tellin' me he 'can't do this.' I said, 'You only have to do this for three minutes longer, then you can do whatever the hell you want. Just don't stop, don.' And he pulls out!"

"What kinda stupidness is that?" I asked. "He already had his penis inside you and he's just gonna stop? What was wrong?"

Charlotte snorted. "Nothin' from my end, I'll tell you that, ma. I was hookin' up the Kegel crunches and everything! When he started to pull out, I tried trappin' the dick in there by flexing, but he got away."

I laughed. The image of Charlotte, flat on her back, trying to squeeze her vagina into imprisoning some poor boy's penis was hysterical. "So what was his explanation?"

"He said he was still in love with his wife."

"Well good for him. True love survives, I guess," I muttered sarcastically.

"I was like, 'I know this. I don't give a damn! Just finish the job, nigga!' So he just up and dipped, leavin' me high and—"

"Not so dry," I quipped.

"Shit ain't funny," Charlotte pouted. "I had to finish the job myself."

"Not the 'massager you abuse for your own purposes' again?"

"Hey, a woman's got needs. It's still a poor-ass substitute for a man, though."

I heard that, I didn't say. I could feel my vaginal walls clinch from the memory. "So why did this freak leave you in the middle of sex like that?"

"'Love made me do it.' What a crock of shit," Charlotte condemned. "No one takes accountability for love. They act like we can't control our emotions."

"We can't," I said. "You can't control who you love."

"Bullshit," she countered, pumping her little brown legs even harder. "I can control my emotions. I can control who and who I do not love."

"Now you're full of it, Char. You can't control who you love. You may be able to control the situations you're in or who you give yourself access to, but you can't control who you love," I explained. "For example, I can say that I don't want to fall in love with a white guy or something and limit my access to them. But I can't say that the possibility doesn't exist that I could fall in love with one. Because you can't control what you feel for other people."

"Well how do you explain women who stay in abusive relationships? Women who get their ass beat every day who stay with their man, who say, 'Love made me do it' or 'I love him; that's why I stayed'? Why is it that love has become this all-purpose excuse from personal accountability for your actions? Or non-action? How do you explain that?"

"I think they're stupid," I said decisively. "I believe that love itself, the emotion, the feeling, is uncontrollable. It's a feeling, which automatically makes it the opposite of control. Now what we do from those feelings is something else entirely. We have control over our actions, what we choose to do in life. Those feelings, like love, merely inform our decisions. That's what I think they mean to say, but it comes out something stupid like, 'Love made me do it.'"

"So you agree with me, that people should be accountable for their actions?"

"Yes," I agreed. "I think that actions are controllable. But feelings are not."

"Bump that, ma—mine are," decided Charlotte. "I think love is overrated."

144

"That, my sista, is because you've never had it."

*

After our workout, Charlotte decided to be a mom and spend some time with the baby. I, on the other hand, went out with Nadine and Rodney, unescorted. We can debate the foolishness of the idea another time. This had been a preset date for the three of us for over a month. We met for dinner at Sylvia's, a sit down soul food restaurant Downtown.

As I sat there watching Nadine coo and fuss over Rodney, my mind began to wonder if she had told him about my recent attempts at Nick. The trips to California. Worse even, did Nadine tell Rodney about Jacque?

How silly. Nadine was my girl, and Rodney appeared to be all too unaffected by my presence. Especially considering he had recently told me that he still loved me. While part of me wanted to pull Nadine aside sometime at work and tell her what I thought of her marrying a man who was still in love with his ex-girlfriend, my better judgment always intervened. Nadine wouldn't believe me, accusing me of still carrying a torch for Rodney, while Rodney would deny it, accuse me of still wanting him, or, even worse, admit to it and break Nadine's heart. No good could come of it.

Dinner itself was a thoroughly nauseating affair. Maybe it was just my jealousy talking but I couldn't stand watching Nadine and Rodney act like such newlyweds before the "wed" part. I'm sure a good therapist could figure this all out for me but I figured I'd save the money and hire a P.I. instead. Perhaps the term was projection, I don't know. For some reason, their happiness made me feel hollow inside.

Once dinner was over, I could not get out of that restaurant fast enough. I hopped into Alexia and headed for home. For the second time in twenty-four hours, a strange mood washed over me and I did something I probably shouldn't have. I picked up the cell phone and called...

"Jerome."

"Who this?"

145

"It's Jasmine." God help me, we know entirely too much what we do...

"Jasssssssmine," Jerome growled, oozing more genuine sex appeal from his voice than ten Chippendales put together. I could just see him laid out on his bed, one hand down his shorts, chillin', his eyes half cocked in the perpetual, weed-influenced haze he always seemed to be in. "What's goin' on witcha, boo?"

Mentally, I cringed. Once upon a time, I had called Nick "boo," a generic term of endearment he had promptly made me retire. Shortly after I did, I realized precisely how generic it truly was when every other man used it on me.

"Not much," I lied. "Just handlin' my business."

"I been watchin' you on TV. Well, at least on the weekends," Jerome said. "You know I can't be gettin' up that early durin' the week. You know how I be stayin' up late, workin' on my music."

His music. I tried not to laugh. Jerome was an aspiring booty shake rap artist. I had listened to some of his stuff before and it was okay at best. But true to his native ATLien roots, Jerome would stray from the high energy, Luke-style booty bass beats and try to prove he could actually spit lyrics and rap, as Atlanta bass artists were wont to do. And, of course, they all sucked. All a good booty shake song had to do was have a high energy beat, a crazy ass hook, and be disrespectful to hos. Jerome couldn't even accomplish that simple mandate. But what did you expect from a guy I'd met at the World Club whom I fucked just two days later?

"Of course," I humored him.

"So whassup wit ya, boo?"

"I've been thinking 'bout ya." For all of five minutes, negro.

"You know I been thinkin' 'bout you, boo. Thought I wasn't gon' hear from you again," he accused.

You almost didn't, I didn't say. It had been two months since our last tryst. As empty as the experiences would be, physically, Jerome never failed to disappoint. Attentive and always tall as a flagpole, with an ass so tight, it could turn coal into diamonds. "My bad, Jerome," I apologized.

"Naw, man, my feelin's hurt. You need to make that shit up to me," he bargained.

Another wonderful trait about Jerome was that you could

always see him coming a mile away. I believe Charlotte's name for him was "Marblehead." "How do I do that?" I played along.

"Come see me."

Bingo! That took all of what, a minute and a half? If they ever wanted to make a complex man, they would have made him a woman. "You still live over there by Howell Mill Road?"

"Naw, man. I'm over by my cousin's house off Bankhead Highway."

Bankhead? Dang it! This booty call was a little further out than expected. I turned onto the onramp for I-75/85 South. Great. I was taking a trip to the hood.

*

From pulling up to the address he gave me in my Lexus LS 430, I should have listened to the bad feeling in the pit of my gut. Not to sound like the privileged priss I was but here I was, smack dab in the projects, a few streets away from Atlanta's Bankhead Highway at eleven at night. Several blocks away, the notoriously ghetto fabulous nightclub "The Bounce" lay dormant only because it was a Monday night. Come Friday nights, there was a freeze-dried hair stack and two gold teeth minimum for entrance. A battleship of a Cadillac (sporting flossy rims and purple ground effects, no less) rolled by with the windows down, car full of blunt-smoking brothas nodding their heads to the bouncy Lil Jon beat. What the hell was I doing here?

Having come this far, I figured I couldn't back out now. I marched up to the front porch of the public housing duplex and rang the doorbell. If I had to traipse through the hood to get it, I was getting some dick tonight, Damnit!

A large, lightskin woman with cleavage the size of North Georgia, answered the screen door. She was on the phone with one hand and cradled a crying baby in the other. Magically, she was able to balance a cigarette between her thin lips. She squinted at me. "Yes?"

"I'm here to see Jerome."

"Oh. Aw'ight." Without moving from the screen door, she hollered into the nether regions of the house, "JEROME!"

I blinked a few times. My eardrums may have popped.

"Wait righ' here." She disappeared from the screen door.

Here was my chance to run, yet I didn't take it. I could be pretty determined when I fixed my mind on something.

Two minutes later, Jerome came to the door. Blue-black dark skin and a body by Jake, Jerome stood in the doorway looking chiseled from black marble. He was still in his work outfit of unbuttoned coveralls and just a wifebeater. Jerome was a mechanic. He was good at fixing things.

Showing no overt pleasure from seeing me, he simply said, "What you waitin' fo'?"

For your black ass to invite me in. My, he was forever the gentleman.

I stepped inside into a mini-Bosnia. Phones rang, babies cried, a TV played videos from BET Uncut, and a radio blared Atlanta bass music. The air was oppressed by the heavy smell of hot wings, hot sauce, and cigarette smoke. If I weren't so full, I actually might have liked it. Thankfully, Jerome steered me clear through the kitchen, through a living room/child's bedroom, and into his shoebox of a room. The walls were covered from head to toe of Jet Beauties of the Week. I had forgotten how extremely visual Jerome was.

The man wasted no time. The second the door shut to the mayhem outside, Jerome peeled out of his wifebeater, revealing his rock hard abs. That wasn't a six pack, that was an eight pack! Without my doing, my blouse was on the floor seconds later. He dropped his coveralls. Damn, I loved those ribbed, black Calvin Klein boxer briefs he wore! His kissing me was a thin excuse for him to reach around and unhook my bra. Before I knew it, I was pushed up in a corner of the cramped, twin sized bed, Jerome's hands scurrying up my legs. He pushed up my skirt and removed my panties. So much for foreplay.

As he continued to kiss me and ready himself for entry, I tried to block out the noise, the smell, the environment. I tried to disappear inside my mind, turning my body over to feeling. I opened my eyes just long enough to make sure Jerome put the condom on, and then retreated back to my imagination.

And feeling. Let's just say Jerome wasn't subtle when he entered. A gasp escaped me, forcing my eyes open. He grinned, as if I had gasped from how big he was or something. I had gasped because he'd just dug up in my flowerbed without wetting the ground first. My body slackened as did that area down there, eventually. Against his best efforts, I gradually accepted him inside of me.

Inside of me. As he began throbbing and grinding against me, occasionally remembering to suck a nipple now and then, it just struck me that this man was now a part of me. We were joined at the coochie. My eyes wide open, I realized that I didn't want to be joined to this guy for anything. Not even the sex at the moment, which was going okay, I guess, was worth "joining" with Jerome for any stretch of time. When you joined with someone, you shared space, gave them a piece of you as they gave you a piece of them.

I wanted nothing Jerome had to give me, not even the sex I had called him up for. I didn't love him. But I know whom I did.

"Stop."

Jerome just growled his sexy little growl and kept going, as if that would overrule me.

"Stop," I said a little louder.

"Oh, boo…You make me feel so good…"

This ain't about you. It's never been about you. "I said stop, Jerome."

"Mmm…don't stop me now, boo…You feel too good…"

Oh, I know this cat wasn't gonna turn this into a date rape… "I'm going to tell you this one last time, Jerome," I said calmly, as he pulsed in and out of me. "Stop."

Jerome closed his eyes and groaned.

"GET THE FUCK OFF OF ME!!!"

With two hands, I flung Jerome off—and out—of me. Somehow, the condom slipped off as he tumbled backwards, flying onto the bed. I scrambled out of its way like the coochie grenade it was.

"Goddammit, you don't listen, do you?" I hissed, hurrying back into my clothes.

"How you gonna do me like that, boo?" he whined. "How you gonna let me in and then just kick me out? That ain't right."

"No, Jerome," I said, clothes on, opening the door. "This ain't right."

149

*

Sometimes going to work early in the morning had its advantages. One of them was that I could promptly get busy and try to forget about my reversion to Slutty Ways yesterday.

Slutty Ways was the seven-month stretch of time I spent shortly after Nick rejected me via The Phone Call last year. Charlotte, happy to have seen me stoop to her level, naturally came up with the moniker to describe the funky period of denial and hurt I was going through, which I unleashed upon the unsuspecting black Atlanta male populace. While Charlotte still swears I had sex with at least fifteen men during that stretch, the number was closer to six. Seven if you count that dude I met in Jamaica—which I don't. What had brought me out of Slutty Ways was what, I hoped, was bringing me out of them now—work. With the rising ratings and exposure, I figured one of WAGA's up-and-coming anchors shouldn't be carrying on around town like I had been.

Stubborn as I was, I don't regret that confused, emotionally turbulent time, either. Sometimes you can't know what good is without indulging in a little bit of bad. The whole period had confirmed what I readily knew—that I wasn't cut out for casual sex. While that didn't stop me from indulging in it selectively, it kept me from letting everyone take a turn on my knob.

If work could save me once, it would save me again. No more Jacque. No more Jerome. No more brothas with names that start with J.

I was off the air by ten. Out of makeup by ten fifteen. Checking my messages by ten seventeen. Calling Aaron Moore at ten nineteen to confirm. That crazy ass white boy had done it again. For free, too; I only had to promise to be the mother of his children. On the line with my travel agent at ten twenty-five. Heading for the airport in Alexia by ten forty. Flying out to Cali at eleven forty-five. Again. The reason why?

Love made me do it.

April's showers came early. It was March in New York and the city was already a submersible flotation device. On this

150

particular day, it rained with the fury of a black man trying to catch a cab in Downtown Manhattan at night. That was why he didn't hear the Beemer pull up to his townhouse driveway.

Jacque answered the door in a tank top and shorts. While it was wet and cold outside, Jacque was nice and warm inside. He had been studying Advanced Managerial Finance for a test the next day. This was his senior year at Columbia and there was no way he wasn't going to finish on time.

"Nia?" The man was genuinely surprised. "Come on in."

Nia was soaked. Nia was crying. Nia was drunk. Jacque quickly found out the last one when she tried to sit down on the couch. Her butt missed the couch by a good sixteen inches.

He kneeled down next to her on the floor. "You alright?"

"No!" Nia's breath smelled like Jack Daniels and Coke, more Jack than Coke. "Where's Jasmine?"

"She's not here," Jacque said of his girlfriend, her sister.

"Why not?"

"Because she's not," Jacque said slowly. "Have you tried her apartment?"

"She wasn't there. That's why I came here."

That wasn't an entirely uneducated guess. In the three years of their relationship, Jasmine virtually split time with Jacque between her apartment in Bay Ridge and his rented townhouse in Clinton Hill. "As far as I know, she's not coming over tonight. I've got a test to study for tomorrow."

Nia seemed drunkenly dejected. Her normally attractive features were dampened by Mother Nature and her attitude. "Oh."

Jacque felt for her. "What's wrong?"

Nia wanted to disintegrate from shame. "My boyfriend's cheating on me."

Jacque was floored...uh, literally. "Cheating on you?" It didn't seem possible. "Vince?"

Her head fell back and hit the floor gently, making a soft thud. Jacque leaned over to help out. He had a feeling this explanation was going to be a long one so he had better get her out of these wet clothes.

Nia, on the other hand, didn't seem to mind Jacque's peeling her coat off her. "I've never been cheated on in my life. Ever. I've never cheated on anybody in my life. I had my opportunities, you know!"

"I know, I know," Jacque said soothingly, placating the drunk. He hung up her jacket and hat.

"No, you don't know! I'm a good girl! I'm the type of girl that men marry and be happy with!"

"How many drinks did you have?" Jacque inquired.

Holding up six fingers, Nia continued, undaunted. "It wasn't supposed to be like this! We were supposed to be getting married soon and be happy and…and…I fucking hate him for doing this to us!"

"Would you like some coffee?" Jacque offered, heading into the kitchen.

"No!" she snapped.

"It's Colombian," he enticed.

"Okay." The drunkard struggled to sit her tail down on the couch.

As the coffee began grinding and chewing, Jacque sat next to his inebriated visitor. "So what're you going to do now?"

The pretty, butter pecan features of hers battled to maintain composure. It was as if she wanted to cry but had been all cried out. After six rounds of crying in your own beer, it was understandable.

For the first time in the three years Jacque had known his girlfriend's sister, she looked vulnerable. Scared even. It was like her life was over, over at twenty-five because this one, foolish man had failed to love her right. A woman that fine should never be alone.

Soon enough, the coffee was ready. Nia absorbed it in gulps, slurping it down like Gatorade. Problem was this petite-sized black woman was not much of a drinker, so when she got drunk, she got blasted. Coffee was a joke to her system right now. Nia's depressing little drunk-chick vibe still swirled around her shaken little form.

After an hour of babysitting her towards sobriety, Jacque gave up. She was too lit to drive back home. He told her to go kick off her shoes and lie down in his bed. Unfortunately, his girlfriend's big sister was gonna have to spend the night. All the better, Jacque figured. The senior set up shop with his papers and all outside the bedroom in the living room. He needed to pass this test tomorrow.

By one thirty in the morning, Jacque called it quits. He was tight.

Gingerly, Jacque entered his room to hear Nia lightly snoring. Quietly, he got himself ready for bed while she slept. His was a roomy queen size bed so he decided to slip into the opposite side of the bed and go to sleep. Nia was so upset and distraught and drunk she had to be knocked out for the night. She was.

In the morning, around five A.M., Nia woke up to find a very tall, very thick, light brownskin young man lying next to her. In her hurt, emotionally warped little mind, something told her that this was Jasmine's boyfriend lying right next to her. Somehow, that didn't stop what happened next.

Nia, still feeling hungover, kissed Jacque. She woke him up with a kiss. Used to receiving morning love, Jacque responded in kind, his eyes closed, allowing his mind to go free with Jasmine.

Only it wasn't Jasmine. By the time Jacque opened his eyes and recognized that it was not his girlfriend he was kissing on, her sister had already stripped down to her bra and panties. As she manipulated his tongue, Jacque couldn't help but be a guy for a moment and admire Nia's body. Although he loved Jasmine, he hadn't seen much of her recently, due to his hunkering down to finish his degree on time and her having a new temp job down at a law firm in Downtown Manhattan. He missed this closeness, this affection, this…What was that!

The next thing he knew, Nia was on her hands and knees, slurping up Jacque's most personally persuasive instrument. He wanted to tell her to stop, that she was his girlfriend's sister. But he couldn't. Right when he had finally gathered up the gumption to stop her—or at least slow her down—Nia adroitly dragged her tongue from his thighs up to his mouth, as slow as sensually possible. All protest Jacque had was quickly buried beneath her tongue. She helped his hands slide off her small sized panties and made them disappear.

Good sex must have run in the family. Jacque was a captive of the cat. Nia rode, dipped, arched, and danced her body to complete orgasm. Fully committed now, Jacque actively made sure to pleasure her, from sucking on her nipples to slurping up her neck. Just when he felt about to lose control, he pulled out, erupting all over his bedsheet.

Nia grinned a silly little smirk of satisfaction. Vince wasn't the only one who could cheat. She rolled over to go back to sleep.

So did he. Jacque, of course, felt what every man feels after a meaningless ejaculation. He had never cheated on Jasmine before and never wanted to again. It wasn't worth it. He would be proven right.

Needless to say, Jacque flunked his test. In more ways than one.

9

"NICK...THIS IS YOUR FATHER."

For a man who made his living through expression, Nick offered none. Just the same steely-eyed glare I had been overly accustomed to seeing these past few weeks.

I did not fly all the way out to California for this. "Aren't you going to let us in?"

Nick backed away from the door wordlessly, eyeing his father the entire time. As I followed Nick Senior in the door to Nick Junior's house, I, too, was still fascinated by the elder Nick—and I was the one who had found him.

Okay, actually Aaron Moore had found him. I swear, that crazy-ass white boy could find a virgin in a whorehouse. All I had given him was a name and last known city of address—Richmond, Virginia—and Aaron Moore had tracked him down.

Ironically, Nick's father lived in the quiet San Fernando Valley suburb of Sylmar, about forty-five minutes north of Nick's Playa del Rey home. I had found his house on a placid, orderly, tree-lined street in a new housing development that screamed suburbia. Minivans outnumbered kids on the street. Pumpkins and other Halloween decorations dotted the odd porch. I'd parked my car behind his unassuming Volvo stationwagon.

That was essentially Nick Senior's existence in a nutshell—a Volvo stationwagon. Safe, dowdy, boring. He was remarried to a slightly younger white wife. They sponsored three mixed kids, with one more on the way, I gathered from the swell of her belly. He was a Volvo salesman, for God's sake. This six-foot one, mustached, unassuming, slight whip of a man was the spitting image of his son. Or was that vice versa?

Either way, I had spent the night over there, talking to Nick Senior, getting to know him a little better, informing him of my plight. I had convinced him that his son was getting ready to marry the wrong woman, that I was the right woman, and that if my presence out here in California, some twenty-five hundred miles from home, didn't prove that, then nothing would. His redheaded wife had regarded me with sympathy. She knew a little something about loving someone at all costs, no matter what the world would think. Even better, Nick Senior had agreed to accompany me this morning, to confront his son, the one he had not seen in some twenty-seven years. It had taken a guilt trip of epic proportions—and the absolute sincerity of my quest—to convince him to come. I mean, how could the father of the man I loved not want to ensure his son's eternal happiness? I had Nick Senior positively convinced it was me. Nick Junior could not miss the boat, or set sail on the wrong one.

Showing up this morning on Nick's doorstep had taken guts from both of us. It had taken guts because we both loved Nick so much.

Would Nick take this into consideration? Probably not. I watched him keenly as he paced the living room like a caged tiger. I didn't know whether to stay proud of my bringing together a father and son or to feel bad for having upset Nick so much. The Junior one.

Several times Nick looked to say something to me but thought better of it. Finally, he said, "You don't need to be here, Jasmine."

Although I had kinda wanted to sit in on the reunion, I could understand. "I'll be back in two hours."

Nick growled, "Make it one."

*

Since this entire trip was on my dime, I drove a rented Bonneville around to kill time. As I am a girly girl, I headed over to Fox Hills Mall in Culver City to do a little window-shopping. Maybe it would be shopping-shopping. I had an air of confidence about this one. If Nick's father couldn't convince him, for goodness sake, who could?

I slid into one of my favorite stores, Victoria's Secret, and tried a few things on. I found a cute, lacy, forest green bra and panty set that I tried on. I gazed at myself in the mirror—tall, pecan, slim, and sexy. My curly dark hair framed the edges of my pretty, smooth face. My stomach was still as flat as its nickname, The Table. Even though I still could use a little more butt, I was still a damn fine catch.

My cell phone rang and I knew who it could only be. "Hello, Nadine."

"Where the holy heck are you!!!"

She was outraged, as she should be. I had taken off after work yesterday, not to return for work this morning. Nadine had rained voicemail messages to my cell phone as early as two-thirty A.M. Pacific time. I had kept my cell phone turned off all day until I had left Nick's house and decided to check my messages. So I couldn't blame the woman for her use of "holy heck" today.

"I'm in California," I coolly explained.

"Again?" Nadine screeched. "Woman, what is wrong with you?"

"Nothing. This time, I did a good thing. I got—"

"Why won't you let that boy alone?"

"Nadine, you don't understand—"

"Well you understand this," she shot back. "You're fired."

My heart froze. Standing there in the Victoria's Secret dressing room, I felt fear and humiliation flood my body. I had never been fired from any job before, much less while I was half-naked. "Fired?"

"Yeah, you were, for about ten minutes this morning. Alex wanted your head in a hand basket. I convinced him not to. With the upcoming HART Awards, the fact that Polly isn't ready yet, and…"

"The fact that you're my friend?" I finished hopefully.

"That was the last thing on my mind," she snapped. "I swear, talent can, and will, only get you but so far!"

"Look, Nadine. I have a gang of vacation days I haven't even touched. Just consider this one of them."

"You coming back tomorrow?" she demanded.

Our connection on the phone began to waver. Nadine was beginning to break up. "I think so."

"You think so? You better think your tail onto a plane, h—"
Her call was dropped.

Good, I thought, immediately shutting off the phone. I hope
I didn't have to come back tomorrow. It would be nice to spend
all night tonight making up with Nick for the first time in some
six years. And this would be a nice little outfit to do it in, too.

I changed back into my clothes and marched up to the
register. I smiled confidently. "I'll take 'em."

*

Ninety minutes after I had left, I drove the Bonneville up to
the curb outside Nick's house. Surprisingly, I found Nick Senior
sitting outside on the porch. Seeing my car arrive, he bounced
up and came on over.

"What're you doing outside?" I asked quizzically.

"Let's go get something to eat," Senior suggested, sliding into
the passenger seat.

"What's wrong?"

"Let's just go get something to eat," he negotiated. "I'll tell you
over lunch."

I shrugged and we were off.

Of course, Senior had to pick the mildly expensive
Cheesecake Factory for lunch. And, of course, this frugal Volvo
salesman probably expected the lunch for the both of us to be on
me. After watching the man order a steak, I skimped by ordering
a chicken salad. There was no way I could expense this one to
WAGA.

Once the food had arrived, my curiosity would stay at bay no
longer. "Well?" I pressed.

"Nick hates me," Senior declared dramatically. "He said he
wants nothing to do with me."

"But didn't you tell him what you told me? Didn't you
apologize and all that?"

"I did. I told him how deeply sorry I was for hurting him and
his mother twenty-seven years ago. How I had squandered all of
our money and just wasn't a very good dad. How I was sorry
that it was the reason why his mother left. I told him how I count

158

it as one of the greatest mistakes in my life," Senior said with enormous remorse. The man was sincere. "But he didn't care."

I sank back in my chair, astonished.

"He said that it was curious timing for me to want to show my face just after he's secured a movie deal," Senior continued. "I told him that it wasn't like that, that it was your idea to bring me to him."

"Uh huh," I said numbly.

"Then he said that impressed him even less, that it took a woman he didn't even love anymore to bring me to see him."

"He said that?"

"Nick wasn't through. When I said that, as his father, he should at least listen to me, to hear what I had to say about being with you, he came back with 'You haven't been a father to me all my life; why the hell should you start now?'" Senior stopped just long enough to rub his eyes. "He was brutal."

My heart did a brief arrhythmia. Who was this man? Who was this spirit parading around in the skin of the man I loved? This was not like Nick to be so out-and-out rude—not just to me, but to everyone. How could he treat his old man like that after not having seen him for four-fifths of his life? At the very least, you'd think he would want to get to know him, find out what he's been doing all these years, to at least listen to what he had to say. Instead, Nick had rudely shut him down, just as he had done to me.

My mood darkened, my brow angry. I had no idea Nick was capable of such disrespect.

"I am so sorry, Nick," I apologized darkly. "I will have a talk with your son."

"Don't bother," the elder Nick said. "He's angry, he's confused, yet he thinks he's gotten it all figured out. He hasn't forgiven me yet. Hopefully, one day, he will. That's a lot of hate to carry around in your heart. The heart wasn't meant to hate; the heart was made to love. I don't know if there's that much love left in his heart."

There was, I knew there was. And I would be damned if I went back to Atlanta without having made him show it.

*

It was a long ride out to Sylmar and back. The largely silent drive gave me a chance to brood and harness my anger. After I had dropped Nick Senior off, I decided that it was time for the gloves to come off. No more Ms. Nice-Ex-Girlfriend. Time for some tough love. If you love somebody—and I truly did love Nick—you have to tell them when they're messing up. I couldn't imagine a time when Nick's emotions could be more screwed up than now. It was one thing to reject me, especially when our relationship was still fresh in his mind, but to discard his father out-of-hand? That pained me just to hear it. Something was wrong with the man I loved, and I was determined to fix it.

So with that mindset, I slammed on the parking brake before exiting the Bonneville outside Nick's home. The late afternoon sun still hung high in the sky as it glanced off the waters of the Pacific Ocean less than a mile away. Despite my mood, I decided that this was the perfect setting for a confrontation. I could care less if his heffa was home or not—I had something to get off my chest.

I pressed that doorbell like it was the nuclear Button.

When Nick answered the door, I shoved right past him into his house with all the subtlety of Bill O'Reilly. Before he could ask the same question, I beat him to the punch, grandstanding in the middle of his living room: "What are you doing?"

"What am I doing? What are you doing?" volleyed Nick. "You're the one in my house!"

"Look, Nick, I'm only going to tell you this because I love you—you're fucking up."

"I'm fucking up?" he crowed incredulously, shutting the door. "Who the hell told you to go find my father? Huh, Jasmine? Who gave you the right to intrude on my personal life like that, any more than you already have, I might add!"

"It's not an intrusion, Nick. I was trying to help you."

"The only way you could help me is by staying the hell outta my life!"

I shook my head. "You don't mean that."

"Stop trying to tell me how I feel!" he yelled. Immediately, Nick shifted it down a gear. He even allowed a small sardonic

160

laugh. "Isn't this ironic. Now you're telling me what I think and feel when I used to do the same thing six years ago."

I sighed. The man had a point. "I'm not telling you anything you don't already know."

"You aren't?" Nick hissed. "Since when did I say I was still in love with you?"

"You didn't have to. Your kiss did."

"A kiss you started."

"But a kiss you finished." I sidled up to Nick carefully. His emotions were so volatile right now, I had no idea if he would even let me get this close to him. "Do you believe I love you?"

"I believe you believe you love me."

"Please don't be difficult, Nick," I said breathily, close to his face, defusing him with my mixture of presentation and feminine wiles. "Do you believe I love you?"

Losing most of the edge in his voice, Nick said, "Yes."

"Do you believe that if I loved you, I would always want what's best for you?"

"Yes."

"So why won't you believe me when I say that I'm the one for you?"

"Because you're not." Nick turned his back on me, taking a quick trip around the couch. "Jasmine, just give up! This is a battle you cannot win. I don't love you."

"But I love you."

"I don't care!" The full fury of his eyes was upon me. "I don't care and I'm tired of dealing with this shit! I never asked for you to kiss me in that church! I never asked for you to stalk me all over Southern California! And I never asked to see my father! You violated whatever trust I ever had in you!"

"Babyluv, I—"

"Don't you 'Babyluv' me! I'm not finished," he snapped. "I am tired of saying this, Jasmine. I don't know how more clearly I can make this: GO HOME. I DON'T LOVE YOU. Period. End of story. Next chapter.

"People who love you don't harass you. People who love you don't try and upset your life. People who love you don't show up on your wedding day—in the middle of your freakin' wedding—and try to talk you out of it!

"People who love you are supportive. People who love you keep loving you no matter whom you love or what you do. People who love you let you live your life. They don't judge you, they don't disparage you, and they don't hurt you! Jasmine, can't you see that by your doing all of this you are hurting me? You've ruined my wedding, pissed off my fiancée, stressed out my sick mother, and are endangering my career. You don't love me, Jasmine. You've never loved me. You've only loved yourself."

I was stunned. Against my better instincts, I attempted speech. "But I do love you—"

"You love the image of me, the image of us. You have revisionist history, Jasmine. You see our past relationship, our faded love, how you want to see it. What we had was, for the most part, beautiful. But it wasn't perfect. And even if it was perfect, no perfect love is worth all this abuse, Jasmine," Nick reasoned. "I have tried everything with you. I've been nice about it. I've been mean about it. I've been indifferent. I've been standoffish. I've been flat-out rude. My wife-to-be—" I cringed at the word "—has been mean, physical, and rude. I just don't know what I'm going to have to do or say to make you believe that I don't love you anymore. I don't love you anymore. I love someone else; I love Tabitha. I love Tabitha, and I am marrying her. I don't love you anymore, and I never will."

"Never?" I croaked.

"Never," he affirmed decisively. "So what will it take, Jasmine? What will it take for you to get the hell out of my life forever? What will it take for you to finally move on with your life?"

I was shaking on the inside but I wouldn't show it. Or at least I don't think it did. "Kiss me."

Nick's eyes shot heavenward. "Not this crap again, Jasmine! That won't prove a damn thing!"

"You asked what it would take for me to get the hell out of your life, to finally move on, and this is it. Kiss me. If you can kiss me and not feel something, anything for me, then I'll leave. I will never bother you again."

Nick's face contorted to rage briefly, then, oddly, relief. "Is that it? I can kiss your ass goodbye?"

"That's it." I was nervous. A lot rode on this gamble. It had kinda worked three weeks before in the church, but now I left a lot up to what I truly believed was our chemistry. I mean we were made to love each other.

Without further ado, Nick grabbed the sides of my face and forced his lips onto mine. I tried to slip my tongue inside but Nick's closed lips prevented me. Then, inexplicably, his mouth relented and let me inside. I explored. I relaxed. I revisited my old stomping grounds. Nick's mouth felt warm and familiar yet different. Like so much these past six years, things had changed. For whatever reason, his mouth did not feel the same as it did three weeks ago.

This kiss couldn't have lasted even ten seconds before he broke away. He smiled at me generously. My eyes turned hopeful. The kiss test had worked!

"Goodbye, Jasmine."

My whole world crumbled in a single two-word sentence.

"Jasmine if you love me, if you ever loved me, please just leave me alone."

As Nick escorted me to the door, I couldn't bear to turn around. If I turned around, my emotions would start leaking from the eyes. This wasn't just rejection; I had gotten used to rejection lately. This was banishment. Whereas I had once been the queen of his kingdom, I wasn't even allowed throughout all the land.

Once I made it onto the porch, I did dare take a look, a last look at the man I truly loved. Nick didn't smile, gloat, or ridicule me. His face was sadly dispassionate. If there were a twinge of compassion there, I didn't see it. If there were a twinge of compassion there, Nick wouldn't let me see it. His eyes said it all. It's over, Jasmine. Go home.

As I settled into the seat of the Bonneville and drove away aimlessly in the general direction of the Westin Hotel (I guess), I settled into the most unsettling realization of all. I loved him. But I was not made to love him.

The Phone Call

So much rested on this phone call. I didn't even know if he would still be home. But before I could answer Rodney's question, I needed to know the answer to mine.

On the fourth ring, Nick picked up. "Hello?"

"Hi."

I could tell he was shocked, like the wind had been sucked right out of him. To his credit, my ex-boyfriend used only a hint of sarcasm. "To what do I owe this honor?"

Even though it felt odd to hear his voice for the first time in three years, I pressed on. "I heard that you were leaving Chicago."

"Two minutes later and I would already have left," he informed me. "How did you find out I was leaving?"

I grimaced. "Mia."

"Oh, so you're talking to her now?" Nick inquired pointedly. The fact that I had not spoken substantially in many moons to my best friend was still a sore spot for me.

"No, not really. But she did tell me about you."

"Why would she do that?"

I grew quiet. Mustering all the humility the situation required, I said, "Because I asked her about you. I called her to ask about you."

"Not Mal?"

"Malloy wouldn't talk to me," I said. "He told me that I had done enough to ruin his boy's life."

Nick snorted. "How did that make you feel?"

A pause. I felt so small right now—and deserved it. "Like he was right."

This time, Nick fell silent. Somewhat anxious, he asked, "Jasmine, why did you call?"

If sighs were water, I could have exhaled an ocean of feeling for that boy. "I miss you."

"I'll say it again," Nick reiterated. "Jasmine, why did you call?"

"I love you." Hell, it was the truth. I did love him. Even after all this time.

"Jasmine..." Nick sounded doubtful.

Be honest, Jasmine! Be honest! "I love you, Nick. I'm so sorry that I hurt you. I'm so sorry that we didn't work out, that I didn't work out. I loved you then and I love you now."

"Then why did you not want to marry me?"

"Because I was stupid. I was young. I didn't know any

better," I explained dismissively. "I was scared. I just didn't think things through." True, true, and more true.

"Jacque?" Nick asked bitingly.

"Maybe." I felt like I was on dangerous ground. "I mean, I hadn't even seen him since the summer you and I got together, but the possibility that I might have still had feelings for him at the time raised some questions in me. Marriage is kind of like a conviction—you have to be sure beyond a reasonable doubt."

"That's original," Nick snarled. "Especially coming from a woman."

I had to go for broke. "Look, Nick, I know things are different now. I know we're both different people now. I know I had a good thing and I blew it. I know that and understand that now. But I know in my heart that I still love you. I do. And I know that if we work at it, we could be together again, we could love each other again, perhaps even...even marry each other."

Nick was surprisingly rigid. "That wouldn't be me proposing, that's for sure."

Trying to turn his statement into a joke, I tried using the playfully nasal nerd voice Nick used to love. "Staaaawp it!"

"I threw the ring in the lake," he said, obviously trying to be hurtful.

"I don't care," I replied immediately. "I want us to start all over, from scratch, and rediscover what it's like to love each other." All this was so true. That was what I wanted! But was it working?

"Wh...I...We don't even live in the same place. Do you even know where I'm going? What I'm doing? I don't even know where you live anymore."

"I'm still in Atlanta," I said. "I've been working for WAGA-TV for two years in a glorified intern position and I'm not happy. I've got a damn degree in Communications, a degree that took me seven years to get, and I'm still doing the crapwork of the production coordinating staff. I know you're moving to San Diego and I'm willing to move there and get my own place, just to be near you. I'll take some entry level job at a TV station, bust my ass like I did for two years at WAGA, and in two years in San Diego, I'll either be in front of the camera or running the show behind it."

Come clean, Baby J, come clean! "We can do this, Babyluv! We can do this! I'm willing to go where you'll go. I wanna be where you're going to be. I want to be with you again, Nick. I want to know what it's like to truly love someone again, and not to have to relive that feeling through cold and distant flashbacks."

I could tell Nick was moved, but I wasn't sure how much. "What would Winnie say about your moving to San Diego to be with me?"

"I don't care what Mama would say. She hasn't supported me since I moved down to Atlanta, so why should I expect her to support me now? I don't care how she feels about you, Nick. I'm the one who's in love with you. I don't care what anyone else thinks." Listen to me, Nick! Just listen to me!

Nick was stunned. "Where's all this coming from, Jasmine? After all this time?"

"Remember how you used to tell me about the difference between need and want? That adults go for what they need and not just what they want?"

"Right."

"Well I need you, Nick. No man has compared to you, to us, to what we had four years ago. I mean that. All I've done these past few years is compare every guy I've ever gone out with to you—only to find them painfully lacking.

"I was too young to realize that you were everything a good man should be! I was so young, and naive, and vain that I thought all guys would be as good to me as you were. Nick, listen to me. I'm admitting that I made a mistake. A huge, terrible, big mistake. I cannot tell you how sorry I am for hurting you. By hurting you, I hurt myself. I miss you and I love you, Nick. I want you back."

"Just like that? You want me back?"

"I want you back," I declared, with even more determination the second time. If only Nick knew how much I had at stake, how much I put on the line to do this. How there was my boyfriend, Rodney, who had just proposed to me last night, and how I had to tell him "I have to think about it." What was with me and that damn line? How my girls Charlotte and Nadine were already picking out china patterns when I told them about Rodney's proposal. How this nagging, persistent memory, like a scratch at the back of the throat that refused to heal, made me pick up the phone and call him today. If only Nick knew how much I wanted this, needed this, needed him, and wanted him, he would say yes. He had to know I still loved him. And no matter what his emotional situation was as he moved to San Diego, he had to know that he still loved me.

"You want me back, but you don't need me," Nick quibbled.

"I need you, Nick."

"It's been so long, Jasmine..."

"I love you, Nick."

"But I don't love you."

That statement sank like a stone to the bottom of my spirit.

"Jasmine, I did love you. Very fiercely, at one point. I wanted to make you my wife. I had envisioned my whole life with you. I was so in love with you, I lost a piece of my soul in you. I couldn't see past you. But, evidently, you could."

Not anymore, Nick!

"There's a part of me that loves you, Jasmine. There always will be. But I don't love you now. Love is an action verb. I actively stopped loving you three years ago. I used to have dreams about you, about us, about our shared history. But it's over now, and so are we."

No we aren't, Nick!

"You want me to save your life. Just like Bleek Gilliam in Mo Better Blues, you think that by marrying me, I can save your life. You're unhappy with your job, with your family, with not having someone who romantically loves you, perhaps even unhappy about being twenty-nine and unmarried. You think that by being with me again, we can somehow approach what we had before I proposed to you."

We can, Nick!

"But that's all in the past. We should leave it there. Like the saying goes, the past is prologue. 'Those who live in the past are cowards.' Yes, it hurt me that you rejected my proposal. No, I don't wish away all the memories I have about you, about us. I keep them, treasure them, and reminisce over them at times. But

I do not live in them. And you can't either. It's over, Jasmine."

No, Nick, no!

"I'm not saying all this to be mean or to get revenge. We're bigger than that. I'm just being honest with you. To date, you have been the greatest love I've had in my life. I will always remember and love you for that. But it's time to move on, Jasmine, because I already have. I can't save your life any more than I can love you now. I can't. Only you can save your life and you can do it by loving yourself. Thank you for thinking of me, Jasmine, but you are not what I need right now. I'm sorry."

My damn heart hurt. My damn head hurt. Probably kind of like the hurt Nick must have felt four and a half years ago.

With a dignity I didn't know I had at the moment, I said very maturely, "Good luck, Nick. I hope I see you on TV or in a movie someday."

"Good luck to you, Jasmine," he responded similarly.

"Nick, I—" I stopped herself. The Fifth, The Fifth. Just take the freakin' Fifth.

The tears started welling in my eyes, emotion leaking out in my voice. "Goodbye."

"Goodbye."

With the press of a button, I was out of his life forever. Or so he thought.

10

I HAD A BEESTING WHEN I was nine. I remember the event like it was yesterday. I was running around in a park in Toronto with the other kids on a field trip during summer camp. I grew tired, slid in the grass, and had the back of my right knee land on a bee. Not only did the unsuspecting insect sting me, but also I ended up crushing the sucker. Not that I bothered to think about that as I was bawling my eyes out from this beesting, which turned out I was slightly allergic to. I mean if you wanted to hear world class wailing, you would've showed up at Exhibition Park that day around 1:45 in the afternoon. I cried as if my life depended on it, when it really didn't. Hell, as far as I was concerned, it did. How was I to know?

Tonight, I cried with the force of a thousand beestings.

I had no idea I would, that I could, react so badly to Nick's harsh words. I was stoically fine in the Bonneville, driving with statue-stiff posture as if my moving an inch would throw me from the car. Just as my mother had taught me all my life, I maintained my composure like world peace depended upon it.

Inside the hotel room was an altogether different story. My wails would make downed buffalo envious. To top it all off, I had cramps. Bad ones. I didn't always get cramps every month, but when I did, look out. I always carried an emergency bottle of extra strength Midol in my purse. I popped three of those bad boys in my mouth and crawled under the covers. Let the cramps come get me. I'd rather die from menstruation than a broken heart.

After an hour of crying, struggling to watch reality television, then crying some more, I did the unthinkable. I reached over to my cell phone and dialed a suburban New Jersey number. I made The Call.

"Hello?"

My sobbing would not relent.

"Hello?" she repeated. "Who's this?"

Crying gave way to stunted breathing.

"Who is this?" she asked, a bit angry.

Sniffling under a rainstorm of my own tears, I eeked out, "Mama..."

"Pooh?" Winnie asked. This did not sound like her thirty year-old daughter.

Forming coherent sentences was a little beyond my ability right now. "Mama...he...I...I'm in pain, Mama..."

She was shocked as I was shocked. I hadn't spoken to my mother in one, maybe two years. Nia kept me up to date with her movements, as Winnie had finally moved out of that Bay Ridge section of Brooklyn home we had grown up in. She had moved to a slightly bigger house across the Hudson in Englewood, New Jersey, a three level joint with two levels full of crap. I had been there once, before we had fallen out for good, and wondered at how she could essentially live on only one level of a three level house, filling the other two levels with all of our childhood junk. Besides her overwhelming disapproval of my life in Atlanta, living away from the nest, I couldn't point to one singular thing that had started the sangfroid between the two of us two years ago. But I could tell where and when the seed of it was planted.

"What's wrong, Jasmine?" she asked firmly, in control. "I can't understand you."

"He...he said he doesn't love me," I cried. "He told me to get out of his life forever..."

"He who? Rodney?"

I cried a torrent of tears. I boohooed more than I did on the first plane ride back from Cali. I was in so much pain, I could barely breathe for crying. I knew what I said next would touch off a nuclear winter of discontent. "...Nick..."

"Nick?!" I could hear my mother's blood boil, almost taste the bile she had on her tongue for him. In that moment she took to figure things out, I knew that vein of her on her forehead pulsed with the intensity of lights in Times Square. I expected a cold harangue on common sense, a tongue lashing for the ages. I expected a rebuke that never came. "Where are you? Atlanta?"

"LA," I sniffled.

"California?" Winnie sighed. "I'll be out there first thing tomorrow. Where are you staying?"

My mother was coming? Okay, the moons must have been aligned or something because I did not see that one coming!

"The—I'm at—the Westin on Century—uh—um—Century Boulevard. Room 203," I stammered nervously. Out of my world of hurt, I suddenly felt a little bit foolish. Our first reunion in two years was going to happen out in California over a boy?

But a boy who had hurt her daughter. "I'll be out there first thing tomorrow morning. Don't go anywhere. And try to stop crying, Pooh."

I'll also try to stop the sun from shining, while I'm at it. Still, I was amazed. Mama was coming to see me in my time of need. Just when you think you're old enough to have your parents figured out, they throw you a curveball and show you just how much they do care.

"Yes, Mama."

*

That night, Mark called and left a message. I didn't answer my cell phone because I didn't recognize the number. Okay, that was a lie: I didn't answer the cell phone for the rest of the night period. I didn't want anyone to hear me like this.

Charlotte called, too. Her message said that she was nervous about her audition a week from today in LA. If only she knew I was out here...Maybe she already did. Maybe Nadine went ballistic and called her before speaking to me. I really could have cared less. That beesting for a heart I had was not going away.

I stayed up all night, the tears finally dried, but in a permanent state of morose. You know the state: your face feels as fresh as dried plaster, you've come accustomed to the taste of your own mucous, and you look like someone just sat on your grill. I felt so lost, as if the last eight years had been for nothing. When you're only thirty years old, you hate to think that you wasted almost a third of your life loving somebody who didn't love you back.

In my permanent state of morose, I went through all the appropriate motions. I was mad at Nick, mad at myself, mad at God, mad at Jerry Springer for putting on a "special edition" of "When Lovers Don't Love You Back" just for me. I was mad at my sheets for being too white. I was even mad at Eddie Murphy in Boomerang because for me, unlike for him, there would be no coming back around. And so I fell asleep, mad at the world and everything in it. If I knew you at the time, I'd be mad at you, too.

I was surprised at how quickly Winnie got to LA. It seemed like only nine-thirty in the morning when I heard her knock at the door. Slowly, I crawled out of bed and opened up the door. Opening up that door was like opening up a past life. I instantly reverted to my mother's daughter, little ol' Jazzy Pooh with pigtails or the French braid. "Hi."

With a sigh, Winnie embraced me in the doorway before marching right in. As I shut the door, I did a visual inventory of my mother. Winnie wore a presentable pale blue blouse, slacks, and a nice pair of Gucci flats. For the most part, she looked the same—light skin, small salt and pepper afro, bespectacled face that gave her the look of an intellectual.

And she was a very smart woman. Winnie worked as a mathematician for a pharmaceutical company for over thirty years. She made crazy bank and invested wisely. I'm proud to say that Mama went to MIT for undergrad. If I had an ounce of book sense rather than common sense it was genetic rather than learned.

When my mother had entered the room, I immediately felt twelve years old. Not since my breakup with Jacque eight years ago had I needed my mommy to save me. Mama was remarkably civil about it. Usually by this point, she'd be dancing in the middle of an "I told you so" fest.

Calmly, as was her nature, Mama sat in a chair across from my unruly bed. I, myself, looked a mess, too—hair everywhere, eyes red and swollen, with my nose raw and cherry colored. I looked like Cupid had just whupped my ass. Mama examined her beat-down looking daughter. Devoid of intonation, she said clearly, "So why are we here?"

I couldn't lift my eyes for shame.

"Nick, right?" she said acidly.

A little history was in order here. Mama hated Nick. No, that wasn't it; hate wasn't a strong enough word. Mama loathed Nick like Republicans did the truth. Mama despised Nick like I did triflin'-ass brothas with corny game when my feet hurt. Mama hated Nick like the Ku Klux Klan did black men with white women. Mama hated Nick like she had invented the word.

Less than a month into our relationship eight years ago, Nick had dinner at Mama's house with Nia and me. It was the first time he had met Mama. Let's just say it would be the last.

My eyes still couldn't bear the scrutiny so I kept my head down.

"Pooh, I'm talking to you," Mama spoke patiently. "I did not come three thousand miles to have a conversation with myself."

A cleansing sigh. I tried to strike my nerve up.

"Talk to me, Jasmine. Please." My mother sounded so...motherly. It was as if all of the fallout from my having moved to Atlanta years ago against her wishes had all gone away.

"I love him," I confessed quietly.

"I know," she acknowledged through gritted teeth.

"I love him and he doesn't love me back." I could make a mouse sound like Rage Against the Machine right now. "It hurts."

Now it was Mama's turn for a sigh, a very motherly sigh. "I know, Pooh, I know."

Mama glided over from her chair next to me on the bed. She held my hand. Mama was holding my hand. "You don't think I know what that feels like, but I do. Your father made me feel that way."

Ah, the Playboy of the Western World. Mr. Jet to this and Concorde to that. Mr. I'm-too-busy-to-raise-a-family. I held about an even keel of contempt yet fatherly respect for him, just enough not to hate him. While he never cheated on my mother, he was the one who broke up our family by filing for divorce. He enjoyed jet setting around the country for his corporate exec job more than he loved his family.

"I have always loved your father. Even back at UPenn when we were just junior undergrads dating from two totally different fields, I loved him. When I got pregnant with Nia halfway through senior year, I loved him. When we married that summer with me six months pregnant, I loved him. When we had you, I thought I'd die for loving him so much. And when he stopped loving me, I still loved him."

Mama stole a moment to gather her thoughts. I sat there amazed. It wasn't every day your mother recounted the story of her love life with shockingly plain-faced truth.

"I do know what it's like to love someone who no longer loves you back. It has to be the most painful, humbling, humiliating feeling in the whole wide world."

"Tell me about it."

"Especially when there are children involved." Mama shook her head sadly. "The saddest day of my life was the day we left Toronto. I thought my heart would never heal."

Wow. Now Mama was speaking my same brokenhearted language. "And did it?"

"No. And it never will."

My balloon of hope deflated.

"Listen Pooh, that crack in my heart is like the crack in a simple sidewalk—it exists but life goes on. It has to. What has happened to you, what has happened to me, has been happening to every woman since the dawn of time. What's happening to you now is what practically defines us as women. What makes us stronger, what makes us women, is that we survive, move on, and eventually learn to love again."

"But I've never loved anyone like I love Nick."

Just the simplicity of my statement rocked Mama into a whole other frame of consciousness. Her whole tonality changed. "Jasmine, go home. Your friends, your job, your life is waiting for you in Atlanta.

"I admit, Pooh, that I've never liked Nick. Believe me, moments like these do not make me like him any more. But what I really don't like is that boy just isn't smart. I saw that a long time ago. No matter how much he loved you when he came to the house for dinner that one time, the boy was not very smart to challenge my love for my daughter in my very own house. It wasn't very smart of him to insult me and walk out. And it really wasn't smart of him to make you choose between him and your family."

I knew all about the Dinner from Hades; I was there. And your point is…

"I say all that to say this: When you stomped out of the house after him that night, I was surprised at the level and depth of your emotion for him. You had never allowed a man to come between you and family before. When you stomped out of the house I really didn't like him because he made you make not very smart decisions. And they weren't very smart because I knew, some day, I would have to come to you and say this. I don't like Nick, Pooh, because he makes you dumb. And you, Jasmine Selene, are not a dumb woman."

That hit home like John Henry's hammer.

"I did not raise dumb daughters. Go home, Jasmine. Be smart."

I reached over to embrace my mother. I was so sorry both our stubborn prides had kept us apart for the past few years. I was even more sorry that it took a sorry-ass man to bring us back together.

I said something I hadn't said in years. "I love you, Mama."

Exhaling slightly into my back, Mama said, "I love you, too, Pooh."

She disengaged herself and stared at me. "Go take a shower. You look a mess. I will not have my daughter going home looking a mess."

I smiled. Presentation, presentation. "Yes, Mama."

When Jasmine had slipped inside the shower, Winnie slipped inside her daughter's purse. As expected, Winnie had found Jasmine's Palm Pilot and quickly accessed the information in it.

Which explained her presence here. As she pulled up the rental car to a well worn curb in Playa del Rey, Winnie sucked her teeth in disdain. The house was pretty, contemporary, and instantly rivaled the home she had in Englewood. With all of the determination of a Sherman tank, Winnie steamrolled to the front door. Pity that she would never tell her daughter about this visit.

A young, light pecan brownskin woman answered the door. She looked about two semesters out of college. "Hello?"

"Yes. I'd like to speak to Nick, please," Winnie demanded politely.

"And you are?"

"A former acquaintance who would like to speak with Nick."

The woman eyed her suspiciously. "He's a little occupied right now. I'm Tabitha, his fiancée. Is there anything I can help you with?"

"Yes," Winnie said crisply. "You can go get Nick. That's 'what you can help me with.'"

Tabitha started like she didn't know whether to begin arguing with this woman or to simply obey. The authoritative tone in Winnie's voice, however, made her choice easy. "I'll, uh, go get him. Um, would you care to come in and sit down?"

"No, I'll wait right here," Winnie responded tersely.

"Right. Hold on." Tabitha drifted off, thoroughly perplexed. Winnie stood there stiffly, examining her nails. Perfect, of course. Once again, she would give this young man a lesson in class.

Nick arrived at the door, seemingly alone to Winnie's knowledge. When his eyes fixed themselves on her, all color drained from his face (and that's a lot of color).

Inside, Winnie triumphed. Already, she was inside the young man's head.

"May I help you?" Nick grimaced.

My, there's a lot of that going around. That made it easier for her upcoming, unrehearsed, off-the-cuff speech. "Actually, you could, but I think you already have. You could help me by never, ever contacting my daughter again."

Nick made a motion to speak, but Winnie cut him at the knees with an index finger. "Wait. I'm not done. I do realize that my daughter has become somewhat more proactive in recent years, especially when it comes to you, so I can assure you that if you never contact her again, she will never contact you again.

"Because, see, my daughter isn't a good woman, she's an exceptional woman. She's the kind of woman that men dream of and mothers adore. My daughter is the kind of woman who is loyal to a fault—her own—but has the nerve and strength of character to stick to her beliefs and feelings even when they are unpopular or inconvenient. She is the kind of woman who will put everything—her family, her friends, her job, her very life—

behind her so long as she believes in whom she loves. While this isn't always the smartest thing to do, it is one of the most honest, admirable qualities in a human being I have ever witnessed, and it makes me proud to call her my daughter.

"Also, because she is an exceptional woman, you do not deserve her. Quite frankly, I never believed you did. I found it sad and disappointing that of all the men in this world she could possibly love, she chose to love you. Yet she did. She put you above everything else in her world, including the opinions of her own mother, just because she believed so much in you and your love. And eight years later, how do you repay her? By breaking her heart.

"I know my daughter hurt you several years ago, and your reaction to her advances is understandable. But what I don't understand is why she would even want you back in the first place. For my daughter to publicly put herself in the position she has—pining away for a young man who is en route to being married, risking her job, her friends, her disapproving family, and her mental and physical health—demonstrates a startling amount of loyalty and love to a person who couldn't even find the chapter in the book of Life on both of these subjects.

"You may think that you are simply paying her back, teaching her a lesson, or perhaps it is as simple as the fact that you do not love her anymore, but know this. Know that this woman, my daughter, loves you with everything she has and everything that she hasn't! And if you can't even simply acknowledge that concept, to accept her love politely and graciously and go on about your life in the manner of a young man who once gave a damn about her well-being, then you are even worse than being undeserving of my daughter's infinite love: you are unlovable. You could not ever love anyone fully, period.

"So to save you and her the embarrassment of having to find that out, you can just relax and stay out of my daughter's life forever. Because now that my daughter realizes all of these things about you, she won't ever bother you again. Just make sure you don't ever bother her. Understand?"

Feebly, Nick nodded.

Winnie turned to leave, but stopped short. "What makes me

sad about all of this is that love in this world is so awfully hard to find. True love is almost impossible. For better or for worse, with my blessing or not, my daughter loved you, truly loved you. Had you married her, she would've made you the perfect wife. Her loyalty, love, and commitment are unlike that I've ever seen. Just for those qualities alone, whether I liked you or not, I would have accepted you because she chose to love you. And based on the strength of her choice, to be with you forever, and all that forever entails with Jasmine, you would have had my blessing."

A rueful, cryptic smile took hold of her. "But now we'll never know."

Winnie walked away, leaving a shell-shocked Nick picking up the remains of his emasculated pride. She shook her head as she settled into her rental, turning the key to the ignition. A big sigh. Something she had always wanted to say was finally lifted from her shoulders. She shifted into drive, leaving the beautiful Playa del Rey residence behind, a picture perfect purplish-gold sunset framing it all.

"Now we'll never know."

11

TALK ABOUT NO REST for the weary. I returned home around nine that evening, jet-lagged and ready for bed. Of course, my answering machine and cell phone were blowing up with messages. I suppose it felt good to know that I had friends and people who cared and worried about me, but my biggest objective was hitting the sack. That would prove a challenge in itself.

The messages also reminded me of the life I had left behind. Although only gone a couple of days, I felt like I had been on the outside looking in for the past couple of weeks. A message from Charlotte detailed the elaborate wedding shower/bachelorette party she had in store for Nadine, whose upcoming nuptials were now only three days away, on Sunday. One from Nadine not only called me on the carpet, demanding my presence or my resignation tomorrow morning at five A.M., but also reminded me to go pick up my bridesmaid dress. That woman was amazing. I was in awe at how she could shift gears from professionally reaming me out to playfully addressing me like a girlfriend as easily as changing lanes on the 85 at night. Nadine threw in a reminder about the HART, that the ceremony was only a week and a half away. There was also a cautiously worded message from Rodney, calling to make sure I was all right. I guess Nadine's paranoia would soon be legally branded into his consciousness in three short days.

So before I made it to bed, I decided to make one short call to my girl Charlotte, to bring her up to speed. I could easily imagine her reaction to what I would tell her.

"Hey, girl."

"What up, ma? Where you been? A sista's been incognegro, huh?"

I sighed. "I went to Cali."

"Again?" Charlotte screeched. "So did Movie Star invent a new way to say no?"

"Something like that." I frowned. "Movie Star?"

"You know how be I namin' these foolish men. He's been without a name for too long."

"Right."

"So...what happened?" she prompted, that edgy Brooklyn voice of hers intruding the way that accent did.

I gritted my teeth. Just how much do I tell Charlotte? True, she was my girl and all, but I didn't know how much of her self-righteous man bashing mixed with romantic defiance I could take today. As much as I tried never to compare the two, I would never censor my thoughts around my former best friend Mia.

"He invented a new way to say no," I deferred.

Char gave her "Men" snort. "I know you didn't just take that. You figured out another way to make him say yes, right?"

"No. I pretty much just took the 'no' and ran with it." I crawled into bed, now in a pair of shorts and a long tee. The covers were drawn up to my chin. "Then I went back to my hotel room and cried a new water supply for the City of Los Angeles."

Patiently, yet a bit exasperated, Charlotte commiserated with "I'm sorry."

"Don't be. Mama came out to talk to me."

"Yo, you mean Ma Dukes? She came all the way from New Jersey to holla at you?"

"She took care of me, got my head screwed back on straight," I admitted. "As far as reconciliations go, this was a pretty good one. We had a long talk, a good one. My mother's back and now Nick's out of my life—for good."

"He's out of my liiife," crooned Charlotte, à là Michael Jackson. "Great for you, ma!"

Although I was fine with the decision and how I had arrived at it, the hole in my heart still couldn't match her enthusiasm. "Well, it's a start. It's all over now. I'm putting Nick behind me for good."

"That's tight, J. Now you soundin' like the assertive, award-winning journalist, and all-around ass-kicker we know and love!" Char approved.

Yeah. That's exactly what I am, I thought sarcastically. I was sure that if Char said it enough, I'd eventually start believing it. "Alright, alright, alright. No need to be gassin' me up, girlfriend. What's goin' on with you? How's Mr. Issues?"

"On another newsstand," Char dismissed. "Someone else can pick him up and try 'reading' him. He and his broke-ass chick deserve each other anyway. How you gonna love a lifetime underachiever like his McDonald's manager of an ex-wife is beyond me."

"More like 'How you gonna love a lifetime underachiever like his McDonald's manager of a wife over you,' huh?" I laughed.

"That too," she agreed. "Actually, I'm startin' to cut peeps off. I dunno, J. I've got a real good feeling about this audition next week. I think I'm gonna knock it out the box. I don't think I'm gonna be around here long."

"Good. Keep that confidence up, and I'm sure you'll do fine."

"I have just one request."

"Which is."

Charlotte's voice was small. "Come with me."

"Back to Cali? Oh no no no!"

"Then you say yeah yeah yeah yeah yeah!" Char responded, this time invoking Destiny's Child. "C'mon, J! I need the support! And if you're really over Nick, it won't bother you to go back out there. Consider it a test, a challenge."

You'd think we have been friends all our lives the way Charlotte knew how to tweak my emotions. Going at my pride head-on yielded spectacular results. "I'll think about it," I demurred.

"Good enough. We leave on Tuesday night."

"Right," I said sarcastically. "Is Nadine real mad at me?"

"Mad? Naw. She called me a few times, looking for you, but she sounded concerned more than anything. But other than that, it's been straight LPS."

"LPS?"

"Little Princess Syndrome," Char explained. "Her head is all wrapped around this wedding coming up, I'm surprised she even knew you were missing."

"It's her job to know when I'm missing," I said. "But still, she's buggin' out about the wedding?"

"No, she's obsessing about it. Driving everyone crazy about it. You know we have a rehearsal tomorrow night, right?"

"No, I didn't know that."

"Well now you know, ma. And please, please, please do not forget to pick up your dress! That woman will go crazy if you haven't at least tried it on to make sure the alterations fit," Charlotte warned. "Our girl wants her wedding to be perfect."

"It will be perfect," I assessed with a sigh. "It's Nadine's life, not mine."

*

Ready for a tirade of the ages, I stepped towards Nadine's office at five A.M. the next morning. I was already outfitted by in a sharp gray suit top while I wore jeans underneath. Tyrone had, once again, done a fabulous job on my makeup (ladies, to look this good, you betta "call Tyrone!"). I looked great, I felt great, I was bright and alert. Jasmine Selene was at the top of her game.

Then I stepped foot into Nadine's office.

"Shut the door," my boss advised. I obeyed. "Have a seat."

Once again, I obeyed. Not a good start. Her head was bowed as she sat at her desk, filling out some paperwork. I made amends. "Morning, Nadine."

"One second," she growled.

Dang. Was this the woman for whose wedding I was a maid of honor? Keep it up, Nadine, and you can find your own way down the aisle…

Finally, Nadine stopped writing. She held up what she was working on. "You know what this is?" She spat it as more of a threat than a question. "It's the recommendation for your application to Fox Headquarters for Fox Nightly News. Do you want to hear what it says?"

"Do I have a choice?"

"No," Nadine vetoed, launching into her reading. "'Jasmine Selene is as bright and capable a talent as any I have ever had the pleasure of producing and working with. In as little as sixteen months, I have seen her star rise from production coordinator assistant to one of Atlanta's most watched, most respected, and most skilled anchors. What she has accomplished in her rookie year of broadcasting borders on legendary, and her learning curve is unmatched. I would stack her against any anchor in the Fox Network."

I glowed from the inside out. "Go on."

Nadine shot me a look. "'Yet for all of her on air acumen, Ms. Selene is equally as unprofessional off the air. Although she has had lively and informative input on script sessions from time to time, she has been known to skip entire days of production without any advance warning to the production staff; she has taken liberties in producing pieces that would have been found objectionable to any other producer were it not for my personal friendship with her; and she has proven to be stubborn in everything from pursuing stories to resisting management's insistence upon taking vacation time.

"'While I have the highest respect for Ms. Selene's on air skills and demeanor, her off air personality may be a force to contend with. The fact that I consider her a personal friend makes this recommendation of her cloaked thoroughly in truth, as I have objectively displayed all of the qualities that Jasmine Selene brings to the Fox Network as on air talent.

"'I do recommend Ms. Selene for the lead anchor position on the upcoming show Fox Nightly News, but I do so with reservations. I think it should be noted that most of these reservations have been issues that have been raised within the last month and may not generally reflect Ms. Selene's consistently professional manner. However, should it be necessary, I would love for the opportunity to expound upon my views at the above address. Thank you for the time and consideration of WAGA-TV Atlanta's candidate for the position.'" Nadine put the paper down and affronted me with her eyes. "Signed, Nadine Montgomery."

I didn't know what the appropriate response would be right now after such a character assassination. I also didn't know if I was talking to my boss or my friend. Can you truly have a boss as a friend? Or, better yet, can you keep a boss as a friend? Well hell if I was going to sit around here and take this missionary style. If I was going down, with her sending in that flaming rejection of a recommendation to Fox Headquarters, I would go down swinging. "What're you, proud of yourself or something?"

"It's the truth, Jasmine," Nadine answered.

"It's character assassination! You know that's not how I am!"

"It's the truth and you know it. Ever since Nick came back on the scene, your common sense has turned to oatmeal!"

"Oh, here it comes...Go ahead and tell me, Nadine, Miss Bosslady, how my personal life has affected my professional life. Go ahead and tell me how wrong I am for all of the choices I've made in my heathenistic little life. Go ahead and tell me how much better life would be were I Nadine Montgomery, a sheltered, thirty-year old virgin who has experienced life only through the news I report to her, and not through any experience of her own!"

Nadine held onto a shred of her calm, but just a shred. "Alright, I will go ahead and tell you. Your personal life hasn't affected your professional life—it has destroyed it. Had you not showed up today, honey, we would've shipped your behind out to Warner Robins or Tifton, and let you report on cow manure fertilization levels of local crops. And I'm not going to tell you how wrong you are for all the choices you've made outside the path to God because that is not for me to say. What is for me to say is that were you open to more spiritual instruction in your life, you might have made some different choices in your life that might have made you a little happier than you are today. And as far as my life being better than yours...Just the fact that you even imagined such a concept tells me all I need to know. Get it together, Jasmine."

"Get it together?" I howled. "Why don't you get your own man, Nadine! Why is it that your past two boyfriends have both been my leftovers! You don't think I didn't know about you dating Brian Richardson over at WSB shortly before your 'departure?' You don't think Brian and I still talked, even though I kicked him to the curb two years ago? Oh, you'd be amazed at what he will tell you after a few drinks at the reception for the National Association of Black Journalists convention! You wanna hear the book on you, Nadine? You wanna hear what he told me about you, Miss Montgomery?"

Nadine rolled her eyes. "If it'll make you feel better, you go right ahead."

"Because I know I'm right in the eyes of the Lord..." I know what you're thinking right now, trick! I wanted to holler, but knew it could cost me a friend and a job. Well, what I had to say next might do that for me anyway.

"You really should try getting a man of your own and quit digging through my trash, Nadine, because maybe then one of 'my men' would be able to keep your little secret. Miss 'I'm a Virgin.' You're a virgin, my ass. Literally."

Nadine shot me a look so dirty, I could shower for a week. "You need to shush up, honey, before you get your feelings hurt."

"No, I won't 'shush' this time. I've sat around and listened to your hypocrisy off and on ever since we became friends, after you moved to this station. I've seen and heard you preach like the PK you truly are about abstinence and all this hootie hoo, just to hear about you giving up the ass to Brian!"

Uppercut! It was on now!

"I never, ever had sexual intercourse with Brian Richardson!" Nadine huffed, flustered.

"Oh, that's right. My bad," I faux-retracted. "If you're talking about inserting Tab A into Slot B, he didn't do that. But he did stick Tab A into Slot C!" You dirty, hypocritical, sanctimonious, frontin' ass chick!

Shame flooded Nadine's face at the same time she tried to save it. "I do not acknowledge what it is you're talking about!"

"Oh, of course you wouldn't acknowledge it. But we both know that when you wouldn't let Brian in the front door, he took the back door—and you let him!"

Enraged, Nadine said, "Why you jealous, manipulative, lying—"

"Say I'm lying!" I dared her. "Say it! Say it loud and clear so God can send you straight to Hell, with gasoline draws and a window seat!"

Although her dark skin was well into a shade of purple now, Nadine did not—could not—say anything.

"If you can say right now, in all honesty, in front of me and God that you did not have anal sex with Brian Richardson, then I'll drop it," I challenged. "But I know you can't say that, and you know why I know? I know because Brian has no reason to lie to me. But even if he was just being a dumb male about it and

185

bragging a fabrication, I know it happened because I kicked his stupid, freaky ass to the curb when he wanted to stick his dick in my poo-poo hole, and I wasn't havin' it!"

Nadine squirmed around like live bait, which she was. "Honey, we're at work…"

"Fuck work!" I declared. "The door is closed. We're all adults here. I got issues!"

Seizing the opportunity, Nadine volleyed back, "You sure do. Let's talk about you for a second, Jasmine!"

Look at her try and misdirect the conversation. "Don't change the subject! You let Brian Richardson put it in your ass and that does not make you a virgin!"

"Whereas you, on the other hand, will sleep with anything with three legs and a smile?" she charged. "And now, how desperate are you? You see me getting married to yet another fish you threw away so you go running back to an ex-boyfriend of yours who does not want you. Charlotte's told me what's up. How many times the boy gotta say no? How many times are you going to humiliate yourself at the hands of a man? Then there's Jacque. He proposes to you, tries to make amends, and you diss him, too! How many times are you going to realize that maybe there isn't something wrong with the men you turn down. Maybe there's something wrong with you!"

"Okay, Oprah's lovechild, let's hear it. Please tell me, Dr. Phil, what the hell is wrong with me!"

"Get over Nick! Leave the poor boy alone! Have some freakin' dignity and go about your life!" Nadine shouted. "Give up this ridiculous obsession with The One That Got Away and move on! Have the courage to love someone new! Quit flying out to Cali and risking your job for this man who does not want you! Stop being an emotional coward!"

Damn that stung. And you know how I felt about beestings.

"So I should be like you, huh? Duck life head-on and hide behind the church and work? Chase after awards like the HART as if they were personal validation for leading an unfulfilling, work-centered, overly sheltered life? Go rummaging through Charlotte's black book and see whomever I can catch on the rebound, right?"

"Say what you will about how Rodney and I got together but

you gave us your blessing, and he genuinely loves me. Do you have anyone you can say that about in your life? Oops, no you don't—you threw them all away."

"Rodney only loves you because he—" I stopped myself. I was about to take things too far. I really and truly was. I swore to myself I would never tell her about the ring and Rodney's recent admission to me, and I never would. Who was I to begrudge her happiness simply out of spite? Who was I to wreck her upcoming marriage just days before?

This fight was over. It had to be because I was about to lose a friend. A friend and a job. But more so a friend.

I wanted to apologize but DFP kicked in again. If I could ever just extract Damn Fool Pride from my personality, I'd have been married to Nick with a second baby on the way by now. I can freely admit DFP was one of my uglier qualities but how do you fight your own nature?

So, instead of apologizing, I stood up. "I have a show to do," I remarked acidly, turning for the door.

"Yeah, you go do your show, honey—for once this week!" Nadine hissed.

When I slammed the door, I was mad I didn't unhinge that muthafucker.

I stewed at my desk for the rest of the hour. I was mad about so many things. I was mad that I was back to cursing like a sailor's ho. I was mad that Nadine had brought me down from my professional high and readiness. I was mad that Nadine had called me out in a professional and personal manner, in a way that was more than likely going to cost me a shot at the anchor desk at Fox National. I also got mad at myself for having been so baited into a ruinous argument like the verbal Bosnia I had plowed headlong into. They really shouldn't make "Don't Do Drugs" commercials on TV. They really should make "Don't Do DFP" spots. I'd be their national spokeswoman. Most importantly, I was mad at Nadine for speaking the gospel truth.

I groaned. I was one of her bridesmaids, for God's sake, a co-maid of honor. I think I had just defiled the honor part right out of the title.

I concentrated on getting myself ready for the show at six. Five minutes before airtime, sitting behind the desk next to my co-anchor Richard, a handsome, well-educated blond haired man of forty-two, I achieved a sense of calm that allowed me to function. Inhale, exhale, blah, blah, blah.

"You alright, kiddo?" Richard beamed at me. I must have seemed visibly nervous or something, which was odd for any professional who made their living this way five times a week.

I smiled back at him. I loved it when he called me "kiddo." "I'm fine, Richard. Thank you."

"Great. Let's get 'em." He smiled that smile that won him this job. We were a very telegenic pair. No wonder Atlanta loved us. That's right, Damnit. Atlanta loved me. Screw what Nadine said. Jasmine Selene is on top of her game.

Cameramen shouted instructions, TelePrompTers rolled, lights came up, our intro music thundered in, and we were on the air. Thankfully, Richard led off with some story on DeKalb County police corruption. Wow, what a shocker. That surprised absolutely no one about the South's shadiest police force. We out here called them "Rampart East" after the infamously corrupt LA police precinct.

As I listened to him go on about the story, I readied my concentration for my story coming up. Okay, okay. Baby's mother dumps the baby in the trash can of a Church's Chicken bathroom. Damn! That's some shit, ain't it! I mean, she couldn't have even dumped the kid in a Miss Winners at least? A KFC? I mean a Church's! Made me want to slap the momma.

Okay, okay, focus, Jasmine! Richard was almost done. I remembered some of the fundamentals my Media Broadcasting class back at NYU had taught us about delivery and speech flow. I always ran back to my basics when I had a hard time getting focused.

Richard ended. Time to pick up the ball. I focused on the TelePrompTer. "A one month old baby girl was found in the trash of a Church's Chicken on Old National Highway in College Park last evening," I read.

Having gotten the beginning of the story out clean, I put myself on autopilot, as I habitually did on this job. Most pros did, I'm sure. You tryin' to tell me Dan Rather hasn't thought about getting his Beemer waxed while he was talking about strife in the Middle East?

Something was strange about this time on autopilot. The words were coming out but I labored to do it. That never happened. That was why they called it autopilot. I got angry that I had to focus again. I got angry that I got angry. Wasn't nothing going right this morning, I swear. I felt a little hot under the collar, literally. The lights seemed even brighter than usual, if possible. My heart rate sped up. What was going on?

Suddenly, the world turned into a kaleidoscope of color, a blur of images and varying degrees of light. Just before all sound drowned out, I heard a thud sound. I saw black.

*

I woke up in the hospital. I had no idea how long I had been unconscious, but it must have been some time because there was an IV stuck in my arm. That really unnerved me. I didn't like the idea of being fed intravenously with some needle poking out of my skin. Creepy.

I must have been doped up, too, because my eyelids felt heavy as stones. I could barely make out a large bouquet of flowers resting in a corner of the room. I think the words "I'm Sorry" were printed on a balloon that floated in place above the bouquet. As far as I could tell, I was alone. How depressing was that? I'm stuck in the hospital and I'm all by myself. No one waiting bedside for me, hoping I get well. That thought alone was enough to make me black out again.

*

I think it was morning when I came to again. I guessed that because of the shafts of light hitting me right in the head when I fluttered my eyelids open. The drugs must have worn off because I could move my eyes pretty well. The side of my head felt like Tony Soprano had taken a hammer to it.

This time, a look around the room provided me a peek at my very own indoor garden. It was amazing and eerie at the same time. I didn't know there was that much love for me out in the world to warrant the amount and variety of flowers in my room.

"You up, ma?"

Charlotte! I offered up a weak smile. "Hey, girl. How're you doing?"

"Bump that, ma! How are you doing?" Charlotte hovered over my bed, her beaming dark brown face offering instant encouragement and support.

"I'd be a lot better if they weren't feeding me like a vegetable." I wiggled my right arm with the IV in it. "I hate needles."

"Had no choice. You were knocked out for a grip, J." Charlotte made a face. "Do you remember what happened?"

"No. One minute I was talking about some mother ditching her kid at a Church's Chicken and the next thing I know I'm in here." I shifted myself into a more social position. "Any enlightenment would be helpful."

"Right." Charlotte pulled up a chair by the bed and sat. "You fainted on the air, J."

I blinked twice. "I fainted?"

Charlotte shrugged her eyebrows at me. "You went down like the Titanic. The worst part is—"

I scrunched my face. "It was on air," I finished.

Charlotte gave a hopeful little look. "Well, look at it this way. If peeps didn't know who Jasmine Selene was before, they know now."

I shook my head sadly. "I take it you've seen the footage."

"Everyone has. Repeatedly. It made national news. You tell me the last time you remember hearing about an anchor fainting on air in a major market."

"True." I rubbed my forehead, to find a bump on the side of my face. There were stitches, about eight of them, I counted with my fingertips. I hid them by rearranging my curly hair by the side of my face. "Damn, I must look crazy right now."

"You look a lot better than when you took a face plant off the anchor desk."

"Thanks." I forced myself to stop touching the bruise. "I want to see the tape."

"No you don't."

"Yes, I do."

"Alright then. Don't say I didn't warn you. It's almost time for the noontime news. Ten bucks says your condition leads it off," Charlotte guessed.

My face panicked. "There's media here?"

"Outside the room. They've all been barred. Not even the WAGA folk. Nadine wouldn't have it. I think she reacted extremely well to the whole situation," assessed Charlotte. "She was one of the first people on the scene before they cut tape. She's really taken care of you."

I relaxed, but only momentarily. Nadine. I had said some nasty things to her, even if they were true. DFP or not, I was going to apologize to her the second I was vertical again. "Nadine's a good girl."

"Yeah she is. She even surprised me by not flippin' out on your absence at the rehearsal last night. She almost called the whole thing off because you were up in here."

I was shocked. "She almost called off the wedding?"

"Naw, just the rehearsal. Rodney convinced her to at least just go through the motions. Said that you wouldn't have minded."

Really, I wouldn't have. "Rod knows me well." I checked my watch. "Hold up. Did you say the noontime news?"

"Yeah. It's comin' on in two minutes," Char said. "Why? Whassup?"

"What day is it?"

"Saturday. Day before Nadine's wedding."

I was aghast. "You mean I've missed an entire day?"

"Yeah. Why you think that IV's in your arm? You knocked yourself out good, ma," chuckled Charlotte. She consulted her watch. "And now, due to popular request, we get to watch it in color TV. Again."

Charlotte aimed the remote at the TV and turned it on. Polly was in the middle of the lead story about the apprehension of the Church's Chicken Momma.

"Oo, good. I'm glad they caught that bitch," murmured Charlotte. "Janaya may not have been a planned pregnancy, but ain't no way I was gonna just ditch my kid in the bathroom of the worst chicken place in the South."

"Our next story is an update on one of our own, in the bizarre situation that took place on our very own airwaves yesterday morning," announced Polly. "We turn it over to Gerald

Hampton, reporting live from Georgia Baptist Hospital in Midtown on the condition of our beloved anchor Jasmine Selene, who fainted on air Friday morning. Gerald?"

Bizarre? Beloved anchor? Dang. Polly must be writing her own scripts these days. Didn't sound half-bad. Watch her take my job for good while I'm stuck in this hospital bed.

The station cut to young Gerald Hampton, a twentysomething brotha in a suit, standing outside the emergency entrance to Georgia Baptist Hospital. "Thanks, Polly. I'm here outside Georgia Baptist Hospital where our award-winning weekday morning anchor Jasmine Selene is recovering from fainting on the air yesterday morning during the six A.M. edition of the morning news on WAGA-TV.

"Right now, no one is being allowed inside the room of Ms. Selene except for family, as she remains unconscious from her fainting spell of yesterday."

I touched Char gently on the arm. "Aww. You're family."

Char beamed a sunny smile at me.

"At last report, Ms. Selene had been unconscious for some twenty-six hours, being fed via intravenous fluids overnight. Medical staff taking care of Ms. Selene expect a full recovery soon and her condition is stable."

I was fascinated. All this attention and newspeak was about me. For once, instead of reporting the news I was the news!

"Gerald, is there any word on what may have caused the dizzy spell for Ms. Selene?" Polly asked professionally. I didn't like that she was getting so good at this.

"Nothing definitive, Polly. As far as fainting goes, it could be a myriad of causes. The doctors' best guess is that the faint could have been caused by either dehydration, stress, or low blood sugar."

"Great. Now they've got me as a stressed out bulimic with diabetes," I remarked dryly.

"Another cause that the doctors are considering is exhaustion," supplied Gerald. "After speaking to the producer of the morning show, Nadine Montgomery, we did find out that Ms. Selene had made several trips to the West Coast recently, including one for the Emmy Awards special we aired just two weeks ago. Jet lag could have been a contributing factor to her fainting."

I sucked my teeth. "That's not sexy at all. I got my ass kicked by Jet Lag? That's weak."

"Okay, ma?" agreed Char disapprovingly.

"Very interesting," said Polly, feigning interest. I knew she was faking it because I said the very same thing when I was faking interest in something. Woman probably wanted me laid up as long as possible so she could continue to creep on my job. "Do the doctors have any idea when she may make a complete recovery?"

"They say it could be as early as today to as long as two days from now. It all depends on her," informed Gerald.

"It all depends on her," Polly echoed, ready to shift gears. "Okay, thank you very much, Gerald."

"You're welcome, Polly. This is Gerald Hampton, reporting live from Georgia Baptist Hospital in Midtown Atlanta," he wrapped up.

"Eh, ma, tell me somethin'. Why is it you guys are always thankin' each other on air for just doing your job?" Charlotte asked of me. "I mean my boss don't thank me for filling the printer with paper, 'na mean? I always thought that was a little odd."

"That's a good question. I don't know. It's just something we always do. You got me on that one."

From the TV in studio, Polly said, "For those of you who haven't seen it, we will play for you the exclusive WAGA-TV footage of the fainting spell of Jasmine Selene yesterday morning." In a darker tone, Polly enticed with, "This footage is of a slightly graphic nature and may not be suitable for younger viewers."

I stole a glance at Charlotte. She was oblivious to me, chin in her palm, leaned forward, ready to enjoy her umpteenth viewing of this "graphic" footage.

It started off innocently enough. There I was, looking fabulous in my gray suit jacket, talking about the Church's Chicken Momma when my speech began to slow and become forced. My words came out like a 33 on a 45 RPM record player, like a distorted eight track. Then my head made a slight wobble, my eyes rolled heavenward, and my face hit the desk. Well, ricocheted was more like it, as my face bounced off the desk like a Serena Williams serve, nicking its sharp edge, and collapsing my body to the carpeted floor by the side of the anchor desk.

I had to give it up to Cameraman Steve. As surprising as my face plant was, he always kept me in frame. What a pro!

Cameraman Steve had even zoomed in to my limp form on the carpet, bleeding a small lake from the left side of my dome. Richard rushed in and cradled my head. The set medic flew in from nowhere. Nadine was half a step behind him. An excited, somewhat panicky murmur muffled the audio on the broadcast. Then the footage ended abruptly as a group of people huddled around my unconscious form, with a cut to the multicolored test pattern TV stations put up when they were caught with their pants down.

Polly gave a curt shake of her head. "Chilling image." Then, as if someone had turned the sympathy switch off, she bounced back with, "In other news, the President's newest tax cut was passed by Congress today…"

Charlotte shut it off. "Happy?"

"I had no idea the human head could bounce like that."

"It can't. Yours can," Char kidded.

"Very funny. So why're you up here? Don't you have a new victim or something?"

"Actually, I do have another date with Not-Nick Rick at one. I just thought I'd check in on your dizzy ass first," Char funned.

"Go handle your business," I approved, taking a playful swipe at her arm. "What time's the rehearsal tonight?"

"So you'll be able to make it, Ms. O'Hara?"

"'Frankly, my dear, I don't give a damn,'" I said in my best Rhett Butler voice. "But I'll be there."

"Eight o'clock. And I got your dress for you yesterday. I put it in your bedroom for you."

"Thanks, Char." I grabbed her hand as she stood to go. "You're a great friend."

Charlotte smiled. "You set a great example."

*

194

Four more hours of dozing off, sandwiched around an hour of TV and hospital food, and I was ready to dip. The nursing staff and a very concerned doctor came in a couple of times to check on me. After examining the stitches, removing the IV from my arm, and having me sign an autograph for him, I was good to go. They all departed quickly, leaving me to change out of my hospital gown into my clothes where my butt wasn't exposed to the world.

As I wriggled into my jeans, I took inventory of some of the various bouquets adorning the room. Surprisingly, there was a bouquet from Mia. Not Mal and Mia, but just Mia. For someone I hadn't spoken to in at least a couple of years, I thought that was sweet of her. In my mad dash to the altar in San Diego, it never occurred to me until now that Mia had been in the audience. Yet she had, wisely, avoided speaking to me at my time of most utter desperation. The biggest bouquet was from, of course, Jacque. He loved me, missed me, and hoped I felt better soon, read the card.

For a change, I wasn't disdainful when I read that. Actually, it brought a tender smile to my face. All past history aside, Jacque really did care about me. Maybe Nadine had been right. Maybe my heart needed to thaw out a little and let those who were trying to court me to actually court me. Rodney was a great guy. So was Nick. Jacque, if we overlooked his fidelity problems, was one, too. I had cast aside some great men. Maybe it was time to give one a second chance.

Just after I had put my bra back on, there was a timid knock at the door. Before I could call them in, the door swung open slowly.

Mom.

Nick's mother entered the room slowly, carefully shutting the door. I was absolutely floored. Mom? Here? To see me?

"Mom! What are you doing here?" I asked. Yes, I called her "Mom," just as her son did. She had always treated me as a daughter, so the least I could do was return the favor.

"To see you, dear." Mom looked drastically different from a month ago when I had crashed her son's wedding. Her hair was graying and thinning out. She had lost some twenty pounds. She did not look like her healthy, robust self, or like a woman who should have traveled some three thousand miles via airplane.

Immediately, I ushered Mom over to a seat. I made sure she was comfortable.

"It's okay, Jasmine. No need to fuss over me," she dismissed. "Besides, I came here to talk about you."

I pulled up a chair across from her. "I guess you heard about the fainting, huh?"

"Yes I did. In fact, that is why I am out here."

"What?"

"I took a call from Nick two nights ago. My son sounded very troubled. He said that you have been very aggressively pursuing him."

"I have expressed my feelings clearly to him," I spinned.

"Breaking up his wedding on his wedding day was a pretty clear indicator, don't you think?"

"It doesn't matter what I think anymore," I sighed. "Nick's a grown man and he's going to make grown man decisions. But I think he's marrying the wrong woman."

"And you are the right one? You show him you are the right one by following him to his job, popping up unannounced at his home, and by injecting his father into this?" The entire time Mom interrogated me, her voice was as level as a protractor.

"Whether I'm the right one or not really doesn't matter anymore, right? She won, I lost, it's over."

"It's not about winning or losing, Jasmine. It's about my son doing what's best for my son. It's about who makes him happy."

"That's all I want, Mom. I want Nick to be happy. I want to be the one who makes him happy. I truly believe his happiness would be best served with me. I believe Nick is my soulmate." And there ain't a damn thing you could say to tell me different. "But enough about that. You were telling me why you came?"

"Well, after Nick told me about your latest two trips out to California, how shaken he had sounded, and then I saw your fainting on the air…I just figured it was time for some motherly advice."

I smiled sweetly. What a beautiful woman, what a wonderful mother. I sincerely hoped Nick did not lose her to the cancer. "You could have just called."

Mom adjusted her head, like a peacock pruning its feathers.

"I needed to stretch my legs," she justified. "I get so tired of sitting around the house being sick all the time. I needed a little…adventure in my life." A giggle. "So here I am."

I turned an askance eye to the sixty year old breast cancer patient. "Does Harrison know you're here?"

"Harrison," she said of her second husband with a smile, "is at work. I'm old enough not to ask for a hall pass, don't you think?"

I nodded bemusedly at Nick's heart and soul. I remember when I had first met her, watching the dynamic between the mother and son. He loved his mother more than any woman in the world. Nick didn't need me, didn't need Tabitha—

he needed Mom. And now that he had the money to pay for her experimental cancer treatment Pilotaxln, hopefully he never had to lose her. As long as Nick had Mom, he had all the women he needed in his life. I began to feel a little better.

"Jasmine," Mom addressed me, "I want you to think about something. I am not the wisest person in this world, but perhaps you could benefit from the experience of my years."

I scooted closer. "School me, Mom."

Mom cleared her throat, summoning up her energy. "I know that my son loved you, may always love you in some way, but he's moved on now. It would be in your best interest if you did so yourself."

"Mom, don't worry about me. I'm already knowing," I cut her off. "My mom gave me the same speech before I came back from LA the other day. I'm moving on and I'll be fine."

"Then why are we here? Specifically, why are you in here?" Mom questioned. "I know exactly why you fainted on the air, and it has nothing to do with dehydration or exhaustion or any of that nonsense. It's because your heart is hurting. Your heart is stressed out.

"Jasmine, ever since I've met you many moons ago, when Nick first brought you home for Thanksgiving, I have treated you like a daughter. I could see how much Nick loved you and wanted to spend the rest of his life with you. So it was easy to fashion my mind around you being part of the family. But if my son, who has a heart that would love the world if the world let him, could get over you and find love anew in someone else, then I think you should follow his example and let it go. Live not for the past, but live for the future, Jasmine."

I nodded very respectfully, biting my tongue, as I could see she wanted to go on.

"The amazing thing about life, Jasmine, is its endless possibilities. While Nick did love you at one time, he has moved on. I am very proud of the fact my son was able to absorb the heartbreak of his life to find someone he felt just as passionately about, to the point where he is ready to commit the rest of his life to her. The miracle of any two people getting married is that they feel the same exact way about each other at the same exact time. While he may always love you in some respect, and you him, the timing isn't right. That could be the whole sad truth of it, Jasmine. Chalk it all up to bad timing."

Mom was very persuasive. Maybe she had been a lawyer in a previous life. As humbly and simply as I could, I dispensed some homespun wisdom of my own. "I hear and understand everything that you said, Mom, I do. While 'bad timing' could certainly be the reason, I think that is an excuse. When two people love each other enough, somehow they make things work. Period. The past defines us and the future is not certain. My love for Nick is now and everlasting, whether he wants it or not. I am not going to fight it; I am just going to let it be and live my life. My love is real and unconditional."

That blew Mom back, literally. She fell back in her chair in utter wonder. I think she was dumbfounded that she had actually found a woman who loved her son as selflessly as she did. I was sure Nick had told her the ways and how many times he had rejected me since the wedding, and I didn't care. For me to still have the brave, mature, realistic take on my feelings for her son and how I dealt with them, must have impressed her. I know they did because this was what she said next:

"Either way, Jasmine, I am staying out of my son's love life. I always have," she said pointedly, knowingly taking a jab at Winnie. "I have always thought of you like a daughter. If you want to be my daughter, it's not going to be easy. You're going to have to earn it, and not with me."

To fight my eyes welling up, I gave Nick's mother a hug. I hugged her like it was the last time I would see her, because it was. Nick was getting married a week from today and there was nothing I could do, or would do, to stop it. I loved this woman and would sincerely miss her. "Thank you, Mom. Thank you for being a mom to us all."

Perfection

This was my last night in the Emerald City. Nick decided to wine and dine me at a classy, expensive restaurant that hung out on the edge of Elliott Bay. Ours was a window seat, with a 180 degree view of the Puget Sound, Olympic Mountains, and Downtown Seattle sparkling in the twilight. He encouraged me to order whatever I wanted so I went big. When the waiter arrived with a sizzling, crackling steak, steaming the aroma of cooked meat and butter, I could have filled myself up on the scent alone. Eating it was downright orgasmic.

After the restaurant, Nick drove us over to the ferry. We boarded for a trip to some place called Bremerton. It would be two hours round trip, but I got a chance to see Seattle at night from the water. On the deck of the ferry Nick wrapped his arms around me, shielding me from the wind chill slapping the boat. Set against the backdrop of city lights fading into view, just the two of us, we were love. To paraphrase Wesley Snipes in Mo' Better Blues, "Black people in love; what a beautiful thing."

"Nick."

"Yes, Baby J."

"Thank you for everything. I have had the most wonderful trip."

"Mom says you can come back whenever you like."

That made me smile. "I like her. Tell her I said thank you."

"She likes you, too."

Changing the subject carefully, tactfully, I asked, "Why weren't there any pictures of your father?"

I could feel his body tense up at the question. "I don't know my father."

"You've never seen him?"

Nick held fast. "I don't know my father."

"Oh." I suddenly felt stupid, and quickly orchestrated a subject change. "Seattle is a beautiful city."

"It is, isn't it. I'd like to settle down here, someday."

I didn't want to ruin the moment, so I just let the statement ride. But, somewhere inside of me, I began the process of evaluating the notion. I didn't know if I wanted to settle down here, but some part of me could see myself settling down with him.

When the beautiful ride was over, Nick drove us back to his house. The house was empty. Mom was conveniently spending the night over at Harrison's. A fire was already going in the fireplace while a dozen tiny candles, strategically placed, lighted the living room. A dozen red roses garnished with baby's breath sat upright against the couch, with my name on the adorning card. Some mellow Stanley Clarke instrumental played lightly in the background. I was overwhelmed, completely and thoroughly outdone.

"How did you—" I stopped herself. "Why did you—" I couldn't even speak for the bubble of happiness in my heart and voice. I was reduced to a series of loving sighs for words. "Baby...thank you."

"Come over here, Fineness," Nick invited, easing me over to the carpeted area by the fireplace. "Sit. I'll be right back."

I could hardly wait. Curling my body beside the crackling fire, I took a second look around. Damn. My man had planned all of this for me? When he returned with the two plates of cheesecake, my jaw dropped. Mom had left in the fridge two plates of her infamously delicious homemade cheesecake, topped with an artistic trail of chocolate syrup and a puff of whipped cream. She was as much a culprit in this wonderful evening as her son. Now that was love.

"Eat up, Baby J," he encouraged, still shuttling about like a manservant.

"Aren't you going to join me?" I requested, hesitant to dig in without my lover.

"Yes," he said, settling down across from me, placing a wooden chess set between us. "Do you play chess?"

"A little." I smiled, still immersed in the immense pleasure of the evening. "It's not like I played for the team or anything in high school."

Nick laughed, obviously trying out the image in his

head of me running a chess club. "Let's play, mami."

"Set it up, Babyluv," I approved, mouth full of dessert. "Damn, baby. Did your mom make this?"

"As sure as I made that chess set."

My eyes glowed upon seeing all the individual, uniquely hand-crafted wooden chess pieces assembled on the wooden board. It was all sinking into me, like a golden sunset on a distant horizon. I had fallen so far in love, I could not get up. I didn't want to get up. Nothing Jacque had ever done for me could even come close. Nothing. This was the best night of my life.

As far as the chess goes…well, my baby's not perfect. I creamed him in less then twenty moves, in back-to-back games. His manhood took it well as he put away the chess set and cleared the room, prepping us for the next event.

Patiently, lovingly, adoringly, I quietly observed my man in action. Recording the details to memory, I wanted to make sure that Mia would get a full account of this whole evening.

When Nick was finished cleaning, he guided me to the bathroom. The water was already running with a bubble bath foamed up. I grinned wickedly. Kissing me lightly, Nick slowly, seductively, undressed me as the bathtub filled. Completely naked, I returned the favor, enjoying every touch, every caress my hand could afford. Together, we entered the tub, as I coiled up against Nick's torso. Using a soapy sponge, Nick wiped me up and down with light, caressing, broad strokes, cleaning some of his favorite regions again and again. Mmm…and I let him, too. Teeth clamped to my bottom lip girlishly, I gently returned the favor, delighting at the reactions my touch brought his body. Physically, both of our bodies were aroused, but neither one of us dared to disrupt the intimacy of the moment.

Directly after bathtime was rubtime. Following an extensive mutual drying off period, Nick ushered me back to my guest room. He laid me down on my stomach and removed my towel. I reveled in being naked before my man, how my body must have been calling him. Straddling my back, Nick treated me to a full body massage with my favorite scented massage oil, Plumeria from Bath and Body Works.

I swear this had to be a waking dream. I kept my eyes tightly shut to savor the moment, hoping not ever to wake up. Once Nick finished, I wanted to treat him to a backrub. This was an equal partnership, our relationship. Nick would not hear of it. He instructed me to put on my PJs and meet him downstairs.

Meeting him in the living room, I allowed myself to be led to his bedroom for the final surprise of the evening. Upon entering Nick's room, I gasped. My heart just did a double take. A tear sprang to my eye. Underneath a layer of rose petals laid Nick's bed.

"Lay down," he whispered into my ear.

Biting my lip to ward off the tears of joy, I removed my slippers. As I stretched out along the twin size bed I had now grown accustomed to during Mom's absences, Nick slipped a tape into the VCR. Boomerang! My smile was infinite. The two of us laughed all over each other to Eddie Murphy's exploits until we fell asleep, holding each other.

I woke up four hours later, with Nick still asleep, holding me in his arms. The sound of a door shutting had awakened me. My man, well, he could sleep through a train wreck with him in it. I didn't dare move because I was far too comfortable, and I didn't want to wake him. I began to close my eyelids and go back to sleep.

Quietly and gently, the door to the room opened. Through half-open eyes, I saw Mom peek in curiously, only to smile at our romantic arrangement.

She saw I was barely awake.

She smiled. I smiled.

Mom winked at me and closed the door.

A woman like that did not "wink" at people. She was proud, she was happy. She was Mom, passing the torch of the loving care of her baby from one woman to another. Tonight could not have been any better for me.

Perfection. By Nick and Jasmine.

12

"DON'T STOP, DOO-DOO BROWN! Don't stop, doo-doo brown!"

The nonstop booty bass beat poured through the speakers, rattling our chairs, the floor, and our souls. Near naked men of all nationalities gyrated away to the frenetic Florida booty shake beat. Money was passed like a church collection plate, alcohol flowed like rivers, and lean brown flesh strutted around confidently like roosters in a henhouse. That's right—we were back at the Coronet Club, site of Nadine's bachelorette party.

Nadine couldn't have been more embarrassed as we removed the blindfold off her inside the co-ed strip club. I thought she'd turn into a pillar of salt when she gawked at a brotha stripper who walked by with his penis hanging out. I gave Char a mental high-five for pulling this off. I could be entertained for free just watching Nadine's expressions all night long.

Seeing how I had spent most of the past few weeks in and out of town, the details of the bachelorette party had largely been left up to Charlotte. She did not disappoint. We had exclusive use of the VIP room where only the finest brothas in the club came over to service our every need. Waitresses kept the drinks flowing, evidently running up a tab that Charlotte and I (okay, most I) would have to pay for at the end of the evening. What the hell. I mean, if you're Nadine, you only get married once, right? As far as our crew went, there were about ten of us ladies, a diverse mix of women from work (Angie and me), Nadine's homegirls from Albany (Shereeta and Makeeta), and, shockingly, a few women from church.

"Ladies," Charlotte announced, standing on top of a couch in the plush VIP room, champagne glass in hand. "Tomorrow, we lose one of our own. We lose our sister, the ever-so virtuous

Nadine Montgomery. Tomorrow night, Mrs. Nadine Palmer will be inducted into the annals of womanhood. Tonight, your last night as a single woman, us single ladies all have only one thing to say about your pending nuptials tomorrow afternoon..."

"HELL NO, WE WON'T GO!" we all screamed.

We burst into laughter, slapping five and snapping our fingers, sistagurl-like. Charlotte hugged the bride-to-be, who blushed a new shade of purple that M.A.C. would probably name "Blushing Black Bride."

Charlotte's pronouncement had officially kicked off this party. The ladies cut loose. We were ambushed by sexy men. Lapdances sprung up everywhere like brushfire. The music in the club got even raunchier (if that were possible). The single women drank like there was no wedding tomorrow. Nadine edgily downed two glasses of champagne.

In no time, Charlotte made new friends. One lightskin Adonis named, well, I think his name was Adonis, came back for seconds from Charlotte. After getting propositioned for a dance every five minutes for an hour, I finally wore down and subjected myself to one. The two Amarettos plus two Midori Sours didn't influence my decision at all.

A lapdance is a curious thing for a self-aware, mentally and emotionally empowered woman. Here we had a reverse world where all women held the power. These half-naked boy toys depended upon us for their livelihood and survival. If I asked this gyrating mass of manhood in front of me (named Tricks, no less) to jump on one leg, hold his nose, and lick my navel, he would do it, probably with a smile on his face. Not only that, but as a woman who had been sexually objectified since the age of eleven, I found it a little disconcerting to be doing the objectifying.

But these concerns melted away as Tricks ground his granite hard babymaker against my crotch. By the time the song and Tricks had finished, so was I. I was as moist as a pound cake. I gave him twenty dollars and sent him along his way.

I dabbed at my chest with a napkin. That boy made a sista hot under the collar, lemme tell ya!

"You ready for that raincheck, Fineness?"

I swiveled my head to see stripper extraordinaire Baby Boy!

204

He was still as cut and thick as ever, looking like an Alayé calendar model in the flesh. I smiled weakly, for I truly felt weak. "You remember me?"

"You better believe it. You the only woman who's turned me down that I would dance for for free," he purred.

Jesus! I averted my gaze. I could swear that his penis pouch was twice the size than last time!

"Just work it work it! Just work it now!" hollered one of the "eeta" twins from Albany, enjoying a winding, grinding Tricks. Nadine sat next to them, terrified but amused.

An impish grin took hold of me. "You see that woman sitting over there, drooling at your boy Tricks?"

"Aw, please. Tricks is for kids," Baby Boy scoffed, missing the irony.

I didn't—and laughed. "Yeah, whatever man. That lady right there is getting married tomorrow. I got fifty dollars here if you go over and give her the lapdance of her life. I got a hundred more if you make sure she don't jump that broom tomorrow."

Baby Boy snapped up the Grant I held out in my hand. "I'll be damned if she gets married after having Baby Boy!"

I smirked uncontrollably as I watched Baby Boy roll over to Nadine and start to freak her down. I knew Nadine would get married tomorrow, no question. I just wanted to make sure she had the best time before she did it.

Charlotte, as could be expected, was drunk and out of control. I watched her grinding up on a guy she had paid to grind up on her. As my ex-stripper girlfriend started to strip down to her bra in perfect time to the beat, I was beginning to wonder just who the hell was getting the dance, Charlotte or the stripper.

Half an hour later, Nadine, flush from having Baby Boy suck a new hole into her navel, recited the words to a popular Luke song, Miami ass master supreme. In fact, she led the charge, screaming the lyrics in unison with the "eeta" twins. Something about them calling him "Captain D."

I found Charlotte sitting next to me, stuffing her breasts back into her bra. She was drunk and tired from all that dancing. It was nights like these when I wondered what kind of mother Charlotte was. I wondered what four year old Janaya thought when she saw her mother stumble into the house in this kind of condition, as Charlotte habitually would from the club on weekends. When Char went out to party, the girl partied.

Out of breath, she affected a goofy smile. "What it is, ma? Look atcha girl. She havin' the time of her life. I bet she ain't never had this much fun before!"

I gave Charlotte a gentle hug. "Good call, Charlotte. What can I say? Strippers throw the best bachelorette parties."

"Ex-strippers," she slurred. "Whew! I'm tired."

With that said, Charlotte threw her head back and passed out in the seat next to me. I shook my head once. Amazing.

Nadine wandered over as soon as the song, and her open club karaoke rendition of it, was done. She plopped down in the seat next to me, her face alive and bubbly. "Oh my goodness, if Rodney saw me now, I don't think he'd marry me!"

"Trust me, Nadine, what he's going through right now for his bachelor party is probably ten times worse," I assured her.

Nadine frowned. She didn't like the sound of that. Momentarily, the same bubbly goodness affecting her general mood washed over her. She shrugged indifferently. "Well, ye without sin may cast the first stone!"

Nadine hopped up to her feet. She sang out in full Georgian drawl, "And they some sinners in this house! If you see them point 'em out!"

My head was in my hands, I was so amused. When I stopped crying from laughter, I turned to Nadine to say what had to be said. "Nadine, I'm sorry."

Nadine stopped bouncing her head to the bass booty beat. "I'm sorry, too, honey."

I didn't want to recap what had happened in the slightest. I put DFP on the bac kburner and closed it all out with, "Friends?"

"Sistas. For life."

*

There was nothing like a good old fashioned Southern wedding to make you reflect on how lonely and jacked up your love life was. These and other random thoughts floated in and out of my consciousness as I played co-maid of honor at Nadine's wedding the following afternoon. The ceremony took place in a medium sized church in Decatur, filled to the rafters with people. The decorations of the whole event were off the chain, considering Nadine had hired celebrity wedding specialist Dez Tucker to lay it down.

Privately, I thought it comical how Charlotte struggled to stay upright and presentable throughout the ceremony. The length of the proceedings didn't help either. She should've thought about that before downing that sixth Jack and Coke last night.

We were visions in our lavender purple ankle length bridesmaid dresses, garnished with white gardenias in our hair and on the bosom. My curly hair was pulled back, with a few sensuous curls dangling from the back of my head. Using minimal makeup, as not to overshadow the bride, I was presentable enough to see my girl jump that broom, now that the stitches were out. Charlotte, too, despite her slight, curious, hangover sway, at least looked the part of the maid of honor.

When it comes to weddings, I like to just gloss over the highlights. Lingering on the details only depressed me, reminding me that I'm thirty years old and without a boyfriend. Nadine looked beautiful, positively radiant, in her deservedly white dress and veil. Rodney had never looked better, outfitted in a gray tuxedo with tails, matching that of his groomsmen. It warmed my heart to see his brother, newly out of jail, as one of Rodney's groomsmen. The exchanging of the vows was fairly standard except the bride and groom had small addendums to read. When Rodney said to Nadine, "I will dedicate every single day for the rest of your life to making myself the best husband to you I can be," I truly believed him and wished them well. Bon voyage, Rodney.

After they had said the "I Do's," kissed, and literally jumped over a broom, they walked out under a hail of applause and camera lights. As everyone mobilized to head off to the reception at the Downtown Atlanta Hilton, the bridesmaids and groomsmen stayed behind with the bride and bridegroom to take official wedding pictures with the official wedding photographer. Nadine smiled like the happiest woman in the world, which she was. Today was her day, her world; we were all just paying rent.

At the reception, I did my best to stay close to my girl, Charlotte. I wasn't exactly in a mingling type of mood. Brothas treated weddings like the meat markets they were, hoping to parlay the air of aging desperation from women like myself into a hookup or a night of emotional, wedding day blues-induced sex. As I avoided the gaze of yet another hopeful male wedding guest, I, somehow, lost Charlotte. Okay, I knew how. Charlotte was just being Charlotte, flirting with the free, testosterone-producing world. I was on my own.

No sooner was I on my own than did I run into Brian Richardson. Either he had some nerve or Nadine truly was a saved Christian woman. Brian looked nice, as usual, so I wasn't all that impressed. The man made enough money to keep himself up, that was for sure. We shared the same dentist and dermatologist to the stars, so I knew if he could afford them, he could afford to stay sharp. We chit-chatted about nothing before I took the first available pause to formulate an excuse and slip away.

Unfortunately, with Charlotte still engaged in macking down every man in sight, her leftovers came my way. After having met four of Charlotte's "Eleven Types of Men" at the club in LA, I must have met the other seven in the space of an hour here at the reception. I dismissed Mr. Thug Life and Mr. Ghetto for obvious reasons. I had evolved past that stage of my life when I became an adult. Mr. Intellectual seemed to have it going on: book smart, had a very good job, and I could tell he would care about how I felt and would always return calls and pages. But I could also tell he wasn't very street smart, would be boring as hell, and probably couldn't make love worth a damn. Mr. I Have a Job got played to the left for the simple reason he thought he was all that just for having a freakin' job. Hello, this is Atlanta, people! All good black men down here have jobs. Even the not so good ones, I thought, thinking briefly about triflin'-ass Jerome. I also dispatched Mr. Nice Guy and Mr. Best Friend, respectively because I could tell Mr. Nice Guy secretly wanted to be Mr. Thug Life while Mr. Best Friend, although the ultimate gentleman, would turn out not to be about crap neither. And if either of those bastards cheated on me, I'd have to put their balls in a blender.

Mr. I Don't Have a Girlfriend had an interesting take on his game. He was very complimentary, and I could tell he would be the type who would take me out all the time and show me off to all his friends. I liked that because I could arm charm my man with the best of them, too. But if he was too quick to proclaim he didn't have a girlfriend, as this man was, I could tell that he probably did have a girlfriend whom he's been with since the second grade. Not only did he have Ole Girl, but he probably wouldn't get rid of her or even tell me about her until I had fallen in love with his triflin' tail. I politely took his business card and drifted away, discreetly dropping it in the trash once out of eye's view.

The amount and quality of candidates made me feel as lonely as could be in the crowded Hilton ballroom reception area. Half of young, attractive black Atlanta was here, and I didn't feel like I connected with any of them. Back in high school, I had predicted I would've been married by twenty-five, twenty-six tops. Here I was at thirty, thirty for crying out loud, without so much as a boyfriend, being the maid of honor (an oxymoron if you ask me—ain't no honor in being single and alone) at someone else's wedding.

I let that thought sink like the heavy stone it was. It wasn't as if I hadn't had opportunity to get married. Nick had asked me and I had said no because of Jacque. Rodney had asked and I said no because of Nick. Jacque was giving out rings like toaster ovens at a white sale, and I said no because of Nick.

Or did I? What the hell was it that had happened between Jacque and I a week ago? Why did I sleep with him, after all this time apart? Did I still, somewhere subconsciously, still love that cheatin'-ass Negro? Was Jacque truly reformed? Could I ever trust him again? Could I ever trust him with just a simple second chance? Should there be a statute of limitations on carrying a grudge?

Whatever it was, I knew one thing: I did not want to die alone. Before I died, I wanted to experience the joy and consistency of a long term, lifelong, monogamous relationship. Even despite my romantic miscues in these past thirty years of my life—hopefully the first third of my life—even I deserved at least that much for the last two-thirds.

Right then and there, I made a vow to myself. The next time love was staring me in the face, the next time someone truly claimed to love me, I would at least give them a chance, to give the love a chance. And wherever it might take me, the relationship, and its feelings behind it, I would be brave, open-minded, and honest with my feelings. Nadine was right. It was time to stop being an emotional coward.

"Hey, Pretty."

Shit! I had no idea it would start so soon!

"Jacque?" I turned to face Jacque, nattily attired and, evidently, crashing Nadine's party. "What're you doing here?"

"The same thing you are. I'm celebrating the union of two souls in holy matrimony," he answered smoothly.

"Funny, I didn't see your name on the list," I remarked coolly.

"Fine, Pretty. Go ahead and bust my balls. But I really came to see you."

"Shocking," I said as dry as the martini in his hand. "What do you want, Jacque?"

My attitude confused him. He didn't know what to make of a woman to whom he had proposed and slept with who still kept him at arm's length. "Is everything okay, Pretty?"

"Everything's fine, Jacque," I lied tiredly. "What do you want?"

Jacque rested his martini glass on the nearest table. "Well, Jasmine, it's been three weeks, hasn't it?"

"Yes."

"Over three weeks, actually. Do you remember what I had asked you?"

"Yes."

"And have you given my proposal some thought?"

"Yes, but I—"

"Don't say another word. Hold on," Jacque negotiated.

I was a bit frustrated. I knew what he was doing, asking me a series of "yes" questions so I wouldn't say no to the big question. Don't think I haven't used the tactic before on men myself. But still, it wouldn't work. It shouldn't work. I knew I was vulnerable and I didn't want to have to deal with this right now. In the quietly emotional state that weddings always put me in, I could say yes to skydiving without a parachute if he asked sweetly enough.

What happened next felt like it happened in slow motion, I swear. Jacque reached into his pocket and pulled out a black, felt covered box. A ring box. He dramatically opened the box up to reveal drama of its own. It was a ring, a big ring—no a huge ring. I was no amateur gemologist like Charlotte was, but it had to have been at least six carats! My ring finger buckled under the weight of it as Jacque slid the ring onto my left hand. Almost on cue, as if someone had tripped her precious stones alarm, Charlotte whipped her head around from several feet away to see the rock on my hand that shone like an indoor sun.

Gallantly, Jacque dipped to one knee, my left hand turned insurance risk in his hand. "Jasmine Selene…Will you marry me?"

I trembled. I had no idea what to think, how to think. All I knew was that Jacque had not only proposed to me twice but also the ring had gotten bigger each time he did. If I held out a third time, he might just buy me controlling interest in DeBeers.

The whole room stopped. Nadine, who was over on the dance floor dancing with her new husband, even slowed her roll. All eyes in the room were upon us. I swear, this was like a scene straight out of that movie The Best Man. I was on the spot, in the spotlight—homecoming for a news anchor—yet I squirmed under its glare.

My hesitation did not deter the never-more-earnest-in-his-life Jacque. From his kneeling vantage point, Jacque added, "Please make me the happiest man in this universe and the next. Marry me, Jasmine."

My face was contorted with conflict. This kind of moment may never, ever again happen in my life. I had loved him once; I could love him again. Perhaps I had always, somehow, still loved him, which explained that night a week ago. Which explained why I had said no to Nick five plus years ago. But why the hell was I thinking so damn much? Just say yes, girl! Just. Say.

Yes.

I fixed my mouth to say the word "yes" when Jacque said one

last thing: "I was made to love you."

I dropped his hand. "What?"

I had to have heard him wrong.

With all the sincerity of a first-time politician on his nascent campaign trail, Jacque repeated himself. "Jasmine…I was made to love you."

No. No he wasn't. Jacque wasn't "made to love me," and I resented the implication. Actually, I hated the manipulation. He couldn't have come up with that on his own. He must have had help. I stole a quick glance in Nadine's direction to see Mrs. Palmer beaming her approval. Go on, she said with her eyes.

Then it all crystallized for me. "No, Jacque. I was made to love Nick."

I left him there, and the reception, on bended knee.

Charlotte quietly applauded to herself. Atta girl, she thought triumphantly, and in spite of herself. Damn, that ring was big!

She shook off the cobwebs of the moment as soon as she saw a humiliated Jacque get back to his feet, without the ring and the girl. Charlotte had overheard the proposal exchange. She made her way over to the dance floor with fire in her eyes. She had beef.

"Nadine. I'd like to speak with you for a moment," Charlotte announced, accosting the newlyweds on the dance floor.

"Can it wait, honey? I'm kinda dancing with my hus-band here." Nadine beamed at him, who beamed at her, and they instantly made enough artificial sun to power a space station.

"Naw, it can't wait. Honey," Charlotte tossed in, for good measure.

"I'll be right back, baby," Nadine cooed at her groom.

"I'll be right here, baby," Rodney cooed right back.

Charlotte snatched Nadine and steered her out into the hallway outside the reception room.

"Hey, hey, easy now. This is an Oscar de la Renta," said Nadine.

"Look, I don't care if it's a 'Guess Which Friend Fucked Ya,' what you did back there was not cool!"

Like anyone else, Nadine did not respond well to being cursed at. She matched Charlotte icy tone for icy tone. "What are you talking about, woman?"

"I'm talking about you having Jacque embarrass Jasmine in the middle of your wedding reception!"

"What? I did no such thing."

"You invited him. I know you did. If you say you didn't, I swear to God I will smack you silly," Charlotte threatened.

"So what—I invited him," Nadine allowed. "That doesn't mean I told him to propose to the girl here."

"But it's obvious you fed him lines. You told him what to say, Nadine!" Charlotte accused. "'I was made to love you?' Are you kidding me? Only Nick would ever say something like that to Jasmine and she knows it! What the hell were you thinking?"

Nadine decided to gain some ground on this conversation. As far as she was concerned, she hadn't done anything wrong. "I was trying to help my friend out. I know she still has feelings for Jacque; she has to. Otherwise, she never would've made such a big deal over his proposing to her in the first place."

"That still didn't give you the right to go and encourage him to propose to her! You can't even justify that!"

"Yes, I can!" Nadine, well, justified. "I want to see my friends, my gurls, happy. Jacque is a good brotha, a very good catch, and obviously loves her very, very much. What the heck is wrong with trying to get two people who care about each other together?"

"Because that is not your job!" Charlotte would have screamed that at her if she weren't so tired from last night. "As a friend, your job is to advise and offer support, not to go out and meddle in other people's lives!"

"I wasn't meddling. I just wanted to see Jasmine happy," Nadine pouted.

"Maybe she is happy!" Charlotte stopped, took a breath, and composed herself.

"I just wanted her to have what I have, that's all."

Charlotte could have been mean and said, "She's already had what you have now," but she didn't. Nadine's intentions were good, just wildly, wildly askew from Jasmine's reality. So Charlotte took it upon herself to school her.

"Look, Nadine, I understand now that you were trying to do a good thing, I do. A lot of women are haters, who will sabotage relationships with men just so they won't lose a friend. Jasmine is not like that. I'm not like that, and you are not like that. I also understand that you have always been a Jacque champion, and, in doing so, you have completely ignored the first rule of friendship: Always take care of your friends first. Havin' your little powwow, prep session, or sit down with Jacque, only to embarrass our girl and humiliate the man is not takin' care of your friend first. When it comes to love, you can't just try to mix and match people like Uno cards. You've got to let love seek its own course. If there is love for some people to be found, even for my jaded little self, then we will find it, experiencing it on our own terms. And no degree of manipulation, meddling, or help will make this happen. Do you understand?"

Nadine nodded numbly. "I didn't mean to be a bad friend."

Charlotte sighed, finally embracing Nadine. "You're not. Don't worry about it. You would have been a bad friend only if she had said yes."

13

GOIN' BACK TO CALI? I don't think so.

So went the LL Cool J song and myself, as I found myself on a plane heading out to California for the fourth time in five weeks. I had enough frequent flyer miles that the next time I came out here (hopefully for that Fox Nightly News job) would be for free. That is provided the network didn't fly me out first class, of course.

This time, however, the trip had absolutely nothing to do with me. Charlotte had requested my presence and I was riding along for moral support. It was the least I could do considering she had been down for me the first time I came out to LA.

This time, there would be no brooding, moaning, or pining. No chasing, lying or stalking. This trip I would be entirely at Charlotte's beck and call, to make sure she had everything she needed for her audition. And after the audition, well, we would see what LA really was about. I gave myself a mental note to call Mark after the audition was over. And my trip was totally authorized by WAGA this time, as I used some vacation days that management had been "insisting" I take. With Nadine off on her honeymoon to Aruba and my fainting spell national news, I was given a wide berth around the station's management. WAGA didn't want to be known as the place where anchors went to work themselves to death, on air.

We had left Tuesday night, touching down about one o'clock Wednesday morning, Pacific. Once again, the Westin would be our headquarters as I listened to Charlotte recite her monologues one more time. Both contemporary pieces from movies that came out last year, Charlotte had more than mastered them. She would be fine.

After her final run through at two in the morning, we

stretched out in our double beds with the lights off. Char couldn't sleep because she was just too nervous. I couldn't sleep because I just couldn't.

"Calm down, Char. You'll do fine," I assured her.

"Get outta my head, ma." I could feel her smile even if I couldn't see it. "I'm not exactly nervous. I'm just ready to start this new chapter of my life, that's all. I'm anxious."

"You'll be fine."

There was a brief silence as Charlotte calculated her next thought. "Why did you keep the ring?"

I grinned sheepishly. "I forgot. I left in the heat of the moment."

"Yeah you did, J!" Char laughed. "I still can't believe you left that poor boy on his knee like that! You a trip, girl!"

"It's not something I'm proud of, turning down three proposals in my lifetime. A girl should be so lucky even to get one."

"True that," Charlotte agreed. "But what you did took courage."

"What?" Now I was truly confused. I thought by turning Jacque down I lacked it.

"What you did was courageous. I don't know too many thirty-year-old women secure enough in themselves to turn down a proposal from anyone, especially from ballers like Jacque. It takes courage to stand for what you believe in, to never settle, and to accept love only on your terms. As my ma would say, you an 'odd bird,' Jasmine," said Charlotte. "See, what I hate about life, what I hate about most people in life, is that they settle. They settle on some bullshit. And then five, ten, twenty years later, when that shit blows up in their face and they have to take a do-over on their lives, they look back at the point where they settled and wish they hadn't. As long as you have peace in your heart and you know what you did was right, then you gon' be alright."

"Well looky here," I teased. "Words of romantic wisdom from Flatbush's favorite female mack."

"Why do you think I've been a 'female mack' for so long?" Charlotte sniffed. "That's because I refuse to settle."

"Really? Well what are you looking for in a guy?"

I could hear her shift around in the bed, getting comfortable. "I don't know, really. But when I find it, I'll know."

I sucked my teeth. "Don't be one of those females who complains about the lack of good men when you don't know what it is you want in a man."

"Please, ma. Have you ever heard me complain about a lack of men?" Charlotte responded. "Besides, I'm gonna make acting my man. I'mma do me. I'm gonna go into this audition tomorrow, knock it out the box, and live my dream. Watch me."

I smiled. "I will."

*

And you know what? That's exactly what she did. From all reports, Charlotte went in there, owned the room, and had the agents fighting amongst themselves over who was going to represent her for what. To see Charlotte's squealing, excited face as she emerged from that building on Wilshire Avenue ninety minutes later, I could feel nothing but joy for her.

This much I was able to decipher between excited breaths: The agency loved her, they had signed her, and she got the commercial job. It was a recurring role in a national spot for L'Oreal, one that was sure to pay her hundreds of thousands of dollars next year alone. Charlotte had walked into Ben's agency unrepresented and had walked out just ninety minutes later with a film/TV agent, a theater agent, a commercial print agent, and a TV commercial agent. They wanted her to move immediately to LA, to which she was more than happy to do.

Talk about living your dream. She did her.

To celebrate, I let Diva Fashionista take over. We hit the world famous Rodeo Drive under overcast skies, and bought expensive things on credit that we could only wear out at night. We plotted angles on Charlotte's move and immediately collected many of the various apartment magazines for her move.

I was proud of her. I was so, so proud of her.

All my energy was concentrated on keeping the Diva Fashionista shopping and happy when I brushed by a man in the Beverly Center mall.

"Sorry," I said, without bothering to look.

"Pardon me," he said at the same time.

My neck whipped around. That sounded like Nick! By the time my head made it around, the man was heading directly away from me. He was shaped like Nick, but, then again, several black men were. Weird.

*

Our celebration continued into the evening. Upon the advice of Mark, with whom I had touched base earlier in the day, Char and I headed out for the Mayan. The Mayan was in a large warehouse sized building that didn't look like a warehouse. Although we looked cute with our short, tight, celebratory outfits, I was a little shocked at the jigginess of the attire considering the location. Men entering the club wore straight up suits. A club for grown folk. Now that's what I was talkin' about! Dancing with grown folk cost, however. Fifteen bucks at the door, with no Cute Girl Discount.

Once we were inside, we were really feeling it, Charlotte especially. She had a weakness for Latin men so the whole salsa vibe of the first floor grabbed her. I had to admit, I was feelin' it, too. There was a mainstage with a live band in one part of the club while stairs led up to additional floors where everything from techno to hip hop was played.

With the clientele about eighty-five percent Latino, their music was played to the fullest. It was either salsa or get your ass off the floor. I have to admit that I felt intimidated. Bodies were twirling and flying around the dance floor in perfect rhythm to the salsa beat. I didn't want to be embarrassed, especially since Charlotte knew what she was doing. She quickly latched onto a man who looked like the doppelganger of Chayanne, that sexy ass man from Dance With Me, who swept her onto the dance floor.

Not even my reticence could keep a charming Latino gentleman from requesting the pleasure of a dance. I accepted. Relying primarily on my salsa three step, I let the man be the

218

man. I kept up pretty well and had a great time.

In the middle of a spin where I opened out, guess who I nearly spun right into? Nick. Our eyes connected. His flabbergasted look matched mine. I bit my lip as I was reeled back in by my partner. What the hell was he doing here at the Mayan? Was he here with his fiancée? Probably so, seeing how Tabitha was half Dominican and half Cuban herself.

By the time the song was over, I pulled Charlotte out of a throng representative of Greater Latin America, and marched us upstairs. Time for some hip hop.

"What's goin' on, ma?"

"Nothing," I lied. No way was I gonna intrude upon her day with minor details of mine. "Just time to change el ritmo, that's all."

"Word."

*

Thursday would have been a perfect day. Charlotte and I basked in the habitual California sunshine by driving around Bel-Air and its exclusive, secluded homes with picturesque vistas of Los Angeles. Then we went to the Bally's on Bundy in West LA for a workout and a shot at the steam room. We capped off the day portion with a trip to the beach. Like I said, today would have been a perfect day had I not seen Nick at every one of our stops!

I was beginning to think I was cursed or something. I noticed Nick's head bob as the 4Runner breezed by our rented Bonneville this morning at the Bel-Air gate. I almost walked into the opposing door when I saw Nick exit the Bundy Avenue Bally's. Once again, our eyes locked for a brief but meaningful moment. His perplexed face didn't know whether to embrace anger or astonishment. I, on the other hand, began to wonder just how much coincidence I could take. And at the corner of Venice and Lincoln, en route to the beach, Nick's 4Runner nearly left turned into our Bonneville. This was so bizarre I was beginning to wonder if he was stalking me.

I put the thought out of my head. The man's getting married

in two days, I kept telling myself. He is not stalking me. But I had to admit that this would've been the easiest surveillance job in the history of surveillance jobs were I actually looking for him.

Naturally, Charlotte was oblivious to all of this, as she should be. She had only seen Nick in person a handful of times so she missed all the Nick sightings. Determined to keep this her trip, I kept my trap shut. I was a little spooked at how often I was running into that boy. Funny when you want to see someone, you can never get a hold of them but when you didn't want to see them, they were as common as catching a freakin' cold.

That night, we headed up to Mark's house up in the Hollywood Hills. As promised, we were slated to sit in on the weekly Scrabble game at his crib. As I parked my rental Bonneville next to Mark's shiny black Jag coupe, I reflected that this should be fun. I had heard ahead of time that Ananda and her glam-girl, triple word scoring self would not be present. A sista now had a chance to win.

Mark greeted us with loving hugs at the front door. As usual, the man looked good, dressed California casual in a ribbed V-neck pullover and jeans. When he wrapped me up in such a nice, casual hug, I fully appreciated the fact that I could have men as friends and simply leave it at that. I had met this man on a plane, he had turned out to be cool, because of my situation at the time I had stuck him in the Friend Zone, and he had adjusted and become cool with it. Not all men had such manageable egos to take such placement so easily. I wondered if it was a by-product of the fact that he was a Hollywood TV star and met many more eligible, beautiful women than me on the daily. Whatever it was, Mark was a genuinely good guy, and I was happy to be in his home again.

So, too, was Charlotte. Making her butt at home on one of his leather couches, Charlotte began chatting Charlie Sheen up as if she had seen him just the other day. Winning that audition must've convinced her that she finally belonged out here in Hollywood.

I shuttled between the kitchen and the living room, helping Mark with the snacks and such, making myself useful. We chatted casually about his next project, an independent movie he was co-headlining. But what I really wanted to know was what the deal was with the game.

"So where's Robert?" I asked of the missing Robert Downey Jr.

Slightly embarrassed, Mark offered, "Robert's…um…incapacitated right now."

More like incarcerated, I said to myself. "So we're down two tonight?"

"No. Your friend Charlotte can sit in for Robert."

"That's cool." I tossed the salad with tongs. "What about Ananda's replacement?"

"We'll rotate it but she should be on her way." On cue, the doorbell rang. "Great timing. There she is. Could you get that for me?"

"Sure." I drifted into the foyer, curious who this "she" was. All I knew was that there was no way Ananda's replacement could be as attractive and smart as Ananda was. That was my thought until I opened the door.

Great. Beyoncé of Destiny's Child. I'm not even lying.

"Hey. How you doin'?" she greeted me warmly, with only the slightest hint of her Houston drawl.

"Superb," I deadpanned. "Nice to meet you. I'm Jasmine."

"Beyoncé."

Yeah you are, I thought, ushering her in. If there was ever any doubt it was her, Beyoncé wore a tight, tummy baring top, a pair of sparkly leather pants, block heels, and a silver bellychain setting it all off. I smiled ruefully. Ananda had passed the power of the leather pants to her equally as glamorous understudy. I could only hope that she wasn't as smart as her Scrabble-master predecessor.

Naturally, Diva Fashionista gravitated instantly to Beyoncé. Char chatted her up about a new clothing line Beyoncé was pushing. Throughout the course of the games, they were teammates, becoming instant friends. I had just accepted the thought that I would be losing one of my best girlfriends to Hollywood very soon. To see her fitting in so nicely with Mark, Charlie, and Beyoncé, made me feel a little better about the loss. Charlotte was in her element. She truly belonged here. But once she would be gone, it made me wonder where I truly belonged.

*

As I had hoped, Beyoncé's shortcoming, in spite of all of her glammy-ness, was that she was young. Smart girl, but her not having lived as long as we have definitely had played a role in my winning three out of the five Scrabble games. She showed exactly how green she was when she had challenged me on my game-winning triple word score of "tryptophan."

Today, however, would be a day devoted to pure triflingness. We set out for Six Flags Amusement Park at nine that morning, determined to have a good time. Six Flags lay out in Valencia, nestled in a valley in a remote, mountainous part of Los Angeles County. Took us forty minutes to get there but was most certainly worth the drive.

We went on every ride they had there—twice. The park was mostly empty, as it was a Friday morning and the people of LA County had real lives with real jobs. Char and I, however, rode the Superman ride twice, the Batman four times, the Top Gun and Days of Thunder rides ad nauseum, and the Viper roller coaster consecutive times until Charlotte hurled up her popcorn and cotton candy into a trash can. I smirked as I saw her unload into the trash. Wouldn't be a day at the amusement park without someone tossing up their cotton candy.

A rinse job, three swigs of Listerine, and cup of water later, Charlotte hit the rides with me again. I couldn't remember when was the last time I had this much free, unfettered fun. My vacation days started to actually reflect vacation days. We would leave tomorrow afternoon around three, and I would be wholly glad I had made the trip. Supporting my girl had been the best move to support myself. This distraction had cleared my head of all the excess baggage taking up the overhead compartment space of my mind.

About six or seven P.M., we headed back for LA. She who vomited on the Viper must drive us back, I ruled, so Charlotte drove while I read the paper in the passenger seat. I glowed like a little kid receiving an Icee. What a great, fun day. The best part about it was that it had been entirely Nick-free. That had to count for something, right?

I didn't get halfway through the LA Times' A section when I was knocked out, drooling like an idiot. A happy little idiot.

*

We didn't want our last night in LA to be typical, so we avoided the club scene. Instead, Charlotte stopped us off over at a TGIFriday's in a section of unincorporated LA County called Ladera Heights. Ladera seemed pretty cool, as it boasted an interesting cross-section of yuppie black folk, aspiring yuppie black folk, and preening, artistically inclined black folk. It always did my heart good to see our people stepping out of Benz and Porsches, looking fly as all get out. Made me feel like I wasn't the only successful black person in the world, as I often felt in my industry, even in Atlanta.

This TGIFriday's was just such a place. I couldn't remember the last time I saw a TGIFriday's that would valet your car for you if you wanted. A thicket of dressy brothas and sistas coagulated outside the entrance to the restaurant. Char and I waded our way through, inside to the hostess desk. After being notified of an hour wait, we put our names down and swam upstream to the door. We meandered our way outside, trying to figure out what to do for the next hour. A Starbucks next door caught our attention.

"You want to go get some coffee and kill some time?" I suggested.

"Sure, I'm hip."

Seated inside over two café lattes, Charlotte drank in the ridiculously attractive surroundings. Big men, small men, thick men, tall men lounged about, waited in line, and simply sat around, drinking coffee. It went without saying that they were all fine, too; I mean, this was LA. Sociability was encouraged here, as everyone met everyone. The fashion friendly and the fashion fearless sauntered about the place as well, mixing nicely with the rest of the artistically earthy looking clientele, both affecting their own takes on the word cool. I just wished that silly boy with the knotty dreads would take off those damn

223

sunglasses! It was eight o'clock at night!

"So this was the Starbucks Beyoncé was talkin' 'bout last night," Charlotte observed, visually drinking in her fill. "No wonder they call this place Club Starbucks."

"Yeah. Magic must be making money hand over fist," I opined, glancing at a painting against the wall of retired NBA superstar/owner Earvin "Magic" Johnson.

"Thanks for comin' with me. I couldn't have done it without you, ma," she thanked me.

"Yes you could have, and you would have. Don't doubt the limits of your own ambition. You're a talented, special girl," I told her. "Sky's the limit for you."

"Thanks, ma."

"So how does this work? When are you moving?"

"Next week. I'm flying back out here a week from yesterday." Charlotte unfolded my paper from earlier and began to skim it.

"Next week? Dang, that's soon," I whistled. "So what's going to happen with Janaya?"

Charlotte took a sip from her latte and continued to scan the paper. "She's gonna stay with her grandma."

Say what? "Don't you think Janaya should be with her mother?"

She put the paper down, addressing my eyes seriously. Char wasn't mad, just serious. Plainly, she said, "I don't know if you've noticed, but I'm not that great a mom."

"Well, I guess you wouldn't win Mother of the Year, but who would in your situation?" I offered democratically.

"Let's be real here, J. I am a twenty-seven year old single mother of a four-year-old child. Janaya wasn't exactly what we would call a planned pregnancy. While I do love my little girl, I can't say that I love being a mommy. That may sound horrible, but it's the truth. I'm a young woman who has always had dreams and ambitions long before Satan and his 'just lemme put the head in, mami' ass came and ruined them. Mama Royer loves that little girl as if she were her own. She won't have any qualms with my leaving her to raise Janaya."

But I do! I wanted to shout. "I don't mean to sound judgmental at all, but aren't you ducking responsibility? Taking and caring for a child is a huge responsibility that you can't just shirk off onto another person."

Charlotte's eyes narrowed. "Were you in labor for thirty-six hours, Jasmine? Were you awake at night for six months straight because your daughter would not stop crying? Were you there for your baby's first step, her first words, her first boo-boo, and her first doo-doo? Changing diapers, potty training, teaching her how to walk, how to talk...I did all this by myself, Jasmine. Juan—I mean, Satan—did not help at all. You try doing all that alone, especially at an age where you feel like a kid your damn self, and then you can tell me about 'shirking responsibility.'"

My wrists had been effectively slapped. "Sorry."

"Like I said before, I'm not the greatest mother. I know this. There are things I do and things I want to do that keep Janaya from having the best upbringing she could have," Charlotte admitted. "But I love my daughter. I love my daughter enough to turn her over to her grandmother, my mother, who knows a little something about raising a young girl all by herself.

"I can't even fathom trying to raise a baby girl, Jasmine! What am I going to teach her, that all men fuckin' suck? Am I gonna teach her how her daddy is a deadbeat hiding out in Spanish Harlem, with four other kids by three other baby mommas? Just the term 'baby momma' makes my skin crawl because I am one! I can't bring that kind of bitterness into my daughter's life until it has left my life. How do I try and raise a young woman in this kind of emotional climate where I am limited and bitter and stifled by pain? How can I raise a young woman when I'm still trying to raise myself?"

Charlotte had a point. Sometimes, for better or worse, you just had to go your own path. It might not be the best one, or the one most traveled, but you had to be true to yourself. I could respect that. I could respect that because I had done that. "I hear you," I supplied quietly.

"I will still see my little girl, you best believe that," vowed Charlotte. "I just won't see her as much. I am still a young woman with an entire career ahead of me. That much I know I can raise."

Char sipped her latte and returned to the paper. "Besides, that damn lil rugrat loves Granny more than she does me anyway."

I laughed. If not relieved, at least educated.

"Oh shit," she involuntarily mumbled.

"What?"

Charlotte scrambled to recover. "Nathan. Never mind."

"No, tell me," I insisted.

She blinked twice, and then handed over the newspaper. It was the Calendar section, second page, Liz Smith's column. "Suit yourself."

Double dang. There was a quick blurb on Nick's wedding, to be held at Faithful Central church tomorrow at three P.M. How a newcomer like Nick had ended up in gossip columnist Liz Smith's column was beyond me. But also the reality that he was getting married for real, having had the date and time trumpeted proudly and nationally, kinda hit home.

I shrugged, handing the newspaper back to Charlotte. "Good for him. I guess we'll be able to see clips of his wedding on Access Hollywood if they're interested enough."

Char studied my expression before cracking a smile. "Good for you, ma. That's a great attitude to have. C'mon. Let's go see if our table is ready."

On the way out of Club Starbucks, with my head somewhat bowed, rereading the Liz Smith column again, I bounced off of a man coming through the doorway. Barely breaking my stride, I murmured, "Excuse me."

Once outside, I lifted my head and glanced back. It was a stunned looking Nick, staring back at a stunned looking me. Gratefully, I escaped into the anonymity of the TGIFriday's let-out with Charlotte.

*

"Go see him, ma."

"Huh?"

It was night. All the lights were off in the hotel room. Both of us were stuffed and sleepy—overwhelmed by the infamous black person sleeping disease known only as "The Itis." This was our last night in LA. Well, at least my last night in LA, especially if I didn't win that HART and snag the anchor job.

"Go see him, Jasmine. We have time tomorrow before we

leave. Go see Nick and wish him a happy wedding or whatever. Apologize for harassing him and mean it. Be the bigger adult," Charlotte advised. "It'll clear your conscience."

"Who says my conscience needs clearing?" I rebutted.

"Yours. Because you must've seen the boy at least five times while we've been out here and you haven't even said a word."

Dang, that Charlotte was a sharp one! "Alright, you caught me, you caught me. But I didn't talk about him because this was your trip—and I'm over him."

"Great. Tell him that." Charlotte turned over. "Goodnight."

I lay there, staring into the blankness of the dark and the ceiling. I grumbled. "Goodnight."

*

I knocked politely on the door to the deacon's office downstairs, in the basement of the church. It was some two hours before the wedding and last minute preparations were being made. Thankfully, no one from Tabitha's camp had seen me sneak into Faithful Central while en route to the deacon's office. A helpful little five-year-old boy fitted in a tiny little tuxedo with tails had tipped me off. His reward: a kiss on the cheek.

Now, we were way beyond little boys and kisses on the cheek.

When Nick opened the door, I could have sworn he would have slammed the thing on my face if he weren't such a gentleman. If I put myself in his position, I can't say that I could blame him. Showing him my palms, I said, "I've come in peace. I promise. Give me one minute, Nick. One minute, please."

Warily, my ex-boyfriend let me into the room, closing the door. He had to or else his ass would be in a sling if Tabitha found out that my homewrecker self was here at the do-over of her wedding.

"What do you want, Jasmine?"

"When your mom came to see me in the hospital, she mentioned something about you and me and bad timing. So I thought I'd get to you a little earlier this time," I said, trying out a nervous, slight, playful little laugh that failed spectacularly.

"Mom went to Atlanta to see you?" Nick was incredulous.

"I'm sorry. Last week. I thought you knew." She didn't tell him?

Nick shook his head in denial. "Still, Jasmine, what do you want?"

The courage sigh. "I just wanted to apologize for any pain and inconvenience I have caused you and your family. Sincerely. I never meant to hurt you or to bring stress into your life. I am truly sorry.

"I also wanted to wish you good luck and eternal happiness. You, of all men, deserve it, Nick. Congratulations."

"Thank you," Nick said quietly.

"That's all," I said, turning to leave.

I have to admit, I was a little disappointed in myself. How anticlimactic. How sorry and untrue to myself. This was the last time I could ever see this man in person, and this was how I made the exit out of his life? Oh, hell naw!

A step and a half from the door, I spun right back around. I had more to say.

"Right or wrong, whether you feel it back or not, Nick, I love you. I have always loved you and I always will love you. No matter whom you marry, how many kids you have, or where you live, I will always love you. If you cannot love me back, I'm not mad at you. I just wish I could be the one whose face the sun of your love is shining upon. I will miss you.

"But know this, Babyluv, know this one thing. I will always love you unconditionally. Always."

I grasped the sides of his cool, walnut brown face and bestowed upon him the tenderest kiss in the repertoire of tender kisses. I gave him the goodbye kiss.

As I kissed him, I slipped something in his pocket. When I disengaged, I backed up toward the door.

"What's this?" he asked, feeling around in his pocket.

"Consider it a wedding gift."

"Thanks."

"No, thank you, Nick. Thank you for giving me some of the best memories of my life. I will always remember them, and I am a better woman for them. You taught me how to love, and I learned how I deserve to be loved. No one can ever take that away from me. Thank you. I love you."

The door to the deacon's office was shut. Walking away, I could only imagine the look on Nick's face when he dug out a six-carat diamond ring from his pants pocket.

The Ride Home

The moment we were airborne, Char was knocked out. I, on the other hand, had far too active a mind. Talking to Charlotte earlier had gotten the brain percolating on making one last piece to tape and cut for the HART before the final submission deadline of Sunday at six P.M.

Just as I settled my head into my seat cushion, I prepped to force myself asleep. But something kept me up. The glowing color screen from a seatback across the aisle caught my attention. On one of Jet Blue's satellite TV channels, a movie played. I turned on my own personal screen, earphones jacked into the armrest for sound. Guess what movie was to start the beginning of the rest of my life?

Boomerang.

Of course.

14

I DIDN'T GIVE A HOT DAMN if I had worn this dress before. This here was a six thousand dollar dress that someone (else) had paid for, and I would wear the hell out of it tonight. As I glided into the main ballroom of the Downtown Hyatt hotel, I reveled in the grandeur of my strapless, backless, blue Badgley Mischka. With my once curly hair now straightened back into its trademark bob, I buckled knees and snapped heads. I was the bomb, baby!

I had to admit that my date for the evening looked almost as stunning as I did. Charlotte worked a simply red, spaghetti-strapped dress like it was a full time, sweatshop job! Her red pumps almost brought her up to my five feet nine inches of golden brown glamour queen. If they were handing out awards for best dressed, all the other anchors wouldn't stand a chance next to us.

You better believe we were here for the awards. The ballroom was full of Atlanta's finest broadcasters in television and radio, all dolled up and looking better than ever for the HART Awards. Shortly after entering the room, Derek, our five P.M. weeknight anchor, came over and gave me a good luck peck on the cheek. After Brian Richardson had established eye contact with me, I effectively snubbed him by looking away. I came here to win the HART. I looked too dang good to suffer fools gladly tonight.

As far as dates go, Charlotte was the best one I'd had all year. When I had come home two nights ago, I promptly erased all the triflin' Negroes outta my Palm Pilot. Especially tired-ass Jerome. So you can imagine that I would be dateless for this evening. Not only was I glad to do it, but also I'd rather hang with my girl tonight anyway. She knew how much this award meant to me.

While dinner was served, I scoped out the competition. Beverly (and her red hair) nibbled at her salad somewhat nervously. Legendary Monica Kaufman (and her dyed blonde hair) snacked on her chicken pasta casually, as cool as the other side of the pillow. Now it was my turn for a small case of nerves. Kaufman's piece on unwed teenage mother crack addicts was phenomenal, absolutely phenomenal. Despite my recent notoriety and the last minute piece Angie and I had shot yesterday, I wondered if I had enough firepower to take her.

Speaking of that "recent notoriety," several of my colleagues in the industry stopped by to check on my condition. They fawned all over me with an abundance of false concern. At one point during the processional, Char remarked, "Dang, ma. I feel like I'm sittin' next to Marilyn Monroe."

"I'll keep an eye on my skirt," I smirked.

An hour and a half of ancillary awards later, they got around to mine, Broadcast Anchor of the Year. Charlotte grabbed my hands, only to find them sweaty. I literally perched on the edge of my seat.

They played extended clips of the contenders' top pieces after the introduction of the nominees. Beverly Bradley's "Red Dog" tape drew an impossibly astonished gasp at the part when she got shot; interesting considering that everyone in the room had seen it more times than the Zapruder film. Monica Kaufman's tearjerker of a piece on the coke mommas drew broadly sympathetic stares. Monica glowed like the proud journalist she was. And then there was…

"Jasmine Selene, WAGA-TV, Fox 5 News."

The giant projector screen displayed my tape of yesterday. On the screen, I sat on my plush living room occasional chair, dressed extremely professional in a baby blue full pantsuit. Across from me in an identical maroon velvet chair sat four-year-old Janaya in Osh Kosh overalls. Her legs dangled almost a foot off the floor.

The sight of her creamy brown sweetness elicited an unexpectedly overwhelming "Aww" from the audience. I maintained my composure despite gleaming a constellation of pride inside. Charlotte elbowed me. So this was for what I had "borrowed" her daughter for an hour yesterday.

"Good evening. My name is Jasmine Selene with WAGA-TV, Fox 5. I'm sitting here with Janaya Royer, a four-year-old woman from Avondale Estates."

Charlotte shot me a look in real time that clearly read, "Damn right my baby's a woman!"

"Thank you for joining me today, Ms. Royer."

"Thank you, Mith Thelene," Janaya lithped shyly, just as I had coached her to respond. Once she got over her shyness, she would talk rather normally.

"Janaya, I want to talk about your mommy today. Do you know what her job is?"

"She's an actress," the four year old announced proudly.

"Yes she is. A very good one," I confirmed. "In fact, your mommy is so good, she got a very important job to act that may mean that she won't be around as much. How does that make you feel?"

Janaya took a moment before answering. It was as if the little person was investing serious thought in formulating her response. "I'll miss her. I love my mommy, but I know that she loves her job. If her job makes her happy, then I'll be happy."

"Is it important for you to see your mommy happy?"

"Yes!" she exclaimed. "A lot of times, Mommy isn't happy. She doesn't think I see it, but I do. She cries a lot when she's alone. I've heard her say to Grandmommy that it's hard to be Mommy without a daddy."

In the ballroom, I stole a peripheral glance at Charlotte. She sat rigidly in her seat, mesmerized by her little woman's performance on screen.

"Do you miss your daddy?"

"No. I don't know my daddy," Janaya answered simply. "And if he's why Mommy cries so much, I don't wanna know my daddy. We don't need him!"

"No we don't, Angel," Charlotte whispered to herself.

"Do you think Mommy wants a new daddy?"

"I dunno. I think Mommy wants to be happy, that's it. But no one makes her happy. I feel bad for her," Janaya admitted. "I try to be as nice to her as I can, so I won't be a b...b...A...I don't know that word yet."

The audience took the opportunity to burst into short, contained laughter, grateful for a moment of levity.

"A burden?"

232

"Yeah!" she agreed. "So I won't be a burden to her. I want Mommy to be happy, and I don't think she's very happy. Sometimes, when Mommy comes home, she's been drinking. Grandmommy says that people drink a lot to hide their hurts. I think Mommy hurts a lot. That's why she drinks."

"If Mommy has to leave to take that acting job, how will you feel?"

Janaya sucked her teeth, eminently imitating her mother. "I'll be fine, silly! I just want Mommy to be happy. If she has to leave me to be happy, then I'll be happy. I love Mommy."

That line right there broke my heart, on screen and in real life. I must have watched that scene at least a dozen times since taping it yesterday, and Janaya's brave, fearless, tender, young little heart broke mine every single time. Screw what Charlotte or Nadine had said. Giving up of yourself so entirely that someone else could be happy…Now that was courageous.

"And I'm a strong black woman!" declared Janaya forcefully, thrusting her right fist in the air.

The audience tittered, half crying and half laughing.

I turned to the camera and wiped a very, very real tear away before closing it out. "This is Jasmine Selene of WAGA-TV, reporting on the triumph of a single black mother—and her strong black woman."

The applause was deafening when the footage went off and the lights went up. Charlotte, who sat right next to me, clapped louder than the rest, the remains of a tear down the right side of her face. All of her shortcomings as a mother were forgiven by the person who counted most: her daughter.

It took a full minute for the applause to die down. But when it did…

"And the Heritage Atlanta Radio and Television Award for Broadcast Anchor of the Year goes to…"

*

"Jasmine Selene!" Charlotte howled into her broomstick-cum-microphone. She fell to the floor, rolling around on the carpet, almost in epileptic seizure.

233

I rolled my eyes. "I was not that bad."

Charlotte stopped rolling. "Ma, you were worse! I coulda sworn everyone's heart skipped a beat when you swooned getting up!"

"I was in shock," I defended meekly. "I was just so happy. And surprised. And happy!"

"Well eat a banana or something before you go to another one of these HART things, okay?" Char advised. "If you so much as trip over your own shoelaces, everyone's gonna think you're gonna faint again."

"Very funny," I said, going back to my job. I was helping Charlotte repack two nights later for her trip to California. Sistagurl was staying with me the night before so she I could drive her to the airport in the morning. She really didn't have much, outside of clothes, of course, as she was forever the Diva Fashionista. I suppose she just wanted the company, which was fine by me. My HART had bought me a few more days off. Polly was becoming increasingly reliable and Nadine was a changed woman.

Nadine was back from her honeymoon to Aruba the day after the HARTs. In her deliriously happy-married-devirginized-loosened up version of her old self, Nadine had given me a few more days off to celebrate our win. Even though, in all reality, it was a four-year-old girl who saved both our tails, and made my career.

"I appreciate the shoutout you gave us from the podium," Charlotte acknowledged. "You didn't have to say all the kind things you did about me or my daughter."

"It's the truth. I couldn't have done it without y'all," I said, speaking gospel truth. "I just hope I have, someday, as special a little girl—a little woman—as you do."

"Yeah," Charlotte sighed, bursting with parental pride. "She'll be pimpin' 'em by the time she's twelve. Just like Mommy."

My doorbell rang. Heading in that direction I shot back, "I'm glad someone thinks you're a role model." Opening the door, I said, "He—"

Nick.

On my doorstep. In Georgia.

Thank goodness I was fresh out of faints.

"Hi, Jasmine," Nick said simply.

My eyes started involuntarily tearing. Something had to give because I was speechless.

"I was wrong. You were right. I will always love you, Jasmine. Unconditionally and always."

He held out a ring box.

A ring box. I was still speechless.

"I was made to love you."

I opened up the box. A brand new, beautifully flawless, one-carat diamond stared right back at me.

I couldn't take it anymore. I hugged him so hard, I nearly dropped the ring and its box. I started sniffling and breathing uncontrollably.

As I crushed the life force out of him, Nick timidly asked, "Uh, is that a yes this time, Jasmine?"

I pulled myself off him just far enough to cup his beautiful, dark brown face in my hands. I could've slapped it just as hard as I could have kissed it. Fresh.

I nodded my head, bouncing it enthusiastically with a smile. "Yes, Babyluv. Yes!"

We hugged again, until Nick peeled me off just enough to slip the ring on my finger. It fit perfectly. It was made for me—just like him.

I kissed him and hugged him and kissed him and hugged him, before dragging him into the house.

Almost oblivious to the world and everything in it, I was barely aware that Charlotte had watched the whole thing unfold from a corner in the living room. Then I noticed a rare smile of pure, heartfelt joy and happiness exude from her, as she wiped away a tear. Right then and there I could tell that Charlotte, the realist, became…gasp…a romantic!

EPILOGUE

Ours was a small, simple ceremony. Conspicuously absent was the media, perhaps because of the locale of our nuptials.

We were outdoors at the cemetery Mom was buried in on an overcast Seattle day in December. Unfortunately, Mom did not live long enough to see her son get married, so we chose to get married here, where she could see it. Her grave was a mere three feet behind the minister, Nadine's father, Reverend Montgomery.

Two weeks after Nick had announced to his mother and the world our engagement, Mom died peacefully, in her sleep. Nick took it extremely well, like the strong young man that single black mother had raised before marrying Harrison.

The guest list was real simple. On Nick's side, it consisted of Malloy, Craig, Robert, and Harrison. On my side, it consisted of Charlotte, Nadine, Rodney, Mama, Nia, and, yes, Mia. My former best friend was there not just to accompany her husband Malloy, but also to work and repair our friendship with me. I was glad. I had missed her so much. Even my father was there, taking a break out of his busy schedule to bless us with his presence. At my request, Nick's father was also there. Considering we were getting married on the grave of his mother, Nick was extremely civil to his father. Nick had lost a mother; Nick Senior had lost a former wife. Humanity had lost a great, caring woman.

And somehow, in the midst of all this emotion, I was about to gain a husband. Here came my part, the part I had waited over thirty years for:

"Nicholas Andre Jackson, do you take Jasmine Selene Thomas as your lawfully wedded wife, to have and to hold, from this day forward, for better or for worse, for richer or for poorer, in sickness and in health, to love and to cherish, till death do you part?"

Our eyes locked, our souls meshed. For eternity. "I do."

"Jasmine Selene Thomas, do you take Nicholas Andre Jackson as your lawfully wedded husband, to have and to hold, from this day forward, for better or for worse, for richer or for poorer, in sickness and in health, to love and to cherish, till death do you part?"

Sho' nuff. "I do."

"For as much as Nicholas and Jasmine have consented together in wedlock, and have witnessed the same before this company of friends and family, and have given and pledged their promises to each other, and have declared the same by giving and receiving a ring, and by joining hands...By the authority vested in me by the State of Washington, I now pronounce you to be husband and wife."

Wow. My dreams never got this far. I was too ecstatic to remember what to do next.

Which was Reverend Montgomery's job. "You may now kiss the bride."

We kissed to the greater glory of the universe, and to Mom.

*

We were together, lying on the couch, casually watching Nick's favorite show, SportsCenter. I rather liked the show, too, as I liked sports but was mediocre at playing them.

We were also in his newly bought house in LA's posh chocolate suburbia of Ladera Heights. Despite her protestations, Nick had given the house in Playa del Rey over to Tabitha. It sucked as an exchange for a lifetime of happiness with my man, but it would have to do. Besides, I didn't feel right living with my husband in a house he had planned to live in with someone else. Our house was nice, quiet, and comfortable. We could afford it, as principal photography had wrapped on Nick's Sand Adventures. He had just accepted a new role for a million-five, based on the strength of his white hot buzz from a rough cut of the summer popcorn flick.

Also it didn't hurt that Jasmine Selene was the lead anchor on Fox Nightly News debuting in January.

So on this chilly December evening, we stole a quiet moment together before our trip tomorrow morning to Barbados.

We were together. We were alone. I was finally home.

Nestled in his arms, wedding bands on our fingers, I felt as secure as I could ever want to feel. I could ask my husband any and everything because he was my husband. So I asked the most obvious question I had dared not ask until now, for fear of blowing this wish of a dream away before it had become reality. "Why did you come back to me?"

Internally, I coiled at his potential response.

"I love you, of course," he said, giving me a quick kiss. "I always have and realized that I always would. I realized that less than fifteen minutes after you had left the church. But what really put it over the top was Mom."

My eyebrows perked. "Really?"

"Your mother sent mine a letter—certified mail, return receipt requested, signature required. She wanted to make sure Mom received it. I will always remember what she said in the letter, one that Mom read to me in the basement of the church with less than half an hour to go to the ceremony, when she could see in my eyes that I was having doubts. I will always remember what your mother had written because just the fact that my mother was meddling in my love life was landmark. I will always remember what your mother wrote because it helped change my life:

"'I don't understand this strange obsession my daughter has with your son, nor do I approve of it. But, for the first time in her life, I see that she is consumed by a person, a goal, by something that makes her want to improve herself. While I do not like your son very much, that kind of dedication and loyalty should not go unrewarded. I could care less if she married your son. But I care everything about my daughter's happiness. Rest assured that your son could not do any better nor find a finer person to be with than my Jasmine Selene. If he chooses to ignore these facts and not be with her, the loss most certainly will be his.'"

"Wow." I smiled on the inside. Vintage Winnie.

"Then Mom simply says to me, 'Handsome, I want you to be happy. She makes you happy. Follow your happiness.'"

"That's it?"

"That's it. Then I went over to tell Tabitha, let her hit me once real good in the mouth and in the balls, and then high-tailed it out of the church."

During the commercial break, I changed the channel to Lifetime via the remote. On the channel was a commercial fo

L'Oreal, starring Charlotte, looking more glam and beautiful than Ananda and Beyoncé put together. With uncanny timing, the commercial was ending and Charlotte spoke the exact words I was thinking, as she pitched the company's tagline with an alluring pout:

"Because I'm worth it."

*

Before our honeymoon could start, we had to revive our nuptials the right way, in a romantic setting. At sunrise, holding hands, Nick and I renewed our three-day-old vows before a priest on a flat, sandy Barbados beach. Boomerang, which I had played on my laptop computer's DVD player on the plane ride out here, had nothing on us. If there was a happily ever after to our story, we sure were living it.

I couldn't say that what followed was the most spontaneous thing in the world since I had to be talked into it, quite frankly. Still, I trusted my man, my husband (I still got shivers when I said that to myself), and I would follow him to the ends of the earth, as he would for me.

We stood on the edge of a cliff, about thirty-five, forty feet high, holding hands. Shit, I was scared. I had never gone cliff diving before. Neither had Nick, he claimed, but he was ready to try it. He squeezed my hand.

"Let's go, Baby J. I'll hold your hand all the way down."

I nodded stiffly.

"Okay, on three," he prepped me.

"One, two—" He yanked us off the cliff, hurtling toward the azure blue waters screaming toward us below. Instinctively, I curled my legs under, as did he, into a cannonball to brace the impact.

He screamed, I didn't. I wasn't the most adventurous girl in the world, but even I knew when to shut up, enjoy the moment, and take The Fifth.

We splashed into the water, and into the rest of our lives, together. Forever. For ever after.